Readers love the Coffee Cake
series by MICHAELA GREY

Coffee Cake

"This is a special book in more than one way… I couldn't get enough of Bran and Malachi!"

—Rainbow Book Reviews

"This book is just… OMG awesome! I can't recommend this book enough."

—MM Good Book Reviews

Beignets

"It's a great addition to this series. I hope that there will be more."

—Boys in Our Books

"I so love Bran and Malachi. They are so amazing together."

—Molly Lolly

By MICHAELA GREY

Broken Halo

COFFEE CAKE
Coffee Cake
Beignets

Published by DREAMSPINNER PRESS
www.dreamspinnerpress.com

MICHAELA GREY

Broken Halo

DREAMSPINNER PRESS

Published by
DREAMSPINNER PRESS

5032 Capital Circle SW, Suite 2, PMB# 279, Tallahassee, FL 32305-7886 USA
www.dreamspinnerpress.com

This is a work of fiction. Names, characters, places, and incidents either are the product of author imagination or are used fictitiously, and any resemblance to actual persons, living or dead, business establishments, events, or locales is entirely coincidental.

Broken Halo
© 2017 Michaela Grey.

Cover Art
© 2017 AngstyG.
http://www.angstyg.com
Cover content is for illustrative purposes only and any person depicted on the cover is a model.

ISBN: 978-1-63533-219-3
Digital ISBN: 978-1-63533-220-9
Library of Congress Control Number: 2016915798
Published January 2017
v. 1.0

Printed in the United States of America
∞
This paper meets the requirements of
ANSI/NISO Z39.48-1992 (Permanence of Paper).

For Aaliya, always my favorite.
We're gonna die in a fucking gulag, but it'll be worth it.

Acknowledgments

SPECIAL THANKS to everyone on Tumblr who read and loved this story when it was known as *Buttons on a Coat*. Your enthusiasm kept me writing, and I appreciate you all so much.

AUTHOR'S NOTE

Please kink responsibly.

CHAPTER ONE

MICAH ELLIS was in hell. He was in hell, and there was dirt *everywhere*. He stood very still in the middle of the automotive repair shop, elbows pressed close to his sides, and took small, shallow breaths so as not to breathe in more filth than absolutely necessary.

Why had his car decided to break down *now*? Why today, when he had the Adler Headhunting party with Barrett Frye, of all people, who would find a cruelly clever way to twit Micah about his love handles while congratulating himself on keeping his own slim figure?

And why couldn't the car have had the decency to wait until Micah was close to his usual mechanic, the one who understood how Micah felt about grease and dirt and rust, who kept things neat and tidy and always washed her hands before shaking his?

Worst of all, why was the man working on Micah's car so damn beautiful? He was covered in engine grease and sweat and, oh God, was that a smear of dirt on his *forehead*? He was well over six feet tall, which meant he towered above Micah, and very fit, with blue eyes that gleamed bright under tousled brown hair. Next to him, Micah, with his black hair, dark brown eyes, and strong nose from his Indian mother, felt plainer than ever.

The man wiped his jaw, leaving more dirt behind, and Micah swallowed hard. He couldn't decide whether to be attracted or find a bathroom to wash his hands until they were raw.

He hovered in the middle of the space, and when the mechanic straightened and sauntered toward him holding out one huge—and dirty—hand, Micah took a quick, horrified step back before he could stop himself.

Something flickered over the young man's face, and he dropped his hand. "Devon Mallory," he said. "Looks like your car's decided to take a vacation without you." He smiled, but Micah just glared up at him.

"Do I look like I'm in the mood for jokes? How fast can you fix it?"

Devon's eyebrows went up. "Uh… okay. It's actually a fairly simple fix. It's a worn-out belt, and it won't take long to put a replacement on."

"Fine," Micah snapped. "Get on with it, then."

Devon stared at him for a minute and then shrugged. "Be about an hour," he said, turning away. "You can wait there." He pointed at a small, glassed-in room.

Micah headed in that direction as quickly as he could. There was no one else in the room, which was thankfully much cleaner than the rest of the shop, and Micah perched on the edge of one of the chairs to wait, nerves jangling and brain buzzing so loudly it was hard for him to think.

After about forty-five minutes, Devon ambled in. He gave Micah an apologetic smile as he pulled a heavy logbook out from under the counter and flipped through it.

"Normally Hope'd be in here to take care of you," he said, head bent over the book and shaggy brown hair falling in his face, "but she's out with her little girl today. Measles, I think."

Micah shuddered before he could stop himself. Devon caught the movement out of the corner of his eye.

"Germophobe?" he inquired, one side of his mouth curving up.

"You could say that," Micah said, tone clipped. "Will this take much longer?"

"Shouldn't," Devon said. "Are you new in town? I've never seen you before."

Micah shifted on the hard plastic chair, willing himself to patience. "I've lived in Toronto for ten years and worked for Adler Headhunting for five. The only reason I'm here is because my car broke down on the way to work."

Devon's smile slipped, and he turned back to the book. After a few minutes of writing on a receipt, he pulled out a calculator and punched in numbers, tongue caught between his teeth.

Micah sighed and checked his watch.

"I'm working as fast as I can, sir," Devon said without looking up.

"It's fine," Micah said. "I really shouldn't expect speed from someone who looks like you."

Devon froze in place and then set his pen down very slowly and straightened, narrowing his eyes. "Would you like to repeat that, sir?" he said, his voice dangerously quiet.

Micah swallowed hard but squared his shoulders and met his gaze. "You heard me," he said. "You clearly spend more time working out than you do reading. Can I please pay you and get out of here?"

A muscle jumped in Devon's jaw. "You know what? We're not so desperate for money that we need your business. Take your car and leave the premises, please." His words were sharp, but there was very real hurt in his blue eyes.

Micah stood and smoothed his dress pants, fumbling for words. He'd gone too far. He cursed himself. He hadn't *actually* meant to hurt the young man who was holding his keys out to him as though Micah were the contaminated one, and yet he couldn't figure out how to fix it.

"Look," he began.

Devon cut him off. "Have a nice day, sir."

Micah accepted the keys and bit his lip. Devon turned away immediately to stalk back into the garage bay.

Micah drove to work in a daze, kicking himself the entire way. The rest of the day was a complete bust. He snapped at his receptionist, sat in his office and stared into space for a while. Then he forgot an important meeting and had to make a run for it through the meandering corridors of the building, only to realize he'd left his paperwork in his office and had to go back. When evening rolled around, he was more than ready to crawl into a hole and never come out.

Of course Barrett was at the party and made straight for him.

"Glad you could make it, Mike," he said cheerfully, his predatory gray eyes gleaming.

"Don't call me that," Micah said, more out of habit than hope that Barrett would comply.

Sure enough Barrett just laughed and slung an arm around Micah's shoulders. He craned his neck backward, not even subtle about looking at Micah's ass.

"Packing it on there a bit, aren't you?"

Micah gritted his teeth. *Important client. Don't piss off the important client.*

"It never used to bother you," he said.

Barrett took a sip of wine and smiled down at him. "Yes, well, more to love and all that."

Micah smiled back. Barrett didn't have to know the smile was the result of Micah envisioning the most satisfying way of murdering the copper-haired man whose arm was *still* around Micah's shoulders. He took a deep breath and stepped away, straightening his jacket.

"So that new kid you got for my firm," Barrett said, not seeming to notice, "I have to tell you, Mike, you hit the ball out of the goddamn park with that one. He's cleared a dozen cases for us, and he's well on his way to making us all millionaires."

"I'm glad," Micah said. "I see Myra over there. I should go say hello." He escaped before Barrett could respond.

He spent the rest of the evening longingly eyeing the refreshments table and dodging Barrett, who seemed to make a game of boxing him into corners to talk about work-related things. He couldn't actually eat, not with Barrett hovering nearby, but maybe he could get a drink.

He was halfway there when a hand closed around his bicep and pulled him into an alcove. Barrett loomed over him, his damned eyes nearly aglow in the dim lighting.

Micah stiffened. "Trying to work here," he said, keeping his tone casual.

"I've missed you," Barrett murmured as he swayed closer to take a deep breath.

Micah leaned to the side and fought down fear. "You're the one who broke up with me," he pointed out.

"Maybe I changed my mind," Barrett said. The rich, heavy scent of his aftershave clogged the back of Micah's throat.

"Or maybe you're just bored," Micah said and tried to sidle away.

Barrett grabbed Micah's shoulders and shoved him up against the wall with shocking force. Micah gasped and clutched Barrett's wrists.

"You don't leave until I *say* you can leave," Barrett snarled.

Micah fought the panic that choked him. "I don't belong to you now," he managed. His throat was tight, and he tried to clear it. "You can't... you can't tell me what to do anymore."

"And *you* can't tell me you don't miss it too," Barrett purred. He moved closer until he was pressed up against Micah's body in a long line of heat. Micah could feel Barrett's erection through their dress pants, and he turned his head away, squeezing his eyes shut.

"Look at me," Barrett commanded, and Micah's eyes snapped up to his. Barrett's lips curved in satisfaction. "Such a good little sub," he crooned. "Always so obedient, with your need to be dominated."

"Fuck you," Micah managed, but Barrett just huffed a laugh and dropped his head to nose at the crook of Micah's neck. He was going to be sick, Micah thought with a welling sense of dread.

"Maybe I should put you on your knees," Barrett said, pulling back enough to meet Micah's eyes. "Have you suck me off right here. Would you like that?"

Nausea churned in Micah's stomach, and he was saved by a girl's voice just outside the alcove. "Micah?"

Barrett let go and stepped back as though he'd been slapped, and Micah took advantage of the opening to dodge out into the hall. A young woman smiled nervously at him.

"Myra sent me," she said. "She wants to talk to you about something."

"Of course," Micah said. "Lead the way."

He spent fifteen minutes talking to Myra about her ad agency and the need for new blood as he kept his eyes peeled for Barrett, who never reappeared. Finally he was able to make his escape and very nearly ran for his car.

He slid behind the wheel and was out of the parking lot in a matter of seconds. He almost clipped Barrett's Porsche, which glowed crimson under the parking lot lights, fighting the nausea until he could pull over and press his forehead against the steering wheel.

Finally it receded, and Micah was able to take a shaky breath. He needed to eat something, if there was anywhere still open.

The glowing sign of an IHOP just ahead caught his eye, and Micah pulled into the parking lot before making a conscious decision. Chocolate chip pancakes with whipped cream sounded like just the ticket.

There were only a few cars in the lot. Good. He'd be able to eat in peace and get out quickly.

Looking back, it was probably the universe laughing at him, considering he walked in to see Devon-fucking-Mallory sitting at a table close to the entrance, eating with a single-minded focus.

CHAPTER TWO

MICAH VERY nearly turned around and walked right back out, but Devon had already seen him. Micah squared his shoulders, gave Devon a quick nod, and followed the perky hostess to a booth only a few yards from Devon, who was watching him but hadn't otherwise moved.

Micah slipped into the booth, rested his elbows on the table, and covered his face. *Dear God, who did I piss off so badly in a past life?*

He gave the waitress his order and then sat quietly, praying Devon would finish his meal and leave soon. He was entirely unprepared for Devon to slide into the booth opposite him, set his plate and coffee cup down on the table, and smile at him.

"What—"

Devon shrugged. "I feel like I owe you an apology. I was rude to you this afternoon."

Micah gaped at him. "Are you *serious*?"

"Yes?" Devon said, his brow furrowing. "I kicked you out of the shop. I told you we didn't need your business. I was rude to you, and I'm sorry."

"I basically called you a muscle-bound idiot, and *you're* apologizing to *me*?" Micah demanded. "Do you apologize to your dog when it bites you too?"

"Depends on if I provoked it, but probably," Devon said, and Micah snorted a disbelieving laugh. "Or I would, if I had a dog. Anyway, I'm not saying you weren't rude too, because you were. But I'm the only one responsible for my actions, and I'm sorry I was rude to you."

Micah sat back against the cracked vinyl of the booth and considered him. Devon's eyes were earnest, his broad shoulders hunched as he gazed at Micah.

"I'm the one who should be apologizing," Micah finally said. "I was a total asshole."

Devon shrugged, and his blue eyes danced.

"You don't have to agree," Micah said, but a smile tugged at his mouth, and the sick feeling that had plagued him all day slowly lifted.

Devon's lips were twitching. "We were both dicks. Can we start over?" He held out a hand across the table and then jerked it back. "Shit, you don't like to shake hands. I'm sorry."

"It's the dirt that… upsets me," Micah said. "And you look… clean." Devon did too. His brown hair was still slightly damp, and his skin glowed pink, probably from a recent shower. Micah held out his hand, and Devon accepted it. "Micah Ellis," Micah said. "It's nice to meet you."

"Devon Mallory," Devon said and smiled at him, punching the air right out of Micah's lungs. His eyes were bright with mirth, dimples appearing in his cheeks and his white teeth flashing. Micah couldn't *breathe*. Devon's smile slipped. "Micah? Are you okay?"

Micah feebly waved a hand. "You have no right to be so damn attractive," he informed him, "especially after the way I acted this morning."

Devon's smile widened again. "You think I'm attractive?"

Micah opened his mouth to change the subject or distract him long enough to make a quick getaway, but he was rescued by the waitress, who appeared with his huge stack of chocolate chip pancakes piled high with whipped cream.

Devon's eyes went wide as she set the plate in front of Micah, and Micah reconsidered the possibility of making a run for it. A guy who looked like Devon surely didn't have to struggle when he got up from an overstuffed couch.

But Devon wasn't judging him. "Dude, that looks *awesome*," he said, and he caught the waitress's eye. "Can I get a stack of those too?"

"Sure," she said, glancing at his plate of half-eaten pigs in blankets. "But—"

Devon looked down at his food. "Oh, don't worry," he told her cheerfully, "I'll be done by the time you bring them out."

Micah goggled at him, and Devon grinned as the waitress headed for the kitchen.

"It must be a *bitch* keeping you fed," Micah finally said.

Devon patted his flat stomach. "I'm a growing boy."

Micah couldn't help his laugh. Devon's eyes gleamed, and he picked up his fork and gestured at Micah's plate.

"Eat."

Micah had the fork halfway to his mouth before he realized he'd obeyed without thinking. He narrowed his eyes, but Devon had turned his attention back to his pigs in blankets, seemingly unaware of Micah's internal dilemma.

Finally Micah shrugged and started eating. Devon sent him a smile but said nothing, and they ate in easy camaraderie for a while.

Sure enough, Devon was done by the time his pancakes were brought out, and he dove into them with glee as Micah watched with his mouth hanging open.

Halfway through, Devon looked up and guilt flickered across his face. "Sorry. Sean always says my table manners are terrible. Not that she really has room to talk, considering she can burp the alphabet."

"No, no," Micah said. "I'm just… impressed."

Devon ducked his head and speared another bite. "I work out to burn it back off again," he admitted. "And I don't do it often, but it was a sucky day, and I figured I deserved to indulge for once."

Micah flinched. "I really am sorry," he said to his plate. "I tend to lash out when I'm off-balance. It wasn't personal, I swear. Just me… being me. I'm not a nice person."

"Hey," Devon said. "Look at me."

Micah lifted his eyes. Devon set his fork down and gazed at him earnestly.

"We're starting over, remember? That means no more worrying about what happened. It was unfortunate, but it's done." His dimples flashed as he grinned. "Besides, Mr. Ego, it's not all about you. Other things happened today, you know."

"Yeah?" Micah said, smiling back in spite of himself. "Like what?"

Devon rolled his eyes. "Oh man. So, right after you left, this woman shows up. Dripping furs, a pearl choker, diamond rocks on her fingers, just… ostentatious with money, you know?"

Micah nodded. He knew the type all too well.

"And she tells me that her car should be ready, hurry it along, my good man, that type of thing." Devon snorted and took another bite. "Of course she doesn't bother telling me which car is hers, because apparently I should know who she is."

"Charming," Micah said.

"She acted incredibly offended when I asked her what her name was, but she eventually told me, and I went and found the car," Devon continued.

Micah wasn't really listening. He was too busy watching the way Devon's blue eyes lit up and how he waved his long hands for emphasis as he talked.

Devon was way too perfect, really. Gorgeous, funny, smart, *and* kind? It wasn't fair, and he was sure as hell out of Micah's league.

Micah lost his appetite and set his fork down, and Devon paused in his storytelling.

"You okay?"

Micah lifted a shoulder. "Not really hungry anymore."

"You've barely eaten half of the stack," Devon pointed out. "Are you really not hungry, or is something bothering you?"

"I...." Micah floundered, unsure what to say.

"Do you want to tell me about it?" Devon said.

"I don't even *know* you," Micah protested. "It's not fair to dump my problems on you."

Devon cocked his head. "Sometimes telling a stranger is the best way. I won't judge, because I don't have any preconceived notions." He leaned forward, and Micah gulped, caught in that blue gaze. "Go ahead and lay it on me."

Micah stared at him a moment but finally shrugged. "My... ex. Barrett. He was at this dinner I had to go to tonight for work."

Devon winced in sympathy. "Ugly breakup?"

"Ugly in general," Micah said dryly. "He's way too handsome for his own good—something I didn't realize until I was already in the relationship. He's used to everyone catering to him because of his looks, which is not... my experience."

Devon's brow furrowed. "Are you saying you're ugly?"

"I'm not *ugly*," Micah said hurriedly, "but I'm not on his level. Or yours." Before the last sentence was out, he regretted it, especially because of the way Devon frowned.

"Did he tell you that?"

Micah lifted a shoulder, unsure how to respond. Devon seemed angry, and that made Micah want to shrink in on himself and apologize for whatever he'd said to upset him. At the same time, he wanted to bristle and snap back. Devon didn't know him. He didn't get to pass judgment on Micah's life.

"Are you single right now?" Devon asked.

Micah nodded.

"Good," Devon said. He stood up and dropped cash on the table, enough to cover both their tabs, and held out a hand to Micah, who took it and slid out of the booth, confused.

Devon headed for the parking lot, and Micah trailed behind, still trying to figure out what he was doing.

Devon turned to face him, and Micah froze on the edge of the curb as he stepped closer.

"You are *gorgeous*," Devon said quietly. "I thought so the second you showed up in the shop—a ball of nerves in a nice suit. I wanted to know what you tasted like."

Micah stared, and Devon smiled at him and took another step nearer.

"I can't compare to—" Micah said, and Devon covered Micah's mouth with one long finger. It stopped the rest of his sentence and made him gulp.

"It's not a competition," Devon breathed, and then his finger was gone, and his lips were there, fitting over Micah's in a slow, easy slide. He flicked his tongue along the seam of Micah's mouth, asking to be let in.

Micah clutched Devon's arms as his mouth fell open and Devon pressed inside and took possession in gentle sweeps. Micah's knees were weak and he clung to Devon's bigger frame, helpless to do more than moan shakily and try to keep up. Devon growled and deepened the kiss until Micah was trembling as Devon's long arms wrapped around his waist and pulled him in tight.

When they finally broke for air, Devon rolled his hips forward, and Micah gasped as a very impressive erection ground against his thigh.

"You're really fucking hot, okay?" Devon whispered.

Micah squeezed his eyes shut and struggled for rational thought. "I…. Devon, I… have a question…."

Devon gently moved against him, his lip caught between his teeth, but he looked up at that. "Hmm?"

"I… oh God, I can't *think* when you're doing that—"

Devon slid a hand between them to cup Micah's erection.

Micah's head fell back as Devon squeezed and stroked, rubbing a thumb over the taut fabric.

"What was your question?" Devon asked.

"You're gonna get us banned from IHOP," Micah managed.

Devon grinned. "Worth it. You gonna ask that question or let me have my way with you?"

"Sweet *Jesus*," Micah choked and jerked back, willing himself not to come right then and there like a teenager.

Devon laughed with his head thrown back and his long neck exposed, and Micah had never wanted anything as much in his life as he did the young man in front of him, but he dragged himself back together and cleared his throat.

"Uh... who's Sean?"

Devon caught his breath and managed to bring the laughter under control. "Whew, I needed that. Sean's my sister." He tilted his head, still smiling. "Did you think she was my girlfriend?"

"Your *sister*," Micah said. "I... yeah. Just wanted to make sure I wasn't... encroaching."

"I'm free and clear, just like you," Devon said. "But thank you for asking."

Micah's smile spread slowly across his face. He felt light, effervescent. The horrible day was locked securely away and clean happiness had taken its place. "So what now?" he asked.

Devon shoved his hands in his pockets. "Well, I don't know about you, but I'd really like to take you out. A real restaurant, maybe a movie and a round of mini golf... what do you say?"

Micah shuddered. "No to the mini golf, qualified yes to dinner if I have a say in where we go, and highly doubtful on the movie. Way too much sticky shit on the floor." He braced himself. Devon would see just how high-maintenance he was and walk away. But Devon didn't move.

"It really bothers you, doesn't it?" he asked quietly.

Micah hunched his shoulders. "I'm sorry," he said. "I know I'm a basket case. It drove Barrett *nuts*."

"I think we've established that Barrett's an asshole," Devon said. "I haven't heard anything that's a deal breaker yet, so why don't we play it by ear? What do you think?"

"I think you're too good to be true," Micah said, and Devon laughed again.

"I snore," he said, as if imparting a state secret.

Micah grinned at him, dug for his wallet, and fished out a business card. He scribbled his personal number on the back and handed it over.

"Text or call me anytime," he said.

"I'll do that," Devon said. Rocking back on his heels, he slid the card into his pocket and blew his hair out of his eyes. "I guess I'll see you later."

"I guess you will," Micah said, smiling at him.

He was almost to his car, pulling his keys from his pocket, when he heard rapid footsteps behind him. And then Devon's big hand was on his arm, pulling Micah around to press him up against the car's cold metal frame.

Micah gasped and went limp in Devon's hands. His head fell back with a solid thunk against the roof of the car. The situation was startlingly similar to what had happened with Barrett earlier, but instead of being terrified, Micah had never felt safer.

Devon leaned forward, his breath warm against Micah's skin, and Micah gulped.

"Devon?"

"Couldn't let you leave without a good-night kiss," Devon murmured. And then his lips were on Micah's, his fingers tangled in Micah's hair, and he seemed to be doing his best to memorize the shape and taste and feel of Micah's mouth.

When Devon finally pulled away, he pressed their foreheads together for a long moment as they both waited for their ragged breathing to smooth out.

"You have no idea what you do to me," Devon whispered. Then he disappeared again, leaving Micah cold and alone.

CHAPTER THREE

MICAH WAS almost home when he got the first text.

Home safe?

He pulled into the parking lot and killed the engine. It pinged and ticked as the car cooled, and Micah unlocked his phone to compose a reply.

Just now. You?

He stepped out and climbed the stairs to his condo and got an answer as he was unlocking his front door.

Yep. Warm and cozy in bed.

Micah groaned as he shucked his jacket and hung it up beside the door. "Devon" and "bed" should not be mentioned in the same sentence. He set his shoes on the shelf and wove his way through the apartment toward the bedroom to collapse on his bed with a grateful sigh.

His phone buzzed again after a minute. *In bed yet?*

Micah snorted. *Actually, yes. Why?*

Devon was either a fast typist or using the dictation function, because his reply was almost instantaneous. *Because you looked really tired. You need to sleep.*

Micah stared at his phone for a minute. *Don't need a babysitter, Mallory.*

Thinking that's up for debate ;)

Micah narrowed his eyes and didn't answer.

It wasn't long before Devon texted again. *Hey, didn't mean to offend. I'm sure you're a fully functioning adult.*

Micah sighed and rolled over onto his stomach. He had no idea how to respond.

His phone buzzed. *Still want to eat?*

Yeah. Was thinking Madeleine's, downtown. Know it?

By reputation. Formal wear?

Micah stifled a yawn. *Nice suit will do.*

Friday, 8 PM?

Micah's eyes drooped. He needed to get up, change into pajamas, and go through his nighttime ritual, but he was just so tired. *Yeah,* he managed to type between yawns.

Go to sleep. Talk tomorrow.

Micah was asleep before he could reply.

WHEN FRIDAY rolled around, Micah would have talked himself into believing that he'd imagined the whole thing if it hadn't been for the texts Devon kept sending throughout the week.

He woke up to the first one with sleep creases on his cheek and his hair standing on end.

Morning, Sleeping Beauty.

Micah snorted. *Your standards for beauty are unsettlingly low.*

He didn't get a reply immediately and headed for the bathroom as he waited. His phone buzzed while he was brushing his teeth.

I wish you wouldn't talk about yourself that way.

Micah spat and rinsed.

Not looking for compliments. Sleep well?

Considering was the reply.

Micah padded into his spotless kitchen and pulled out a frying pan. *Considering what?*

The answer was immediate.

Couldn't stop thinking about kissing you.

Micah dropped the frying pan on his foot. He hopped on the other foot in silent agony for a minute, unable to make a noise, and his phone buzzed.

Too much info?

Micah fumbled for the phone, trying to figure out what to say. *More like not enough. Gonna need details.*

He held his breath until the phone buzzed again.

Mostly thinking about the little noises you made. The way you held on to me. How you kissed back like there was nowhere else you'd rather be.

Micah closed his eyes and took a shaky breath.

There wasn't, he replied.

:)

Micah sank to the floor, cradling his abused foot, and whimpered. This motherfucker was going to be the death of him.

THE NEXT exchange came that Wednesday at noon.

Turkey on rye. Possibly the most boring sandwich in the world.

Micah read the text with a smile. *So get something else?*

Can't leave the shop. Dependent on my sister's goodwill for food, and she's mad at me.

Micah's smile slipped. *What happened?*

Remember the rich snob?

Yeah.

I... might've been rude to her when she called to complain about something.

Micah snorted. *Good for you.*

Not quite what Sean said. "We need the money, Devon. You can't go insulting the customers, Devon!"

Micah bit his lip and hit the intercom on his desk. "Norma, I need you to look for a Mallory Auto, down on Seventh Street. Send them two hundred dollars for payment of an outstanding debt."

"Yes, Mr. Ellis," Norma said, her voice tinny over the speaker.

Micah picked up his cell phone. *Just desserts, I'd say.*

That's what I told her! She doesn't agree. Has this weird thing about paying bills, food in our bellies, all that.

Micah smiled. *And you're a lily of the field?*

Oh no, I worry as much as her. I just try not to let her see it. She's got enough on her plate.

Micah pressed the intercom button again. "Make that two hundred and fifty, Norma."

Just the two of you, then? he sent.

Against the world. Well, in Toronto, anyway. Our mom lives in Vancouver. Dad died a while ago. What are you having for lunch?

Micah grimaced guiltily. *Ah... steak?*

There was a brief silence.

I might hate you a little bit right now.

Micah grinned. *I can live with that.*

He put the phone down and tried to focus on work as memories of the way Devon's mouth tasted kept intruding. When his phone buzzed again, Micah nearly knocked his coffee off the desk as he lunged for it.

It wasn't Devon, though. Instead an unfamiliar number with a Toronto area code had sent him a message.

Micah frowned and unlocked the phone to read it.

Hey, gorgeous, you busy tonight?

Wrong number, Micah sent back.

His intercom went off as he put the phone down again.

"Jenny Roberts is on line one for you, Mr. Ellis," Norma said. "She's with that new megastore downtown. They need top-level management for their new location."

"Put her through, Norma. Thank you," Micah said.

THE THURSDAY before their date, he didn't hear from Devon until he was pushing his front door open with a sigh, home late yet again. He hung up his coat, set his shoes on the shelf, and dragged through the kitchen and into the bedroom, where he changed into comfortable clothes and collapsed on the bed.

His phone buzzed, and Micah groped for it, still facedown on the mattress, and rolled just enough to read the text.

Looking forward to tomorrow.

Micah couldn't help but smile. *Me too.*

Hope I don't smell like mothballs. Haven't worn this suit in ages.

Micah's brain shorted out at the thought of Devon, tall, gorgeous Devon, in a suit—bow tie, hair slicked back, broad shoulders and slim waist accentuated by the coat.... Micah muffled his groan in the bedspread.

Pick you up or meet you there? he sent.

Mind picking me up? Devon asked.

Was hoping you'd say that. I should go to sleep. I'm gonna be useless tomorrow.

Devon sent back, *You and me both. I have to figure out how to convince this guy I'm seeing just how hot he is. It's going to take all my wits.*

Micah laughed even as he felt a blush creeping up his neck. *You're ridiculous.*

MICAH SPENT all day Friday forgetting basic functions, including how to answer his phone and respond to e-mails. He was gone before Norma had her desk cleared, and dashed from the building to his car. Freshly clean and shaved at home, he dithered for a while on which suit to wear and finally decided on the pinstripe and his favorite tie—the green one his ex-girlfriend, Kali, had said made his dark eyes stand out.

In no time at all, he pulled up in front of the address Devon had sent him, and butterflies surged in his stomach. He took a steadying breath, climbed from the car, and tugged on his jacket, smoothing his hair back again as he headed up the sidewalk.

He knocked on the door, and thundering footsteps sounded from inside the house. Micah took a step back, his eyes widening in alarm as the door slammed open and a tall, blonde woman nearly fell through. She shut the door behind her and examined Micah.

"Ah...," Micah said intelligently. "I'm... here to pick up Devon?"

The woman's eyes, bright green and laser-sharp, narrowed. "What are your intentions toward my little brother?"

"You're Sean!" Micah said and held out a hand.

Sean accepted the hand and shook it firmly. She wasn't as tall as Devon, but she still towered over Micah. She was opening her mouth to say something when the door opened again. An arm snaked around Sean's neck, and she was yanked back through the opening.

Micah was left gaping on the porch as the sounds of a scuffle erupted from inside.

After a minute, Devon appeared. He straightened his jacket and smoothed his hair back. "Sorry about that," he said and offered Micah a brilliant smile. "Sean considers herself both my mother *and* my father. She can get a little... overprotective. Shall we go?"

Micah cast an uneasy glance at the door. "She's not going to come after me with a shotgun, is she?"

"Doubt it," Devon said airily. "*Probably* not." He took Micah's arm and dragged him down the sidewalk toward the car as Sean opened the door behind them.

"Have him back by midnight," she shouted.

Devon shot her the middle finger without looking, bundled Micah into the driver's seat, and slid into the passenger side.

A little dazed, Micah started the car and pulled away from the curb.

Devon inspected him from across the car. "You look really nice," he said.

"So do you," Micah said. "Not even a hint of mothballs."

Devon's dimples flashed. They rode in silence to the restaurant, and Micah found it hard to concentrate with Devon so close to him. That lanky frame was folded into Micah's small car in a position that couldn't be comfortable, but Devon wasn't complaining. He was just... *looking*.

Micah flicked his turn signal on and shifted his weight. "You're not making this easy," he pointed out.

"I'm sorry, was I supposed to?" Devon asked, grinning. "Maybe I'm just enjoying the view. Oh hey, thanks for the flowers."

Micah blinked, thrown. "Flowers?"

"The lilies," Devon said. "They're very pretty. Thank you."

Micah made a noncommittal noise. Had he sent Devon flowers and somehow forgotten? Maybe he'd told Norma to do it. Hell, maybe Norma had just done it for him without being asked—she was proactive that way. He'd ask her on Monday.

Micah downshifted, and Devon glanced around.

"Oh, are we there already? Pity."

"Not hungry?" Micah asked as he pulled into the parking lot.

"Starving," Devon said, and Micah shivered at the dark promise in his tone.

He parked, and Devon was on him before he could turn the car off. He twisted his long body over the console, gripped the back of Micah's neck, and pulled him into a hungry kiss.

Micah groaned and kissed back. He slid his hands into Devon's hair and held his head steady as they explored each other's mouths. Finally Devon broke the kiss to nibble his way down Micah's neck.

"Been... thinking...," he murmured.

Micah struggled to gather his wits. "Ah... about?"

Devon's tongue dragged hot and wet along the soft skin under Micah's ear, and Micah shivered again, helpless.

"I don't want food," Devon whispered. He pulled back enough to look Micah in the eye. "I just want you."

"*Fuck.*" Micah pressed the heel of his hand against the base of his straining erection. "You're going to *kill* me. I hope you know that."

"We have a couple of options," Devon said as if he hadn't heard him. "We can go back to your place or we can find a hotel, my treat."

Micah shuddered. "My place," he said. "Very much my place."

Devon settled back into his seat and smiled at him. "Home, Jeeves," he commanded, and waved a hand.

Micah arched an eyebrow, but he said nothing as he put the car into reverse and pulled out. He fished his phone from his pocket, unlocked it, and tossed it to Devon.

"Make yourself useful," he said. "Call the restaurant and cancel the reservation so they can give the table to someone else."

Devon obeyed and shot Micah a smile. "Gorgeous *and* considerate," he said as he lifted the phone to his ear. "Stop being so perfect. You're making the rest of us look bad."

Micah just laughed.

THE DRIVE back to Micah's condo went quickly, and they climbed the stairs in silence, with Devon a warm presence at Micah's back and his big hand on Micah's spine just above his ass.

Micah unlocked his door with hands that only trembled a little and stepped aside for Devon to enter.

Devon whistled as he entered. "Dude. This place is amazing. How do you ever tear yourself away to go to work?"

Micah shut the door and went through his usual ritual with coat and shoes, smiling to himself. He held out his hand for Devon's coat, and Devon willingly handed it over and wandered into the living room as Micah hung it up.

Micah glanced around and saw the place through Devon's eyes. Twenty-foot ceilings soared over the kitchen's hardwood floors and granite countertops. The open floor plan gave way to plush carpet in the sunken living room. A built-in couch spanned two sides of the room, and a huge television hung on the far wall. Devon stood in the middle of the space, staring around him.

"That couch looks incredibly comfortable," he commented. "Do you ever fall asleep out here?"

Micah barely managed to contain his shudder. "Sleeping is for bed," he said primly, and Devon grinned.

"I'm going to drive you *crazy*." He collapsed on the couch and stretched his long legs in front of him.

Micah stood on the step, wondering what to do, and Devon held out a hand.

"Come here."

Micah obeyed before he thought about it. Devon caught his hand and pulled until Micah got the hint and swung a leg over Devon's lap to straddle him.

Devon settled his hands on Micah's thighs to keep him in position and Micah swallowed hard as his nerves swamped him. He didn't *know* Devon. What was he doing? He'd brought him into his home, opened his life to him, and Devon could.... Devon could—

Devon cupped Micah's face with big hands. "Look at me," he said gently, and Micah lifted his eyes. Devon smiled again. "It's okay," he said. "We don't have to do anything at all. We could just watch a movie. Or cuddle. I could cook for you, if you like. We won't do anything you don't *want* to do. You hear me? And we can stop at any time."

Micah squeezed his eyes shut and pressed their foreheads together. From this close, Devon's breath ghosted warm across his face. He smelled wonderful—fancy shampoo and a deep, rich aftershave that hinted at piney forests and snow-covered mountains—and Micah took a deep breath and slowly relaxed.

"I want you," he said, his voice almost inaudible.

Devon brushed a thumb across his cheekbone. "Okay," he murmured. "We'll take it slow. Why don't we start with a kiss?"

Micah pressed their lips together before Devon was done talking, and Devon huffed an amused breath into Micah's mouth as he curled a hand around the back of Micah's neck and took control. He dipped inside and tasted Micah's tongue and lips, and Micah let himself melt into it, willingly ceding the reins to him as Devon began to explore.

He unbuttoned Micah's shirt one-handed to slip inside and splay long fingers across Micah's chest. He found a nipple and pinched gently, and Micah jerked and groaned. Looping his arms around Devon's neck, Micah wove his fingers through Devon's soft brown hair.

Devon smiled against Micah's lips. "So responsive," he whispered. "God, I could do this all day."

"Think we could… maybe… do it in the bed?" Micah managed.

Devon pulled back and looked at Micah's face. "Yeah, okay," he said. "We can do that. Lead the way, gorgeous."

Micah suppressed the roll of his eyes as he scrambled off Devon's lap, but something must have shown in his face, because Devon stood up and pulled Micah back around to face him and tipped Micah's chin up with one finger.

"You. Are. Gorgeous," he said, his eyes boring into Micah's.

Micah swallowed hard and took a step back.

Devon sighed. "I'll make you believe it if it's the last thing I do," he said, but his tone was fond, and he gestured for Micah to lead the way.

Micah's head spun as he headed for the bedroom. How had he gone from insulting Devon's intellect to having *sex* with him? Devon braced Micah's hips with both hands, and Micah missed the doorknob on the first try.

Devon breathed a quiet laugh over the back of Micah's neck, his lips gentle against the bumps of his spine, and Micah shivered.

"Everything okay?" Devon murmured, his voice rich with gentle teasing.

Micah managed to get the door open and twisted to glare up at him. "Everything's fine, you fucker. I can't *think* with you so close."

Devon laughed and pushed Micah through the door, across the room—with a sideways glance at the punching bag in the corner—and onto the bed. Micah landed with a bounce, and Devon loomed over him. His eyes were dark with amusement.

"Let's see if we can turn your brain off completely," he said and dropped his head to mouth the tented fabric over Micah's crotch.

Micah whimpered as Devon dampened the cloth with his tongue, and when Devon finally dragged his zipper down and pulled him out, Micah's hips bucked up against Devon's hand.

"Easy," Devon murmured with a smile in his voice. "We'll get there. Let me look at you for a minute."

Silence fell, broken by Micah's ragged breathing, as Devon inspected him, and Micah had to resist the urge to fold his arms across his little belly roll.

"Beautiful," Devon said, and there was nothing but truth in his voice.

A thought struck Micah, and he froze, horrified, and scrambled backward, out from under Devon's body as he fumbled to tuck himself away in quick, jerky movements.

"Micah?" Devon said. He looked worried.

"I… oh God, Devon, are you clean? I don't know how I didn't ask before. What's *wrong* with me? I should've asked—" Micah's breathing sped up and he clutched his knees and struggled to keep his head clear and not let the panic overwhelm him.

"*Breathe*," Devon said. He followed him up the bed but kept a foot of space between them. "I'm clean, Micah. I thought you might want to see my test results, considering—" He waved a hand vaguely. "Anyway I brought them with me." He fished his wallet out of his pants pocket, pulled a piece of paper from it, and held it up. "Look. See?"

Micah took the paper with a trembling hand. Devon was telling the truth. He was clean and had been tested within the past month. He closed his eyes and took a deep breath. "I'm sorry," he whispered. "I'm so sorry. I didn't mean—"

"It's okay," Devon said. "It's *okay*, Micah. Deep breaths, okay?"

Micah gestured toward the bedside table. "My results are in there," he managed between breaths. "I'm… clean. You can see—"

Devon's eyes creased as he smiled. "I trust you," he said. "Micah… can I hold you?"

Micah took a deep, shuddering inhale and finally nodded. "I… yes. I'd like that."

Devon gently pulled him into his arms, and they lay down together on the bedspread, Devon solid and warm against Micah's back.

"Maybe no sex right now," Devon murmured. "I don't think you're in the right headspace for it."

Micah closed his eyes, not wanting to admit to the rush of relief that swamped him. After a minute, though, he twisted enough to see Devon's face. "But later, yeah?"

Devon pecked him on the nose—a quick, dry brush of lips. "Absolutely."

Silence fell, and Micah couldn't remember the last time he'd felt so comfortable, especially considering Devon was practically a stranger.

"So what kinds of things do you like to do in your spare time?" Devon asked. His breath was warm on the nape of Micah's neck.

Micah mostly managed to hide his shiver. "I… oh, I watch cooking shows a lot."

"Yeah?" Devon sounded interested. "Do you like to cook?"

"When I have time," Micah admitted. "I've been teaching myself some traditional Indian recipes, with the help of YouTube and stuff, but it's kinda slow going. I fuck it up a lot more than I get it right."

Devon laughed quietly. "Well, you can practice on me anytime."

"What about you?" Micah asked. "Do you have any hobbies?"

"Baseball," Devon said, sounding amused. "I play for a league here in town."

"Really?" Micah said. He twisted to see Devon's face. "From your height, I would've guessed basketball."

"Most people do." Devon grinned. "But no, never wanted to play anything but baseball. Actually thought about going pro, but I fucked up my arm my second year of college, and that was that—the scouts weren't interested anymore."

"I'm sorry," Micah said, feeling two inches tall.

Devon squeezed Micah's waist. "It was nine years ago. I've had time to adjust. Hey, maybe you can come to one of my games."

Micah stiffened at the thought of all those germs, the open air and the people and the dirt.

Devon patted his stomach. "Just think about it," he said gently.

"Okay," Micah said.

"When did you figure out you were gay?" Devon asked.

"I'm bi, actually," Micah said. "Is that a problem?" He turned to see Devon's face, and Devon kissed his nose again.

"Not for me it's not. How old were you?"

"Twelve," Micah said, relaxing. "His name was Tim, and he had really pretty brown eyes. What about you?" Tim had stolen a kiss from him behind the bleachers, and Micah had gone home floating on air to tell his foster mother, who grounded him for a week.

"Completely gay here," Devon said. "But it took me until college to really figure it out—probably because I was so preoccupied with baseball for so long."

Micah yawned, and Devon nosed the curls at the nape of his neck.

"Take a nap if you like," he murmured. "Maybe we can fool around later."

They fell asleep that way, and Micah felt warm and safe for the first time in far too long.

HE WOKE early the next morning. Devon was still sound asleep next to him. Micah slowly wriggled out from under Devon's heavy arm, holding his breath to keep from waking him up. He tiptoed to the bathroom, took care of business. Then he pulled his phone out of the pocket of his dress pants to check for missed messages and neatly folded the pants on the back of the toilet.

He had one message from Norma reminding him that he had a meeting with Jenny Roberts on Monday and then two more from an unlisted number.

Both were just a row of question marks. They glowed in the predawn light.

Micah sighed, turned the phone off, and left it on top of his pants. He was going to have to talk to the phone company and see if they were having problems.

In his boxers and T-shirt, he padded back to the bedroom and slid back in under Devon's arm. Devon never did more than stir and pull him closer.

Devon definitely didn't snore. Micah smiled and fell asleep again.

WHEN HE woke next, there was a hand under his waistband, circling his cock and stroking it in slow, gentle sweeps.

Micah arched his back and sighed. Devon kissed the back of his neck.

"This okay?" he whispered.

Micah pressed back against him in answer, and Devon gasped as he ground his erection against Micah's ass. Micah reached behind him to grip Devon's hip and pull him closer.

Devon groaned, and his hand sped up as Micah hardened under his attentions. His head fell back against Devon's shoulder and warmth spread through his body—a fire slowly building in his groin. *Yes, take me, own me, turn my brain off, please—*

Devon kissed the back of Micah's neck, nosed his way up it, and then sucked Micah's earlobe into his mouth. Micah turned his head to give him better access and brought his arm up to cup Devon's head as Devon thrust his hips forward and stroked Micah's shaft faster.

He bit down on the lobe, and Micah sobbed a breath and came over Devon's hand in hot throbs, shuddering in the ecstasy that flooded him. Devon eased him through it, murmuring quiet encouragement that Micah barely heard.

When he finally came back to himself, Devon's hips were still moving restlessly against Micah's ass.

"Can I come on your back?" he whispered, and Micah moaned.

"*God* yes, Devon, *please.*"

That was all Devon needed. His hand withdrew, and Micah heard a zipper being pulled down. Then Devon was stroking himself, breathing hard against Micah's neck.

"Jesus, Micah, you're so beautiful. Wanted this all week… couldn't think about anything else…." He groaned again as his hips bucked forward, and Micah squirmed back more until Devon's cock rubbed against his lower back with every stroke.

It didn't take long at all before Devon's breathing was harsh in Micah's ear. "God yes, 'm gonna—" He froze, and wet heat splashed on Micah's skin in heavy spurts.

Finally Devon wrapped an arm around Micah's ribs and tugged him back against him until Micah's ass was securely nestled in Devon's hips. Micah stretched and sighed as Devon kissed his shoulder.

"Thank you," Devon murmured. "That was incredible."

Micah turned his head and caught Devon's lips in a kiss. He was getting twitchy, thinking about the come all over himself and the sheets, and Devon must have noticed the beginnings of his distress.

"Come on. Let's get cleaned up," he said and tugged Micah off the mattress. Micah followed him into the bathroom on slightly shaky legs, his brain pleasantly fuzzy as Devon turned the water on and adjusted the temperature. Then he turned toward Micah to help him pull off his clothes.

"That is a very nice tub," Devon remarked.

Micah blinked, trying to focus, and glanced at his huge bathtub on the other side of the room. "I like space to stretch out."

Devon raised an eyebrow. "We'll have to take advantage of that sometime."

They shared a warm, lazy shower, with Micah clinging to Devon's neck for most of it, content to let Devon soap him up and rinse him off.

When they were done, Devon pulled away enough to drop his head and kiss him. "Hungry?"

Micah nodded as his awareness slowly filtered back, and Devon smiled.

"Do you always go so far away when you come?"

Micah pressed his face against Devon's chest. "When it's good I do," he admitted.

Devon's laugh rumbled through Micah, and he tightened his arms. "I'll take that as a compliment. Let's get dressed, and then you can watch me make breakfast."

"Okay," Micah said. He caught Devon's hand as he stepped out of the shower, and Devon turned back to face him. "Thank you," Micah said.

Devon's eyes softened, and he leaned in for another kiss that Micah returned willingly. "Let's go eat, shall we?"

CHAPTER FOUR

IN THE kitchen Micah curled up in one of his sturdy dining chairs and drew his feet up so he could prop his chin on his knees.

Devon rooted through the cupboards, after a quick glance at Micah to make sure he wasn't crossing any lines. Micah just nodded, still drowsy and a little blissed out, and Devon's smile was affectionate as he turned back to the cupboard and pulled out ingredients.

"Do you eat carbs?" he asked over his shoulder.

Micah snorted. "You've seen me. 'Course I eat carbs."

"Just making sure," Devon said. "In that case I'm thinking pancakes. You've got all the ingredients, except for vanilla, looks like."

Micah waved a languid hand. "'S in the cabinet on the other side of the stove. Who puts vanilla in pancakes, though?"

Devon arched an eyebrow. "*Civilized* people, that's who."

He found the vanilla with a triumphant noise and added the ingredients to the bowl he'd pulled out earlier. Micah just watched, enjoying the way Devon moved—all grace and careful economy, as though he were too used to knocking things over with his long limbs.

"Even if you hadn't told me, I could tell by the way this kitchen's laid out that you enjoy cooking as well," Devon said as he switched the griddle on and turned to stir the batter.

"Figured that much was obvious," Micah said dryly.

Devon frowned. "Are you getting down on yourself again?"

Micah shrugged. "It's the truth," he said. "And I'm not fishing for compliments. I eat too much, and I don't exercise enough. Plus my wicked sweet tooth. Not a good combination."

Devon set the whisk down, rounded the counter, and advanced on Micah with a determined look in his blue eyes. "I have had just about enough of this," he said.

Alarm flashed through Micah and he flinched backward as Devon loomed over him and then dropped to his knees on the hardwood floor in front of him. Micah winced, but Devon didn't seem to notice. He was too busy pulling Micah's legs down and then tugging him right off the chair and into his lap.

Micah gasped and clutched Devon's shoulders as Devon fixed him with a serious look. He didn't say anything, though. He just pressed their lips together and kissed Micah as though there were nowhere else he wanted to be, no one else he wanted to touch, running his big hands up and down Micah's back.

When they broke for air, Micah blinked hazily and Devon huffed a quiet laugh as he curved his hand over the back of Micah's neck to keep him upright.

"You're beautiful, Mike," he murmured.

Micah winced at the hated nickname and immediately wanted to kick himself. Devon didn't know how much Micah loathed the appellation. He hadn't done it on purpose.

Devon's eyes narrowed as he watched him, and Micah swallowed hard.

"Micah," Devon said gently. "You're beautiful."

Micah relaxed and searched his face. Devon smiled at him, his hand still warm and solid on the nape of Micah's neck.

Micah smiled back. "I'm short, I'm chubby, I have a big nose and plain black eyes and hair. I'm… boring."

"You couldn't be boring if you tried," Devon said. "You have this smile—God, Micah, you need to smile more. It's amazing. It lights up your eyes, and I could watch you do it all day."

The smell of hot metal reached Micah's nose, and he jerked his head up just as Devon clearly realized he'd left the hot griddle on the stove. He scrambled upright and nearly sent Micah sprawling.

Micah caught himself on the chair and climbed back onto it, his legs still shaky. He wrapped his arms around his knees to watch as Devon dashed for the stove and poured the first cup of batter onto the pan.

"Sorry," Devon said ruefully.

"It's fine. Do I get animal shapes?" Micah asked.

Devon sent him a grin. "Sure thing. Amoebas are animals, right? You're getting amoeba pancakes."

"Your pancake game is *weak*," Micah said, laughing, and Devon's grin widened.

"Doesn't have to be strong when they taste as good as mine do."

Sure enough, when he slid the first one onto the plate, Micah took a deep sniff and then a careful bite, and his eyes got big.

"Okay," he said, his mouth full. "You weren't kidding."

Devon looked delighted. "I'll make some brownies for you soon. Sean says they're the best in the city." He continued to flip pancakes as Micah relaxed, content to watch. It was nice to just *be* with Devon, who was so undemanding and kind. After one night with him, Micah was already more comfortable in his company than he had been a year into his relationship with Barrett, who'd expected to be waited on hand and foot.

"So why is there a punching bag in your bedroom?" Devon asked.

Micah blinked, startled. He'd forgotten all about the punching bag. He'd been furious when he came home one day to discover that Barrett had installed it in his bedroom without asking him first. His gorgeous high ceiling had an enormous hole in it, all so Barrett could take out his aggression on an inanimate object—when he wasn't taking it out on Micah.

"My ex," he said briefly. "Liked to hit things. I keep meaning to get rid of it."

Devon watched him for a moment but finally shrugged and changed the subject.

Micah nibbled on his pancakes and listened with one ear to the story Devon told. But somewhere in there he dozed off.

Devon touched his leg to wake him, and Micah jolted upright with a gasp. "I'm sorry!" he said. "I was listening, I swear!"

Devon's brow furrowed. "Dude, it was a story about Sean getting drunk and me putting her hand in a bowl of warm water. Relax."

Micah rubbed his face and struggled to calm his heart rate. Devon's eyes stayed fixed on his face, concern creasing his forehead.

"You don't work today, do you?" he asked.

Micah shook his head.

Devon smiled. "Good. In that case, today you're mine."

Micah drew back slightly. "Uh, Devon...."

Devon patted his knee. "Trust me, okay?" He helped him to his feet and pointed him in the direction of the bedroom. "Go get dressed. Decent clothes, nothing too fancy."

Micah dug in his heels and shot him a look over his shoulder. "You coming with me?"

Devon snorted a laugh. "If I do, we're not going to leave the bedroom."

"I repeat," Micah said. "You coming with me?"

Devon groaned. "Fuck it. I'll make the rest of the pancakes later." He turned the griddle off and spun to catch up to Micah, who was already halfway down the hall. Devon caught him right before they got to the door and picked him up to drop him laughing on the bed.

Then Devon was on top of him, lowering his long body until he pressed Micah firmly into the mattress and their lips met.

There was no rush this time around, no hurried dash for the finish line. Time blurred and slowed, narrowing to the slide and drag of hands on skin, the sharp nip of Devon's teeth, his breath hot against Micah's throat. And all too soon, Micah shuddered through his second orgasm of the morning as Devon crooned filthy encouragement in his ear.

Then it was Devon's turn, and Devon caught his trembling hand when Micah tried to reach for him. He lifted it to his lips. "You're no use to me like this, Ellis," he said. His other hand worked steadily as he spoke, and he rolled his hips forward and ground his erection against Micah's thigh. "My God, you're so gorgeous," he growled, and Micah squeezed his eyes shut.

He could almost believe it when Devon looked at him like that, touched him with that sort of reverent wonder that Micah had done absolutely nothing to deserve. And he wanted desperately to hear it again, to understand what Devon saw in him, but Devon had pressed his forehead against Micah's chest, coming over Micah's leg on a choked groan.

Micah held out for a full two minutes—a new personal best—before he couldn't keep the twitch in any longer and Devon lifted his head with remorse in his eyes.

"Shit, I'm sorry," he said. "Let's get you cleaned up."

He helped Micah to the bathroom, and they had their second shower, Micah still high on endorphins and holding on to Devon to keep himself upright.

Devon laughed deep in his chest when they were done. "You are adorable. C'mon. Let's get you dressed, and then I'll wash the bedding while you rest on the couch and come back from wherever it is you are right now."

Micah helped Devon dress him and fumbled for the pant legs until Devon gently set him on the edge of the bed and told him to be still. Micah faded out again then, and he came back to himself curled up on the couch. Devon was nowhere in sight, and Micah sat up in alarm.

"Devon?"

Footsteps sounded on the hardwood, and Devon appeared from the direction of the laundry room. "Hey," he said as he sat down next to Micah, "how are you feeling? You spaced out pretty spectacularly there."

Micah couldn't help but lean against Devon's reassuring bulk, and Devon wrapped an arm around him.

"Can I expect that a lot?"

Micah shook his head, still remembering how to form words. He felt wonderful—light and clean and empty—but it was taking a while to gather his thoughts.

"Haven't hit sub space that hard in a long time," he murmured through a yawn.

Devon was quiet above him. "Sub space?"

Micah froze, and mental clarity rushed in on him with a startling snap. "It's... nothing. Just a word to describe where my head goes. Where did you want to go today?"

"I was thinking the aquarium," Devon said, clearly deciding to let the matter go.

Micah pulled away and peered up at him. "I'm not a fan of fish," he said.

Devon dropped a kiss on his nose. "I think you'll like this."

Micah sighed but nodded.

HE WAS in hell again. But it wasn't dirt that surrounded him this time. It was millions of gallons of water and screaming children on all sides.

In theory Micah had nothing against kids. He even, distantly, wouldn't mind having one or two of his own, if he ever got his neuroses under control. But they were tiny walking germ factories, and every time one dashed past him, he flinched.

Was it a school holiday or a field trip? He neither knew nor cared. But if he didn't leave soon, he was going to have a full-blown panic attack in the middle of the fucking aquarium and probably scar more than one child for life in the process.

Micah's breathing sped up as he suddenly realized he couldn't see Devon. Where had he gone? Had he seriously left Micah to deal with this all by himself? Micah gritted his teeth and started backing for the exit.

Devon settled his hands on Micah's shoulders, and Micah took a shaky breath of relief and relaxed into Devon's body.

"Easy," Devon murmured. "Sorry, sweetheart. I stopped to look at the seahorses. You're safe. I'm here." His breath was warm against Micah's ear, and Micah closed his eyes and swallowed hard.

A child shrieked nearby, and Micah flinched again. Devon tightened his hands, and they began moving, walking toward the wall. They didn't stop until Micah was nearly up against the glass, and then Devon wrapped his big coat around him and cocooned Micah in a Devon-sweet warmth.

"Look," Devon said quietly and pointed with his free hand. "See the manta ray?"

Micah looked where he was pointing, his head against Devon's solid chest as he watched the huge black fish with white spots undulate through the blue water in no particular hurry.

"Keep watching him," Devon said. "Don't think about anything except that ray. Just… watch him swim and let me hold you. Can you do that?"

Micah nodded almost dreamily, and Devon curved his arms around him. He narrated various aquarium facts into his ear as Micah watched the manta ray float around the tank. He found a button on the placket of Devon's coat and absently felt the ridges with his thumb as his mind drifted and calm began to fill him again.

He had no idea how much time passed before Devon let go and he stepped back. Micah glanced around and came back to himself. The kids were gone, and they were alone in the room. Devon smiled.

"Feel any better?"

Micah nodded, stunned. He'd never even noticed the children leaving. "How… how did you do that?" he croaked. "I was about to have a full-on meltdown, and you… stopped it."

"*You* stopped it," Devon corrected. "I just helped. A little. Ready for lunch?"

Micah nodded again, and Devon grinned and took his hand. "I wanted to cook for you again," he said. "But that means going to

Wychwood Barns. Want to wait in the car while I get what I need or come in with me?"

"I'll wait in the car," Micah said. He shivered at the thought of the open-air market. "Why are you being so nice to me?"

Devon stopped and turned to face him, towering above him on the sloped walkway that led out of the manta ray exhibit. "Because you deserve it," he said with honest confusion in his voice. "Because I *like* you."

Micah closed his eyes briefly. "I don't—"

Devon stopped the rest of his sentence with his finger across Micah's lips, and Micah opened his eyes, startled.

"I don't think the aquarium would take kindly to me making love to you right here, so how about you don't finish that sentence?" Devon said.

Micah couldn't help the laugh that bubbled up. "Okay."

Devon tugged him up the ramp, and they passed the open tank where the mantas were available to be petted. Devon cocked an eyebrow at him as Micah watched a manta breach the surface under a little boy's hand and then swim past.

Micah shivered and shook his head. Devon stopped again as they passed through the gift shop, and he dug in his pocket for his wallet. He picked up a soft, stuffed manta ray plush toy and handed it to the cashier with a cheeky grin. As soon as she scanned it, Devon turned and pushed it at Micah, who sputtered as he accepted it.

"You didn't have to—"

"Shut up. I wanted to," Devon said. He took Micah's hand again and pulled him outside as Micah hugged the stuffed ray to his chest.

On their way to the truck, Micah caught a glimpse of a crimson Porsche and stiffened.

"Everything okay?" Devon asked.

"Fine," Micah said, and he quickened his pace. There were a lot of red sports cars in Toronto. It was just a coincidence.

CHAPTER FIVE

MICAH WASN'T actually sure how it happened because it evolved so seamlessly, but one minute he was insulting Devon in the auto shop and the next, Devon was such a big part of his life that Micah wasn't sure how he'd gotten along without him before.

He cooked for Devon, who had a voracious appetite and would eat almost anything. Micah practiced his Indian recipes on him as often as possible, although it was hit-or-miss at times. Still, Devon ate the disasters and assured him they were delicious and even asked for more, and Micah thought maybe he could learn to love this man who laughed at his jokes and touched him so gently, as though Micah were a precious gift he'd never expected to receive.

Devon stayed over more nights than not, and Micah grew used to waking up to the delicious smell of pancakes and bacon. Micah would roll out of bed and follow his nose to the kitchen, where Devon would drop the spatula, scoop Micah up, and kiss him until they were both short on air.

That was one of Micah's favorite things, he decided. They'd been dating for a month, and Devon still lit up like a Christmas tree every time he saw Micah, like he was the only thing Devon had ever wanted. It humbled Micah, left him breathless, and he couldn't get enough of it.

BUT MICAH didn't want to think about Devon. All that did was remind him how much better than him Devon was—how Micah had done nothing to deserve him—and *that* just made him angry.

He was having a horrible day. He'd slept through his alarm, which never happened, so he was already off-balance and scrambling to catch up by the time he got to the office, where he was greeted by Norma with a fistful of messages and a worried look in her kind eyes.

"Barrett called," she said.

The day went downhill from there. He lost an important client due to his distraction, and then the restaurant screwed up his lunch order and Micah found a smear of lipstick on his glass, but not before he'd drunk half the contents.

The ensuing panic attack shut him down for the rest of the afternoon, and when he was finally able to pull himself back together and he gathered his things to leave the office, his cell phone rang and Micah answered without looking.

"Micah," Barrett purred.

Micah's head fell back, and he closed his eyes. His stomach roiled. "Hello, Barrett," he said, keeping his voice even with an effort. "To what do I owe this honor?"

"Don't be like that," Barrett chided. "I've missed you, Mike."

"*Do not call me that*," Micah hissed. He kept the contents of his stomach down with difficulty.

Barrett's voice sharpened. "I'll call you whatever I want to, *Mike*."

"If you're not calling to discuss business, I'm hanging up," Micah said desperately.

"Oh, I am," Barrett said. "I'm thinking of switching account managers, and I'm going to request you."

Micah froze as horror flooded him. "That's... not a good idea."

"Why? Because we have 'history'?" Barrett said, and amusement was rich in his voice. "Please. We're both adults. I'm sure we can look past that."

Micah swallowed hard. "Fine. I have to go now."

"I hear you have a new boyfriend," Barrett said, and Micah's blood turned to ice.

"How—"

"Doesn't matter," Barrett said. "Does he Dom you, pet? Does he pin you down and take what he wants from you, let you worship his cock? Does he hurt you, make you beg so pretty, mark you the way I know you like?"

Micah pressed the back of his hand against his mouth and struggled for air.

"Oh," Barrett said, and his voice was heavy with glee. "Oh, he doesn't even *know*, does he? He has no idea what a sick little slut you are, has no clue that you're gagging for it, that you *want* to be hurt."

Micah hung up the phone and collapsed to the floor to vomit into his trash can. He emptied his stomach in shaking heaves and clung to the cool metal sides of the can.

Devon didn't know. Barrett was right about that much. Devon would run for the hills if he knew how much Micah needed, *craved* domination. He was too gentle, too kind and thoughtful. If he knew how twisted Micah was, he'd bolt and never look back.

Micah sat back on his heels and wiped his mouth with a trembling hand. He needed to go home. He needed.... He clenched his fists. He needed to *hit* something, and he knew just the thing.

He made it home in record time, hung up his jacket, and then shoved his shoes onto the shelf without stopping to see if they were lined up neatly.

A quick stop in the bathroom to brush his teeth and then he was back in the bedroom, standing in front of the punching bag that Barrett had left behind.

Micah balled a fist and drove it into the bag. The starburst of pain in his knuckles shocked him, but he sucked in a breath and did it again with the other hand. Again and then again, he pounded his fists against the sand-filled bag and let the pain center him, imagining it was Barrett's handsome face every time he threw a punch.

His lips were drawn back in fury, and he grimaced as he battered the bag. He lost track of time, unaware of his surroundings until Devon suddenly grabbed his shoulders and yanked him backward.

"*Jesus*, Micah. What the hell?" Devon demanded.

Micah staggered, off-balance, and blinked up at him. "What are you doing here?"

"You told me last night to meet you here after work, remember?" Devon said. "I knocked but you didn't answer, and the door was open. You shouldn't leave your door unlocked, you know. No telling who's out there." He took Micah's wrist and lifted it to examine his bruised knuckles. "Don't you have gloves? What've you done to yourself?"

Micah jerked away. "I didn't ask your opinion, Mallory." He glared up at Devon, daring him to say something else. Devon's eyebrows climbed his forehead but he didn't challenge that. Instead he reached out and cupped Micah's face in one big hand.

"Do you want to talk about it?"

Micah turned his face into Devon's palm for one brief moment, took a shuddering breath, and then steeled himself. "No," he said flatly. "I just want you to fuck me."

Devon's eyes widened. "Uh, Micah—"

"Shut up and get naked," Micah snapped, and began to yank his clothes off. Behind him he could hear Devon taking his shoes off, and he swallowed the revulsion he felt at himself. He would take what *he* needed for once—use someone instead of being used himself, only to be cast aside.

Devon snaked his long arms around Micah's waist from behind and kissed the nape of his neck, slow and gentle. Micah snarled to himself and twisted away. He didn't *want* slow and gentle. He wanted hard and rough and fast, fingerprint bruises on his hips and hickeys on his neck.

"Is that all you've got?" he challenged.

Devon narrowed his eyes, and a feeling of sick certainty settled over Micah. He was going to lose this wonderful man, this gorgeous gift, because he was too fucked-up to deserve him.

"I don't want to hurt you," Devon said.

And that right there's the problem. Micah swallowed hard, crawled onto the bed, knelt on the mattress, and fixed Devon with a sharp look.

"I'll make it very simple, Mallory," he said. "I want sex. So what's it going to take to get you to actually fuck me?"

Devon closed his eyes briefly. Then he slid onto the bed, pushed Micah onto his back, and leaned over him.

"Be still," he growled and dropped his head. He fastened his mouth over Micah's collarbone and sucked hard. Micah arched against him with a helpless sound, and Devon brought his hands down on his shoulders, pinned him to the bed, and leisurely investigated Micah's clavicle with his lips and tongue.

Micah twisted as grief and frustration filled him in equal measure. Devon kept slowing things down, trying to turn what they were doing from fucking to making love, but Micah... couldn't. He couldn't handle Devon loving him right then, not when Devon was going to leave him once he knew the truth.

So he bucked up against Devon's body and ground his hard length against Devon's thigh—pushing, demanding. He *needed*. Why couldn't Devon get that? Why wasn't Devon giving him what he craved?

"Come on," he hissed. "Come *on*."

"Goddammit," Devon snapped as he lifted his head. "Be *still*."

"Make me, Mallory," Micah shot back and squirmed against him as driving need roared through him.

Devon's jaw tightened, and he knelt up on the bed, grabbed Micah's arms, and then flipped him over so that his face was pressed against the mattress. Micah choked back a sob and came all over the bedspread as Devon's weight pinned him down.

Barrett's mocking voice echoed through his mind. *"Does he pin you down and take what he wants from you?"*

Devon was utterly frozen above him as Micah trembled through the aftershocks, just barely keeping the tiny whimpers locked behind his teeth.

Now... now he'll leave me. There were tears on his cheeks, he realized in a distant way, but he couldn't muster the energy to wipe them off before Devon saw them. Instead he lay still, wept into the mattress, and waited for Devon to get up and walk out the door.

But Devon turned him back over with gentle hands, and his worried eyes filled Micah's vision as he thumbed the tears from Micah's face.

"Oh, sweetheart," Devon murmured. "Why didn't you say something?"

Micah blinked. His thoughts were fuzzy and indistinct, and Devon closed his eyes as though he were in physical pain.

"Come on," he said. "You need a bath."

He scooped Micah into his arms, and Micah turned his face into Devon's bare chest, floating on a sea of misery and endorphins.

Devon settled on the edge of the huge bathtub with Micah still cradled securely in his arms as he turned the water on and let the tub fill. Micah kept his face pressed against Devon's skin with his eyes closed and was only vaguely aware when Devon stood up and stepped into the tub. He sat down carefully with Micah held tightly against him. As the hot water rushed over Micah's skin, he took a deep breath and let go of all the sick fury, the nausea, and the self-hatred. He burrowed deeper into Devon's arms and allowed sub space to pull him from his body.

He had no idea how much time passed before he came slowly back to himself, stirring and blinking.

Devon was in the same position, with Micah warm and safe in his arms, and he smiled down at him.

"Welcome back," he murmured.

Micah gazed up at him for a minute. "Why are you still here?" he finally asked.

Devon's mouth twisted. "Because you need me." He shifted his weight into a more comfortable position, stroking Micah's thigh with slow, hypnotic motions under the water.

"You just saw how fucked-up I am," Micah whispered. "Why aren't you running?"

"What kind of person would that make me?" Devon asked.

"Human," Micah sighed.

Devon snorted quietly. "Speaking of that, I need to apologize."

Micah lifted his head, baffled. "What for?"

"I… handled this whole thing wrong," Devon said. Did he look *ashamed*? "I didn't realize soon enough how upset you were, and I shouldn't have taken advantage of you like that."

"Wanted you to," Micah said through a yawn. "*Needed* you to."

"Yeah. I got that," Devon said. "Micah, we need to talk."

Now? Naked in a bathtub, in his arms? *Now* Devon wanted to tell him he was leaving?

Micah tried to pull away and collect himself, but Devon tightened his grip.

"Be still," he murmured, but there was a hint of steel in his voice, and Micah stopped moving. Devon met his eyes. "What happened today?"

"I…." Micah bit the inside of his cheek. "Barrett. He called right before I left work."

Devon's mouth tightened. "Barrett." There was a world of loathing in his voice. "What did he say?"

"Doesn't matter," Micah whispered.

"I think it does," Devon said. "I think it has to do with something I wanted to talk to you about anyway, so can you please tell me what you talked about?"

Micah closed his eyes. "Barrett and I—we had a… complicated relationship."

"You mean Dom/sub," Devon said. Micah recoiled in shock, and water sloshed over the sides of the tub as he shoved away from Devon's embrace.

"You… how did you know about that?"

Devon met his eyes steadily, but didn't make a move to close the distance between them. "You mentioned sub space the morning we had sex for the first time. I did some reading."

Micah stared at him with his mouth open. "You knew," he whispered.

Devon lifted a shoulder. "I suspected," he said. "You kind of freaked me out, that first time, so I did a little research. I'm good at research. I figured out that you're probably a sub, and I learned about sub space and a bit about the Dom/sub scene. I'm not an expert, but I want to give you what you need."

Micah just shook his head. "You can't," he managed. "I'm too fucked-up. Sick, twisted, dirty—" Devon's hand covered his mouth to stop his words, and Micah's eyes went wide.

"Stop right there," Devon growled. "Did Barrett tell you that?"

Micah shrugged. "It's the truth."

"It's so far from the truth they're not even on the same *continent*," Devon snapped, and Micah flinched. Devon closed his eyes for a second and took a deep breath. "I'm sorry," he continued. "Look at me, Micah."

Micah stared at the bubbles in the water.

"*Look at me*," Devon said, and Micah jerked his eyes up. Devon smiled, but there was grief in the lines on his forehead and the tension in his jaw. "Barrett… took advantage of you," he continued. "He told you that you were sick and wrong for wanting this so that he could use you, *take* from you, without you ever protesting."

Micah couldn't think of anything to say.

Devon's eyes softened. "We have a lot of talking to do. Would you rather do it here or dressed and comfortable?"

"Dressed," Micah said immediately.

"You got it," Devon said. "Let's get dry and move this party to the couch."

He helped Micah from the tub and toweled him off with quick, gentle movements as Micah braced himself with his hands on Devon's shoulders, still dazed. Devon dug out Micah's softest pajamas, guided his feet into the leg holes, and eased them up over his hips with careful hands. He settled Micah on the toilet lid, and then the shirt was over Micah's head, and he groped for the sleeves, but his eyes never left Devon's bent head as he slipped thick socks onto Micah's feet.

Micah couldn't resist reaching out and touching Devon's hair, silky soft against his fingers. Devon stopped moving as Micah petted his head in slow, wondering motions. When Micah's hand fell back into his lap, Devon looked up. There were tears standing bright in his eyes, but he smiled and stood up.

"Stay there while I get dressed, and then we'll go talk."

WHEN HE returned, Micah refused to be carried.

"I can walk," he said, and he stood up on legs that only wobbled a bit.

Devon's eyes creased, and if he hovered too close, Micah elected not to see it as he made his way out of the bathroom and through his bedroom—resolutely not looking at the punching bag—and into the living room.

Micah sat down on the couch and wrapped his arms around his knees. Devon stood for a minute, looking indecisive, and Micah looked up at him.

"What's wrong?"

Devon shrugged. "Trying to figure out if you need something hot to drink now or after."

"After," Micah said immediately.

"Okay," Devon said and sat down cross-legged on the couch, facing Micah. He leaned forward and rubbed Micah's calves. The warmth of his hands soaked through Micah's pajamas, and his eyes were fixed on Micah's face. "Ready to do this?"

Micah lifted a shoulder. "As I'll ever be," he said. He was so tired. Why was he so tired? He hadn't *done* anything.

"Here's how I see the situation," Devon began. "You need a Dominant. But Barrett's fucked you up to the point that you're scared to ask for it. You think I'm going to think you're a pervert or something. So you're denying yourself what you really need, and it's been building until it became unbearable and you exploded."

Micah lifted his eyes. "Regular sex is good too."

"I know," Devon said gently. "But you need… more. And I'm offering to give it to you, if… if you'll have me."

Micah stared at him. Devon looked apprehensive. There was a tentative smile in his eyes, but nerves lurked behind them. Finally Micah shook his head.

"You don't know what you're saying."

"You sure about that?" Devon asked. He squeezed Micah's calf. "I've done a *lot* of research."

Micah pulled away and pressed his face against his knee. "I want… perverted things. I'm sick."

Devon tightened his hand. "You are *not*," he said sharply. "I don't care what you want, unless it's sex with children or animals, in which case I'm gonna have to draw a line in the sand."

Micah huffed a laugh in spite of himself. "No. No animals. No kids."

"In that case," Devon said, back to rubbing Micah's legs, "what *do* you want?"

Micah looked up, and Devon gazed back at him steadily.

"Tell me," Devon said, his voice gentle but with a thread of command in it.

"I—" Micah stopped and gulped. Devon waited with his eyes fixed on his face. "I want to be hit," Micah finally managed, his voice almost inaudible.

"Hit… like punched or slapped?" Devon asked.

Micah shook his head. "Like spanked. Not in an infantilizing way, just—"

"Okay," Devon said. "I can work with that. What else?"

"I want you to hold me down," Micah said. Devon watched him with unnerving intensity but said nothing. Micah swallowed and continued with a sinking sense of inevitability, like throwing himself from an airplane and hurtling toward the ground. "I want you to use toys on me. Cock rings, vibrators, restraints. I want you to mark me, leave bruises on me. I want… my brain gets so noisy. It's hard to hear, hard to *think*. I want to be broken down, I want to be able to let go, turn my brain off."

With his thumbs Devon rubbed slow, gentle circles on Micah's calves. "Okay," he murmured. "Okay, sweetheart. And you're willing to let me try to give this to you?"

Micah nodded. Relief and terror choked him in equal parts. How had Devon heard the worst of him and not run? He didn't understand what he was offering. Once he knew—really knew—*then* he'd leave.

"Do you want to lay out the scene before we start, discuss what we're going to do?" Devon asked.

Micah shook his head. "I'd rather... go in blind. I don't want to... know ahead of time. If it's too much, I'll safeword, but I—" He took a shaky breath. "I don't want to think about it. I just want to... let go."

"Okay," Devon said. "Let's get one thing straight." Micah swallowed hard. "There will be no degrading talk during a scene. Or any other time, really, but especially not when we're scening. Do you understand me? You will not refer to yourself in a derogatory fashion, and I will not allow you to speak badly of yourself."

"I can't see myself the way you do," Micah whispered.

"I know," Devon said, and he pulled Micah into his lap, tucked him between his legs, and fit Micah's head snugly under his chin. "That's why I'm going to *show* you, baby."

Micah relaxed against his chest, and tears welled. He sniffed once and gripped the front of Devon's shirt.

"Do you want to tell me what Barrett said?" Devon asked.

Micah shook his head. "Don't wanna throw up again," he mumbled.

Devon tensed. "You threw up?"

"I'm better," Micah assured him and burrowed closer. "Just... really bad day. 'M sorry."

Devon tightened his arms around him. "It's okay, sweetheart. We're going to work it out, you hear me?"

Micah nodded and closed his eyes. He drifted into a doze that way, with his fingers tangled in the placket of Devon's shirt, his head on Devon's chest, and a tentative peace washing over him.

CHAPTER SIX

WHEN MICAH woke up, he was still curled against Devon's chest. Devon's breathing was slow and steady. His big hands were wrapped loosely around Micah's waist as he slept, and Micah lay quietly for a moment.

He'd expected Devon to walk away, to tell him he was a sick freak and that he never wanted to see him again, and instead the opposite had happened. Devon had looked at him, not with loathing, but with something that seemed suspiciously like... love. Micah closed his eyes. It wasn't possible that Devon could ever fall in love with someone as fucked-up as Micah. He was too fundamentally decent. Devon would leave—*had* to leave. No one ever stayed. But Micah would do his best to show Devon how much he was appreciated until that time came.

Holding his breath, he squirmed out from under Devon's arms. He padded into the kitchen and assembled ingredients as the pancake griddle heated. When the batter hit the pan with a sizzle, Devon called out. "Micah?"

"In here," Micah said as he took a *dosa* off the griddle and poured the batter for the next.

Devon heaved himself to his feet and headed straight for him. He wrapped his arms around Micah's waist, and Micah melted against him, taking a deep breath of Devon's sweet smell.

"Mmm, pancakes," Devon said.

"Dosa, actually," Micah said and he reached out to flip it. "Figured *rava dosa*'d be a good dinner. I'm not really happy with this batch yet. I can't figure out what I'm doing wrong, but I think they'll still be edible."

Devon looked blank. "Rava... what?"

Micah grinned. "It's Indian, whitey. Watch and learn."

"So the Indian word for pancake is dosa?" Devon asked.

"Well, sort of," Micah said. "It's a kind of pancake, really. Why?"

"I'm going to call you Dosa," Devon announced.

Micah blinked. "Why?" he repeated.

"Because you're my Indian pancake," Devon said triumphantly.

Micah groaned. "That was so *lame*."

"But sweet," Devon pointed out.

"Okay, fine. It was kind of sweet." Micah laughed. "But mostly lame."

Devon chortled and leaned in to kiss him. Micah lost himself in the slide of Devon's lips on his and had no idea how much time passed before they separated and Micah put his head back on Devon's chest with a contented sigh.

"How are you feeling?" Devon asked. His voice rumbled in Micah's ear, and Micah smiled.

"Better," he said. "Hungry?"

"Always," Devon said and dropped a kiss on Micah's hair.

Micah pointed at the table. "Sit and keep me company while I cook. You haven't given me many chances to spoil you rotten."

Devon obeyed and dropped backward into a chair. "Maybe because I like spoiling *you*." He hooked his long feet over the bottom rung and rested his arms on the backrest. "So I was thinking," he said. "How do you feel about collars?"

Micah dropped a dosa on the floor and stared at Devon.

"That was… that was just mean," Micah said. "*Warn* a guy."

"Question stands," Devon said, dimples flashing.

Micah dumped the dosa in the trash and turned back to the frying pan. "Umm. Collars… collars are good." He cleared his throat and shifted his weight. Then he looked up as a thought struck him. "No leashes, though. Barrett used a leash sometimes. I didn't—"

"No leash," Devon said quickly. "What kind of collar do you want, then? Shall we pick it out together, or do you want me to surprise you?"

"I trust you," Micah said, startled to realize that was true. "Surprise me. Nothing too flashy."

He piled the dosa on plates, added the rava and coconut chutney, and then brought them to the table. Devon turned around in his chair and caught Micah's wrist as he passed by on his way back to the kitchen for drinks, and he tugged until Micah toppled with a squawk into his lap.

Devon caught him and tipped Micah's chin up with one long finger. "Hey," he said quietly.

Micah swallowed, caught in Devon's bright blue gaze. "Hey back," he managed.

Devon's lips curved up. "I'm glad I met you," he whispered and pressed their mouths together.

Micah slid his arms around Devon's neck and held on. Devon's hands on his thighs kept him in position, his thumbs rubbing gentle circles, and their lips and tongues fit against each other perfectly.

When they pulled apart, Devon cupped Micah's cheek. "Have you thought about a safeword?" he asked.

Micah nodded shyly. "Ah… I was thinking… manta ray."

Devon's smile lit up the room. "I like that," he breathed and kissed him again. "You're so beautiful," he said. "The light from the kitchen is haloing you, and you look like an angel right now."

Micah couldn't help but snort at that. "*So* not an angel, pal."

"You are to me," Devon murmured and kissed him again.

TWO WEEKS passed, and Micah started to get twitchy. They'd had sex again, of course, but they hadn't scened yet, hadn't explored the possibilities in front of them, and he was beginning to wonder if Devon had forgotten or changed his mind. Devon hadn't even *mentioned* Domming, and Micah had just about decided that Devon was backing out of the arrangement when he got a text an hour before he was due to leave work.

As soon as you get home, go to the bedroom, get naked, kneel at the end of the bed with your hands behind your back, and wait for me.

Micah nearly dropped his phone. He shifted position in his chair as his cock stirred and he took a deep breath. It was happening.

He couldn't concentrate on work. He told Norma to hold his calls and was debating the merits of going home early when his phone buzzed again.

Don't leave early. Stay right where you are. Do your work, and do your best not to think about what I'm going to do to you. Leave the key under the mat for me so I can get in.

Micah groaned and dropped his head to the desk with a clunk. He wasn't going to survive.

He was a jumpy ball of nerves by the time he was free to leave the office, and sidling past Norma with an erection was *not* an experience he wanted to repeat, made worse when she tried to say something as he dashed by.

"Text me," Micah called over his shoulder and ran for it.

Driving home, Micah was on the edge of his seat, and he nearly sprinted up the stairs to his door and unlocked it with shaky hands. He set his shoes on the shelf, hung his jacket up, and unbuttoned his shirt as he hurried for the bedroom. Safely there, he stripped and put his clothes in the laundry hamper and knelt at the end of the bed.

Silence fell around him. The hardwood floor was uncomfortable under his bare knees, and his ears strained for the sounds of Devon's arrival. It seemed like forever before he heard the front door open and softly close and then Devon's footsteps. Micah closed his eyes and took a steadying breath.

Then Devon was there, trailing a warm hand up across Micah's shoulder blades and drifting up to tangle briefly in Micah's hair and around to brush against his cheekbone.

"Look how good you are," he murmured, "kneeling here waiting for me."

Micah shifted, and Devon slid his hand up to catch in his hair again. "Don't move," he said quietly, but the steel of command was in his voice, and Micah settled back on his heels immediately. "That's my good angel," Devon said, and Micah grimaced.

Devon tightened his hand warningly. "You don't argue with me, remember?" he growled. "No degrading yourself, no disputing when I say nice things to you."

Micah gasped at the tiny flashes of pain in his scalp. "I... yes, sir."

"Don't call me sir," Devon said, but there was a smile in his voice. "Don't call me master either. Just call me Devon."

"Yes, Devon," Micah whispered, and Devon loosened his fingers and petted his hair.

"Good," he said, his voice warm with approval, and Micah sighed and leaned into his hand.

"Stand up," Devon said. "Face me, hands by your sides."

Micah scrambled to obey and got a look at Devon for the first time. He was wearing a long-sleeved gray T-shirt with the sleeves rolled up to display his muscular forearms, and soft, faded jeans that showed off his long legs. Micah's mouth watered, but he said nothing, and Devon's eyes creased in approval.

"I have something for you," he said and pulled a flat box out of his back pocket. "Hold your hand out." He placed the box on Micah's outstretched palm and took a step back. His blue eyes danced with anticipation. "Open it."

Micah lifted the lid, holding his breath. "Oh," he whispered. A leather collar, about an inch and a half wide, was nestled inside—an unbroken circle that appeared to have no opening. Micah lifted it out and turned it reverently. There was a small gold nameplate set into the brown leather, and Micah looked closer. It said "Angel" on it, and suddenly tears pricked at Micah's eyes and he swallowed hard.

Devon took the collar from him. "It closes with magnets," he said. "I got the measurements from one of your shirts. Look." He pulled on it, and the leather sprang apart. Devon raised it. "Do you want me to put it on, or do you want to do it?"

"You," Micah said instantly. "You, please."

He closed his eyes as the buttery-soft leather closed around his neck and snapped into place. It was comfortably snug but not tight enough to restrict his breathing. Devon lightly traced the collar, and his fingers brushed Micah's skin. Micah shivered.

"You look beautiful, angel," Devon murmured. "Any time you need to scene, you put this on, do you understand? If you're wearing it, then I know you need a Dom."

Micah nodded, and his breath came quicker.

"Now," Devon continued, "before we go any further, my safeword is halo. Say yours."

"Manta ray," Micah said.

Devon nodded. "Again."

"Manta ray," Micah said louder, his breath hitching.

"One more time."

"*Manta ray.*"

"Good." Devon stroked his cheek. "So good for me. On the bed, hands and knees."

Micah gulped and obeyed. He made it to all fours, and he could hear Devon methodically pulling his clothes off behind him, folding them, and setting them next to the bed. Only then did Devon slide onto the mattress behind Micah and let his hands wander. He smoothed over

Micah's back, his waist, and his belly that never went away, no matter how many crunches he did.

Micah wanted this. He did. But now that it was happening, he was suddenly terrified. *Manta ray.* Devon's fingers ghosted over his cock with the faintest of teasing touches. They could stop anytime. They could end the scene, have vanilla sex or no sex at all, and Devon would take care of him. Micah knew that.

But he wanted more. He *needed* more. He needed Devon to take control, take over and allow Micah to turn off his brain and just feel for as long as the scene lasted. The lights were low, the room was warm, but Micah's skin still pebbled with gooseflesh, and his breath came a little faster, a little harder. He hid his face in his elbow as Devon's hands roamed over his sides and flanks.

Devon slipped one hand lower, over the curve of Micah's stomach and down to his groin. His fingers were soft and barely there over Micah's half-hard length. Micah instinctively sucked his stomach in, and Devon stopped moving.

"What're you... did you just suck in?"

Micah froze. *Shit.* Devon breathed out and held fast to Micah's sides. His fingers dug into his love handles, and he pulled his hips flush against Micah's backside. Micah groaned as he felt Devon's erection trapped between them—evidence of how much Devon wanted him.

Devon leaned forward and bent almost in half over Micah to nip at his ear. "You're so fucking hot," he growled. He gently pushed Micah down on the bed and rolled him over. Micah stared up at him, flat on his back and vulnerable, and crossed his arms over his stomach.

"Don't hide from me," Devon said. He pulled Micah's arms away and pinned them above his head in one big hand as he leaned down to nose at Micah's little belly roll.

Micah whimpered and struggled against the urge to cover up again, to turn the focus back on Devon and his beauty, but Devon ignored him. He sucked marks into Micah's skin, tasting and teasing as he moved methodically up and down Micah's hated pudge, nibbling and licking until Micah was shaking and helpless and tiny whines caught and lodged in his throat.

Finally Devon lifted his head, his pupils blown. "You are gorgeous," he whispered. "Back on hands and knees, sweetheart."

Micah scrambled to obey, and Devon snugged himself between Micah's legs again.

Micah shuddered at Devon's hands on his hips and ground back against him, and Devon let his mouth fall to the back of Micah's neck to suck a bruise into the skin.

"I was going to draw this out," Devon murmured. "Was gonna take you apart in a dozen different ways until you were out of your mind and begging for me. But now—" He broke off and skimmed a hand over Micah's erection, full and heavy between his legs. "Now I think I'm just going to fuck you senseless."

Devon reached behind himself for the bottle of lube. Micah tensed and dropped his face to the comforter again. Barrett had always rushed this part, impatient to get to the main course and unwilling to take the time to make sure Micah was fully comfortable.

But Micah wasn't going to say anything. Devon was the Dom. Micah would suck it up and allow Devon to take what he needed. So it was a surprise—a *wonderful* fucking surprise—when instead of the head of a cock, it was Devon's finger he felt slipping inside of him, cold and slick.

Micah jerked and Devon spread his free hand across his hip to anchor him.

"Easy," he murmured. "Breathe for me." First one digit, then a second, and Micah made a strangled noise when Devon's fingers curled against his prostate. Micah rocked back on his fingers, and Devon's grip on his hip tightened hard enough to bruise. Micah moaned, reveling in the shock of pain and pleasure commingled.

Devon slipped a third finger in, and Micah *ached* to be touched so much he leaked onto the mattress as he bucked back against Devon's steadying hand.

"Easy," Devon repeated. "Gonna do this right. Make it good for you."

"Please," Micah panted into his forearm, rocking desperately onto Devon's fingers. "*Please*, Devon."

Devon continued a moment, grinding the pads of his fingers against Micah's prostate. But then he drew his fingers out slowly. Micah couldn't stop the whimper at that, at the slide and the sudden, cool lack between his legs. And suddenly, he needed to touch, to taste Devon again.

He pushed up onto his hands and turned his head just as Devon, who must have had the same idea, draped himself across Micah's back, and their lips met. It was slow and sweet, no rush to it, and Micah closed his eyes and sank into it. He wanted to be fucked—*needed* to be fucked—but more. He needed the connection. He needed a reminder that he wasn't alone. He was cared for.

Devon's mouth was soft on his. He took control but wasn't demanding, and Micah ceded the reins gladly, allowing Devon to tilt his head and deepen the kiss at his leisure. Devon brought his hand up to the side of Micah's face and tangled his fingers in the curls on Micah's neck, behind his ear as he ran his thumb in slow, wide circles over Micah's cheekbone.

The angle was awkward, Micah's head tilted back and Devon a heavy living blanket over him, but when Devon fisted a hand in his hair, Micah forgot the crick in his neck, forgot everything but Devon devouring his mouth. His world was the beautiful blue-eyed man who was breaking away, and Micah blinked up at him, dazed.

Devon ran a thumb over Micah's kiss-swollen lower lip, and Micah's mouth fell open under the press and let the digit slip inside.

"Jesus," Devon groaned, his voice wrecked. "On your elbows, angel."

Micah obeyed. The hum in his mind was a dim buzz. All he could hear, all he could feel, was Devon shuffling into position behind him. There was a breathless moment of nothing at all, and Micah pushed backward, looking for contact where there was none. Devon caught his hips, and then Micah felt a blunt pressure at his hole, and he opened around Devon as he slid in. It was a slow, delicious burn and ache that made Micah's lips part silently even as he pushed back harder.

At last, at long fucking last his brain was muted, and all he could feel, all he could process, was Devon inside him and around him, filling him and claiming him, making him *his*.

Micah trembled again as Devon bottomed out and moved his big hands restlessly across Micah's skin.

"So beautiful," Devon whispered when the din in Micah's ears abated enough that he could hear again. "My God, angel, you're so fucking beautiful. Feel so good."

Micah didn't answer. *Couldn't* answer. His vocal cords were paralyzed, he thought vaguely, and he couldn't bring himself to care. Devon set up a slow, steady rhythm. He slid home in strong, sure thrusts, the head of his cock dragging across Micah's prostate with each pass, and Micah bit down on his forearm to stifle the frankly embarrassing noises that wanted to burst free.

This was what he'd wanted. This was what he'd *craved* for so long, and he hadn't thought he'd ever find it. But Devon seemed to know instinctively how Micah needed to be touched. He found every erogenous zone on Micah's body as he slammed deep, over and over again and punched needy whimpers from Micah's throat with every thrust.

Devon settled his hands on Micah's hips again and dug deep to counteract the lube as his movements sped up. Micah writhed back against him. His eyes fluttered shut with the force as Devon's hips snapped forward again. He was close, he knew. Devon curled forward. His breathing was harsh in Micah's ear as his hips stuttered and lost their rhythm. With one hand he pressed down on the back of Micah's neck, pinned him to the mattress, and held him there effortlessly.

Devon let go of Micah's hip and slapped his ass hard. Micah bucked under him, crying out in shock, and came in long, desperate spurts onto the bed as Devon froze above him and emptied deep inside Micah's body with a choked-off groan.

Micah's limbs wouldn't support him. Might never support him again. He collapsed in a limp heap on the bedspread, and Devon followed him down, still buried within him as they sprawled on the satin comforter with their arms and legs everywhere.

Devon breathed in short, rapid gusts against the nape of Micah's neck and stirred his hair with each panting exhale. Micah couldn't remember ever having felt this good, this *right*, with Devon still inside him, wrapped around him, holding him as though Micah was something precious, something breakable and *worthy*.

He made an unintelligible protest when Devon slid out and left the bed. It wasn't long, though, before Devon came back and rolled Micah over to clean them both in quick, gentle strokes. He gathered Micah into his arms then, and Micah went gladly, his face against Devon's chest, smelling clean sweat and aftershave.

"Okay?" Devon murmured.

Micah's eyes wouldn't stay open, but he managed a nod.

"Bath now or later?" Devon asked gently.

"Later," Micah slurred.

Devon took the collar off and pressed a kiss to the top of Micah's head. "Sleep well," he whispered, and Micah slid over the edge into darkness with Devon's arms around him.

CHAPTER SEVEN

MICAH WOKE up in the middle of the night as silent sobs shuddered through him. It took a minute to work out why, and then he realized, as his stomach sank. Subdrop. It had been a while since one had hit him this hard.

Worthless, sick, twisted. No good to anyone. No one will ever love you. You're not worth loving.

Micah pressed a shaking hand to his mouth and fought back the tears.

Devon was sound asleep on the other side of the bed in a boneless sprawl. He couldn't wake him, Micah knew. Instead he slipped out of the bed, tiptoed to the bathroom, and shut the door behind him. He sat down on the toilet seat in the dim glow of the night-light and wrapped his arms around himself, trying desperately to stop the trembling.

Just have to ride it out, Devon doesn't need to know. Don't deserve him anyway, worthless, perverted—

Micah just managed to catch the sob that tried to claw its way out of his throat as he squeezed his eyes shut.

Knuckles rapped softly on the door, and Micah froze.

"Micah?" Devon whispered. "I woke up, and you were gone.... Are you okay?"

Micah couldn't answer around the sob that still threatened to rip free if he opened his mouth. He tightened his grip on his rib cage and willed himself to stay silent. *Go away, Devon, I'm okay. Please don't see me like this. Please—*

The door eased open, and Devon put his head in. His eyes went wide at the sight of Micah huddled in on himself, and he crossed the room in a bound and pulled Micah off the toilet and into his arms.

"What is it, baby? What happened?" he asked. "Did I hurt you? Talk to me, Dosa, *please.*"

Micah collapsed against him and sobs wracked his frame. He clutched at Devon's shirt, weeping desperately and unable to speak. Devon eased them both to the floor and just held him with his back against the bathtub and Micah between his legs.

"Breathe, sweetheart," he murmured against Micah's hair. "Just breathe. I'm here. Let it out. It's okay."

Micah clung to him and shook as the sobs ripped through him. He stuffed his fist into his mouth in a vain attempt to stop them as Devon rubbed his back. His hand was warm through Micah's thin T-shirt, and he just held him until the worst of the weeping had passed. Only then did he pull back enough to see him and pull his own shirt up enough to wipe the worst of the tears and snot from Micah's face.

"Hey," he whispered. "What happened?"

"Sub... drop," Micah managed. A hiccupping sob underscored his words.

Devon looked blank. "Subdrop?"

"'S what... happens—" Micah closed his eyes and took a shuddering breath. "Happens... sometimes after... a scene. Equal and... opposite reaction."

Devon was silent for a minute. "So you're saying that you're paying for the high you get during a scene?"

Micah nodded against Devon's shirt and relaxed by increments.

"What do you need from me?" Devon said.

"Hold me?"

Devon tightened his arms around him. "Of course. For as long as you need, sweetheart."

Warmth stole over Micah as he lay in Devon's arms with his head on his broad chest and Devon's heart thumping steadily away in his ear. He sighed and relaxed a little more. He'd have to explain exactly what had happened, he knew, but for now he was content, warm, and comforted. He was asleep before he realized it, there on the bathroom floor.

WHEN HE woke up, he was no longer in the bathroom. He cracked an eyelid cautiously. They were curled up in bed with Devon's long body molded up against Micah's and his arm draped across Micah's waist.

Sunlight poured in the windows over Micah's bed, and he stretched and yawned. The worst of the self-loathing had vanished, leaving him feeling scoured clean and empty.

Devon tugged him closer, and Micah pressed back against him with a sigh.

"Hey," Devon whispered into his hair. "How ya feeling?"

"Better," Micah said through another yawn, and he squirmed around until they were face-to-face.

Devon looked worried, but he managed a smile. "Had me really freaked out there," he said quietly.

"Sorry," Micah said. "I thought…. Well, I sort of forgot about it, to be honest. And then when it hit, I thought I could ride it out on my own."

"What exactly happened?" Devon asked. "Can you tell me?"

Micah hesitated as he searched for the right words. "It's like—you did research on sub space, right?"

Devon nodded.

"What goes up must come down," Micah said. He lifted a shoulder with a rueful smile. "I go from euphoria, feeling amazing, better than I've ever felt, to worse than ever. Worthless, sick, perverted. It didn't help that Barrett told me that a lot, made me think the drop was how things really were, that the sub space was the lie."

Devon clenched his jaw. "I hope I never meet that fucker," he growled.

"Me too," Micah said. "Prison-jumpsuit orange is not your color."

That startled a laugh out of Devon and emboldened Micah enough for him to lean forward and press a kiss to the corner of Devon's mouth.

"I should warn you," he said, "Doms can have the drop too. So if you hit one, just tell me what you need, and we'll get through it together."

Devon nodded. "How did I not run across subdrop during my research?" he asked. "I've clearly failed."

"Good thing you're such a good mechanic," Micah teased. "You have a fallback career."

Devon snorted a laugh, pushed Micah onto his back, and rose above him, blocking out the sun's rays with his broad shoulders. Micah smiled as Devon's weight pressed him into the mattress, and he slowly ground his hips against Devon's pelvis.

Devon shuddered and gasped. His eyes closed. "That's not playing fair," he managed.

"Who said anything about fair?" Micah countered and took advantage of Devon's distraction to knock his arm out from under him and roll them so he ended up triumphantly straddling Devon's hips. Devon rapidly hardened in his thin cotton pajamas, and Micah spent several minutes rocking against his cock until they were both fully erect and breathing hard. Devon's pupils were blown dark with lust as he stared up at Micah.

"You wanna fuck me?" Micah whispered.

Devon bit his lip and bucked his hips up, so hard he had to be aching, and Micah slid off his lap, ignoring Devon's frustrated growl, to pull his pants off and yank Devon's down around his ankles. Then he was back on top, and he grabbed the lube so he could slick Devon's shaft in quick, sloppy motions.

Devon groaned as Micah positioned himself and sank down. He was still open from the night before, still loose and a little sore, just the way he liked it, and he didn't stop until Devon was fully sheathed and Micah's inner walls twitched and fluttered around Devon's cock.

"Je-*sus*," Devon moaned. His huge hands bit into Micah's thighs. "Feels so good, angel."

Micah lifted up and slid back down. He shuddered at the sensation. "Not scening," he reminded him. "Don't have to... call me an angel right... *ah*... now."

Devon rocked up into him, and Micah choked on a groan as the ridges of Devon's cock rubbed over his prostate.

"You're always my... angel," Devon managed.

Micah whimpered, planted his hands on Devon's chest, and moved slowly and torturously, using Devon's cock to massage his prostate over and over. His hips rolled and Devon thrust up into him in short, sharp bursts. Beads of sweat formed on his clavicle and throat.

"*God* yes, Dev." Micah slid one hand down to grasp his own cock as he fucked himself slow and deep, his head hanging back. He could already feel the familiar tightening in his balls, tendrils of lightning wrapping around his spine. He sped up as his breath caught in his throat.

"Gonna.... Micah—" Devon drove upward, and his mouth fell open as he came in hot pulses deep inside Micah's body.

Micah clenched around him and followed, muscles locking in bliss as he spilled over Devon's stomach. Devon held him upright until he was spent and then pulled him down. Micah sprawled across his chest, distantly gratified to note that Devon was breathing as hard as he was.

Devon ran his hands up and down Micah's sides, as though to reassure himself that Micah was real and not going to disappear. His softening cock slid out, and Micah sighed at the emptiness as Devon pressed a kiss to the top of his head.

"Thank you," he murmured. "Let's go get cleaned up."

"Think… you're gonna… hafta carry me," Micah slurred against Devon's collarbone, and Devon's laugh rumbled through his chest.

"I can do that, but first you have to get off."

"Pretty sure that just… happened," Micah said through a yawn.

Devon groaned. "That was *terrible*." But Micah could hear the smile in his voice, and his hands were gentle as he maneuvered Micah off him and got to his feet. He stretched and popped his back with a satisfied noise.

They made their way to the shower, and then Devon settled Micah on the couch while he washed the bedding.

Micah curled up with a hand tucked under his cheek and smiled as he waited for Devon to come back.

CHAPTER EIGHT

THE NEXT week passed smoothly enough, although they didn't scene again. Micah threw himself into work, pursuing a hot, young rising star in the corporate law world who his client desperately wanted for their firm. He barely even saw Devon until the weekend rolled around.

It had been several weeks since Barrett had called and told him he was switching account managers, and Micah had forgotten all about it. So when Norma buzzed him to let him know Barrett was on the phone, it was a nasty shock.

Micah swallowed hard and cleared his throat before he picked up. "Hello, Barrett."

"Mike!" Barrett's voice was cheerful, and the ambient noise suggested he was in his car with the top down. "Are you avoiding my calls?" He laughed before Micah could answer. "So listen. I'll be down in your part of town next week. What do you say we have lunch?"

"I'm seeing someone," Micah blurted, and then he squeezed his eyes shut in mortification.

Sure enough Barrett laughed even harder. "Don't flatter yourself on my account, Mike. This is purely business. I'm switching managers, remember?"

"Right," Micah said. "Of course. I... guess we could do that."

"Great. I'll be in touch." Barrett hung up before Micah could answer, and Micah sank into his chair with a groan. His brain hummed again, sending up warning signals that it was going into overdrive soon. The stress of dealing with Barrett wasn't helping.

He needed to calm his mind and stop the buzzing, but between his schedule and Devon working overtime, they hadn't scened again since that first incredible time. The suggestive texts that Devon sent him while he was in meetings were torture enough, and Micah was getting increasingly jumpy.

He loved the regular sex, but the itch to sub was welling beneath his skin again—the need to be dominated, to be taken apart and used and put back together—and Micah wasn't sure how to tell Devon what he needed. So finally he decided he would *show* him instead.

He flipped a wave at Norma as he dashed out the door and broke the speed limit all the way home. Devon was coming over, and Micah wanted to be ready.

He took the fastest shower he'd ever managed and was toweling his hair dry when he saw Devon's pickup pull into the parking lot. Micah hung the towel on the rack and dashed naked for the bedroom, grabbed his collar from the drawer, and pelted into the kitchen as he snapped it into place.

When Devon walked in the door, Micah was kneeling naked on the kitchen floor with eyes downcast and his hands clasped behind his back. Devon stopped dead and sucked in a startled breath, but Micah didn't lift his eyes. He just waited and prayed that Devon would understand, would take control like Micah wanted—*needed*—him to.

Devon took his shoes off and moved nearer, and his legs came into Micah's field of vision. "I could get used to this," he murmured as he stroked Micah's still-damp hair, and Micah leaned into his touch and arched like a cat. Devon huffed an amused breath. "Be still," he said.

Micah settled back onto his heels, and Devon petted his hair again. "So good for me." The sound of his zipper being pulled down was loud in the quiet room, and Micah swallowed the rush of saliva that flooded his mouth as his cock went from soft to "Oh yes, God, please."

"Can you snap?" Devon asked, and the non sequitur startled Micah and made him jerk his eyes up.

"I… yes," he said. "Umm… why?"

Devon grinned, eyes dark with promise. "Because your mouth's going to be busy. You want to stop, you snap your fingers. Understand?"

Thrilled and a little terrified, Micah nodded. Devon's eyes softened, and he cupped Micah's face.

Then he pressed his thumb against Micah's lips. Micah's mouth opened with a soft moan, and he sucked on the digit for a minute, his eyes fixed on Devon's. Devon watched him with a look of absorption on his face, his tongue caught between his teeth as he slid his thumb in and out of Micah's mouth.

Devon stepped closer, pulling his hand away, and smiled at the whimper that dragged from Micah's throat. "Patience, angel," he said and pushed his pants and underwear down. His cock stood at attention, heavy and flushed, and Micah licked his lips. "You want it?" Devon asked.

Micah nodded and fisted his hands on his thighs. "Please," he whispered.

"Please what? Use your words, Micah."

"I… please, may I suck your cock, Devon?" Micah managed. He was unable to take his eyes off the clear drop of fluid forming at the tip as Devon wrapped a hand around his shaft and jacked himself in a slow, easy slide.

"Maybe I'll just make you watch," Devon said, and Micah jerked his eyes up to Devon's as Devon arched an eyebrow and stroked himself. His voice was strained, but his composure was still in place. "Maybe I'll jack off and come all over that gorgeous face of yours, angel. Would you like that?"

Micah's mouth fell open. This wasn't *fair*. He wanted to touch, to taste, to swallow Devon down, and from the look on Devon's face, he knew that perfectly well.

Devon worked himself harder. A groan fell from his mouth, and Micah nearly whined. He was so hard it *hurt*. Devon was *right there*, his gorgeous dick scant inches away, and Micah didn't have permission yet to touch him.

He shifted on the hard tiles. "Please," he repeated. "Please, Devon, I—"

Devon cupped the back of his head and pressed his cock into Micah's mouth. Micah made a strangled noise as Devon pushed forward, slowly but steadily, until the head bumped the back of Micah's throat.

"Breathe, baby," Devon said, his voice ragged. "Relax and take it."

Micah took a deep breath and forced his throat to loosen, and Devon slid farther in, until Micah's nose brushed the soft curls at the base of Devon's erection. One of Devon's hands was tangled in Micah's hair, clenched tightly enough to bring tears to his eyes, and with the other he stroked Micah's cheek.

"Jesus," Devon managed. "So beautiful, angel." He pulled back, and Micah sucked in a lungful of air. Devon slid his other hand into Micah's hair, caught another fistful, and effectively pinned his head in place as his hips moved.

Micah's eyes fluttered shut as he worked the head of Devon's shaft with his lips and tongue. He hollowed his cheeks, flattened his tongue, and ran it along the frenulum. Devon pistoned his hips faster, and he groaned, harsh and wrecked. Micah brought his hand up toward his own neglected erection, but he'd barely wrapped his fingers around it before Devon's hands tightened and jerked Micah's head back.

"That's mine," Devon growled.

Micah couldn't respond—his mouth was still stuffed full—but he whimpered, and Devon seemed to take that for acquiescence. He thrust again, and Micah laced his fingers behind his back to keep temptation at bay. He spiraled down the slope into sub space as Devon crowded into every corner of his consciousness, taking him, filling him, *using* him the way Micah so desperately wanted. He was only dimly aware when Devon tensed above him and warm, bitter liquid flooded Micah's mouth.

Working his throat, he swallowed every drop and protested wordlessly when Devon pulled out and his hands loosed their grip. But Devon didn't go far. He kicked his pants the rest of the way off and dropped to the floor behind Micah. Then he pulled him into his arms and wrapped a hand around Micah's shaft to stroke hard and fast.

Micah's head fell back against Devon's shoulder, and Devon pressed a kiss to his cheek. "Come for me, angel," he ordered, and Micah obeyed with a helpless sob, waves pulling him under as he jerked and shuddered his way through orgasm.

Wrung dry, Micah collapsed against Devon's solid frame. They stayed like that for a minute, their harsh breathing the only sound in the room, until Devon moved Micah off him, stood up, and gathered him into his arms. He carried him to the bedroom to lay him on the bed, and Micah sighed as Devon gently cleaned him up and drew the covers over him. Devon touched his lips to the back of his neck as he wrapped an arm around Micah's waist.

"Thank you," Devon whispered. Micah smiled and let the darkness take him.

WHEN HE jerked awake and the subdrop sank its wicked claws into him, Devon was ready and waiting. The second Micah tensed, Devon was on his knees next to him, pulling Micah onto his back and leaning over him until his face filled Micah's vision.

"Listen to me," Devon said, his voice filled with authority, and Micah took a shaky breath, fixed on Devon's eyes with a desperate intensity. "You are not twisted. You are not sick. You are beautiful. You are *good*, and you are worthy. Your brain is lying to you. Do you hear me?"

Micah's eyes filled with tears and his stomach twisted itself into knots, but he managed a nod as he covered his mouth with a trembling hand.

"Breathe, baby," Devon said softly, and the tenderness in his voice was enough to make the tears spill down Micah's face.

Devon slid off the bed and helped Micah to his feet. "Bath time," he said. "I filled the tub earlier, and the water should still be nice and hot. Do you want me to carry you?"

Micah shook his head, still fighting the tears, so Devon put a hand on his elbow and led him into the bathroom. He set him on the edge of the tub, tested the water, and made a satisfied noise. Then he stepped in and helped Micah climb in after him.

They settled with Micah's back against Devon's chest and Devon's arms loosely linked across Micah's stomach.

Micah closed his eyes as the hot water dissolved the tension in his frame. Devon's cheek was pressed against his hair, his breathing deep and steady, and Micah wrapped his hands around Devon's wrists and let go of the nausea and the sick self-hatred that wormed through his gut. As he took deep lungfuls of the steam rising from the water, a slow, cautious peace crept over him.

He didn't deserve this man, but damn if he wouldn't fight to keep him for as long as possible.

CHAPTER NINE

"SO YOU'VE met Sean," Devon said one day as they lounged on the couch.

Micah glanced up at him from his position on his back with his head in Devon's lap. "Yes, and what a thrilling experience *that* was."

Devon's lips twitched. "Can't really blame her. She practically raised me, after all. She's... protective."

"Is that what we're calling it?" Micah said. He dropped a grape into his mouth and raised his hand for Devon to take the next from between his fingers.

Devon accepted, his lips soft against Micah's skin. "*Anyway,* my point was, you've met Sean, but you haven't met the rest of my family."

"I thought it was just the two of you," Micah said.

"Well... blood relatives in Toronto, yeah," Devon said as he ran a finger along Micah's chest. "But just because we're the only Mallorys here doesn't mean we don't have an actual family. Jim Shepherd was our neighbor when we were kids and kind of took us in after our dad died. Our mom split not long after. Jim and Irene got married a few years back. We were ridiculously relieved, let me tell you. The amount of *pining* those two did after each other.... It was pathetic, really. And then there's Hope and her mom Annette, and Yancy. They all want to meet you too. 'It's been three months, Devon, why haven't we met your new boyfriend yet?'"

Micah snorted and handed him another grape. "What about Sean? Does she have a special someone?"

"Yeah, actually, speaking of pining," Devon said. His hand drifted across Micah's chest, seemingly almost of its own volition, and down Micah's ribs toward his stomach. "She and Fallon have been together for... oh wow, it's gotta be over a year now."

"So what's Fallon like?" Micah asked.

Devon laughed. "She is weird, prissy, stiff as all hell, has no idea about social niceties and wouldn't care if she did, talks like an English professor, and is *perfect* for Sean."

Micah caught Devon's wandering hand before it could delve below his waistband. "Wait, whoa. Are we talking about the same Sean here? The one you pranked nonstop growing up? The one who pranked *you*? The one who can burp the alphabet backward *and* forward? The one who has a frankly alarming love affair with desserts? *That* Sean, with an uptight-English-professor type?"

Devon grinned at him. "She's actually a surgeon, but yep. One and the same."

"Okay," Micah said as he let go of Devon's hand. "This I have to see."

Devon snuck his hand under the waistband of his pants, and Micah stretched and sighed as Devon's fingers found and caressed his cock.

"I was hoping you'd say that, actually," Devon said.

"Say... what, exactly?" Micah asked. He was getting hard quickly and finding it difficult to think.

"Well, Jim's having a family dinner next weekend," Devon said. He set up a steady rhythm as he added, "And you're invited."

"I'm... oh God, Devon. Your hands—" Micah pushed his pants off so Devon had more room to work, and he writhed as Devon swept his thumb over the head of his cock to catch the precome and help the glide of his fist.

"It's a barbecue at Jim and Irene's," Devon added as though he weren't giving Micah an incredible handjob.

Micah froze, and tremors wracked his frame as Devon stroked him. "I don't... do well with, oh *God*... outdoor functions," he managed.

Devon stopped, and Micah couldn't hold back the whimper of protest. "Oh. I guess... you don't have to go if you're not comfortable with the idea...."

Micah pushed his hips up, desperately looking for friction, but Devon didn't seem to notice. Micah bit his cheek.

"Okay," he said in a rush, "I'll go." Anything, *anything*, to get Devon's hand moving.

Devon's smile nearly blinded him, and within a few minutes, Micah's back arched and he came on a muffled moan into his hastily wadded-up pants.

He lay still for a minute, blinking at the ceiling, as Devon wandered his hand back up along his stomach and chest.

Suddenly Micah scrambled to his feet, uncaring that he was naked from the waist down, and pointed an outraged finger at Devon. "You... you manipulated me. With *sex*."

Devon laughed. "I didn't think it would work," he admitted. "I'm as shocked as you."

Micah's eyes narrowed, and he crawled into Devon's lap, laced his fingers behind Devon's neck, and pressed their foreheads together.

"You will pay, Mallory," he promised.

"A promise made under orgasmic duress is not actually legally binding." Amusement was rich in Devon's voice as he ran his hands up and down Micah's thighs. "You don't have to go unless you really want to."

"Oh, damn you for being so decent, anyway," Micah said and kissed him. "Of course I'll go. Just... don't blame me if I turn into a raging asshole once we get there. You *know* what being off-balance does to me."

"I know," Devon said and kissed him back. "Thank you."

Micah slid a hand between them to grip Devon's hard length in his tented sweatpants, and Devon's head fell back on a gasp.

"There are more pressing matters to attend to right now." Micah stood and held out his hand. "Like you taking me in the bedroom and fucking me into the mattress."

"Work, work, work," Devon groused, but he followed him down the hall.

CHAPTER TEN

DEVON PULLED his truck up to the curb and parked. He killed the engine and turned to face Micah, who was sitting tensely beside him. "Hey." He took Micah's hand. "They're going to love you."

"They're going to *hate* me," Micah corrected him. "I'm going to be an asshole, and I won't be able to stop myself no matter how hard I try."

"Yes, you will." Devon tugged until Micah scooted across the seat and leaned against him. Devon wrapped his arm around him and pressed a kiss to his hair. "I'll be there, and I'll help you through it."

"Do you *know* how many germs float around at barbecues and picnics?" Micah demanded.

Devon's chest shook as he laughed. "How many?"

Micah floundered briefly. "Like, a *lot*."

"Should I have brought an air filter for you?" Devon teased, and Micah pulled away to glare at him.

"Don't mock me, Mallory, or no blowjobs for a month."

Devon mimed zipping his mouth shut and leaned in to kiss him. "It'll be fun. Trust me."

Micah sighed and followed Devon out of the truck, where he looked up at the house in front of them. It was a big, rambling, two-story affair with a neatly kept lawn. Maybe this wouldn't be so bad.

They stepped inside the immaculate foyer. "Hello the house!" Devon called.

"Back here," someone shouted, and Devon led Micah through the entry hall to a huge, sunny kitchen, where a dark-haired woman in a wheelchair was putting the finishing touches on a tray of deviled eggs while a younger, blonde woman worked on a salad on the other side of the counter.

"Devon, honey, you made it," the brunette exclaimed. She pushed her chair around the counter and stretched up to wrap her arms around him. "Oh, sweetheart, it's good to see you. And you must be Micah." She thrust out a hand, and Micah hesitated briefly but shook it with a smile. "We've heard a lot about you, young man," she said.

"Micah, this is Irene. Irene, this is my boyfriend, Micah Ellis."

A lump rose in Micah's throat at the pride in Devon's voice, and he smiled wider at Irene. "It's very nice to meet you," he said.

"And this is Hope," Devon said. He looped an arm around the blonde girl's neck. "She's the one whose kid had the measles or the mumps or the bubonic plague when you came in the shop the first time."

Hope punched him in the ribs and ducked away as Devon doubled over and wheezed for air. She held out her hand to Micah. "It was *not* the bubonic plague," she informed Devon over her shoulder. "So you're the dick who was rude to my boy, huh?" she said, turning back to Micah.

Micah swallowed. "Ah... yeah. That'd be me."

Hope inspected him with sharp brown eyes and finally nodded. "Don't hurt him again or I'll skin you alive. Got it?"

"*God*, Hope, really?" Devon said. He grabbed her around the waist and flung her over his shoulder as she shrieked and flailed and pounded on his back with her small fists. "I'm a grown man," he shouted over her howls, "and I can take care of myself!" He leaned closer to Micah, keeping Hope's wildly swinging limbs at bay, and confided, "For real, though, sleep with one eye open with this one around."

Micah laughed despite his nerves as Devon carried Hope into the backyard. Micah turned back to Irene, who was leaning out of her chair at a dangerous angle to rummage in the fridge.

"Anything I can do to help?"

Irene came up with a beer in each hand, offered him one, and pointed at a stool. "Sit there and keep me company. How are you at peeling eggs?"

"I'm a fair hand," Micah said. "Have they been soaked in ice water?"

"Oh, the man knows his boiled eggs. I'm going to like you. I can tell already. You can wash your hands in the sink."

When Devon came back, pursued by Hope, Micah and Irene were trading recipes across the counter. They looked up as the two stumbled through the sliding glass door. Devon dodged the fist Hope aimed at him, slid his arms around Micah's waist, and kissed the back of his neck.

"Whatcha doin'?"

"Making myself useful," Micah said dryly as he turned his head for a kiss. He glanced back at the counter just in time to see Devon steal a deviled egg. Micah smacked his hand and Irene burst out laughing. Devon turned betrayed eyes on him and Micah arched an eyebrow, unimpressed. "Not time to eat yet, pal."

"Oh yes," Irene said, still laughing. "I *definitely* like you, Micah. Anyone who can put Devon in his place is worth keeping around." She turned to the stove, chortling, and Micah fought a smile as he met Devon's eyes.

"Between you and me," Devon said, "I kinda like it when you… put me in my place." He winked, and Micah snorted a laugh and stretched up into Devon's space to take another kiss.

Hope made gagging noises from the other side of the counter.

Devon broke away and leveled a faux-sympathetic gaze on her. "It's okay to be jealous, Hope. Bottling up negative emotions is very bad for you."

Micah turned back to the eggs and continued peeling, but his laughter bubbled up as Hope glared at Devon and stalked out of the kitchen with her nose in the air.

The sliding glass door opened again, and Sean bounded in, dragging a slim, dark-haired woman with cobalt-blue eyes in her wake. She hugged Devon and shook Micah's hand.

"So, did the tales of Jim's grilling prowess finally lure you in?" Sean inquired. She grabbed the dark-haired woman and pulled her forward. "Micah, this is Fallon Connors, my girlfriend. Fallon, Micah… um… shit, I don't think I know your last name."

"Ellis," Micah supplied as Devon rolled his eyes next to him. He shook Fallon's hand, and Fallon smiled at him.

"Very nice to meet you, Micah. I've heard good things."

"You clearly haven't been talking to anyone who actually knows me, then," Micah said and smiled back at her. He stood up to wash his hands again so he could continue peeling eggs and then settled back on his stool.

"She's been talking to me," Devon said. "And I've told her all about how amazing you are."

Micah opened his mouth to argue but snapped it shut again and leaned back against Devon's warm chest. Devon's arm tightened around him and he dropped a kiss on Micah's hair.

Fallon turned to Sean. "Do you want a drink?"

"If you're getting one," Sean said. She collapsed into a chair and stretched out her long legs. "Fuck. What a long, shitty day."

"Numbers still not adding up?" Devon asked. He pulled up a stool, reached for an egg, and peeled it as he watched his sister with a worried crease on his brow.

Sean shrugged. "Like they ever do."

"No shop talk during family dinner," Irene said, and they both subsided.

Fallon handed Sean a beer, and Sean smiled up at her. She caught her wrist and pulled until Fallon sighed and settled herself gingerly across Sean's lap. Sean wrapped her arms around Fallon's waist and pressed a kiss to her shoulder, and Micah laughed.

"Runs in the family, clearly."

Fallon looked up with a long-suffering smile on her face. "You too?"

"Devon likes to ambush me," Micah confided.

Devon snorted a laugh from beside him. "Not my fault you're so much fun to cuddle with."

Micah set the last egg in the bowl for Irene and got up to wash his hands again.

"Come on," Devon said. "I want you to meet the rest of the crew."

Micah tensed. Devon wanted him to go outside—out with the dirt and the smoke and the germs and…. Devon held out a hand and waited, and Micah knew he wouldn't force him, but…. He swallowed hard and accepted Devon's hand. The smile he got almost made it worth it.

But he was nervous as he followed Devon onto the back patio. An older, bearded man stood at the barbecue grill, turning meat, while a younger man with a blond mullet lounged beside him with a longneck in hand.

"Jim, this is Micah," Devon said. "My boyfriend."

"Nice to meetcha," the bearded man said. Micah drew back as Jim set down the barbecue fork and held out a hand, but before Micah was forced to choose between taking Jim's dirty hand and being unforgivably rude, Devon smoothly stepped between them and put a beer in Jim's outstretched hand. Micah took a relieved breath as Jim accepted it without comment and turned back to the grill.

"So you were the one who was a dick to him, weren't you?" Jim asked over his shoulder.

Micah sent Devon a plaintive look. "I'm never going to live that down, am I?"

"Probably not," Devon said. He rubbed Micah's back, his hand warm and comforting. Micah leaned into it as Devon turned him toward the other man on the patio. "And this is the illustrious Yancy," he said.

Yancy toasted them with his beer bottle. "'Sup, dudes?" he said cheerfully. "Pull up a chair and tell me all about yourself. Dev tells me you're some big-name headhunter?"

"I'm not a big-name anything," Micah said as he settled on the edge of the chair beside Devon. "But I *am* a headhunter, so I guess that part's true. What about you? What do you do?"

"Little as possible, most days," Yancy said and took another swig of beer. He grinned at Micah, who smiled back.

DEVON KEPT his word. He stayed close to Micah at all times and ran interference, especially with Hope's two-year-old daughter, an impish blonde child named Maryann, who developed a strange fascination with Micah and would have climbed in his lap several times over if Devon hadn't gently intervened each time. Micah was strung taut, but Devon must have warned the others about his hang-ups, because no one said a word, and Micah managed to keep the snippiness under control.

They were finished with dinner and getting ready for dessert when Devon slung an arm around Micah's shoulders and pulled him in close to press his lips to Micah's ear.

"I'm so proud of you," he breathed.

Micah smiled and leaned against Devon's side.

"So proud of you, in fact," Devon continued, "that I think you deserve a reward."

Micah glanced up at him.

"I bought you something," Devon whispered. "It's on the bedside table at your place. Make it through dessert and a little more small talk and it's all yours."

"What is it?" Micah asked.

Devon's eyes creased in amusement. "You'll see. But it's something I'm going to use more than you."

Micah crossed his legs and swallowed hard. The rest of the evening was a blur, and yet it seemed to take forever for Devon to stand, make their good-byes, and hand out hugs to everyone.

Finally, though, Jim and Irene waved good-bye to them, and Devon and Micah made their way across the lawn toward Devon's truck.

Micah buckled himself in, and Devon reached across the bench seat to squeeze his knee.

"I told you you'd do fine," he said as he started the engine and pulled away from the curb.

"Apparently distracting me with promises of sex toys works wonders," Micah said, his lips curving. "Don't know why I never thought to try that before."

"What makes you think it's a sex toy?" Devon asked, but his grin ruined the question. "Okay. It's totally a sex toy. And we're taking it for a spin as soon as we get home."

"Drive faster," Micah said.

Devon laughed. "Getting pulled over and ticketed isn't going to do either of us any good. Patience, love."

Micah blinked and watched Devon's profile in the dim light of the dash. Devon didn't even seem aware of what he'd said. He was focused on the road and traffic, his big hands loose and easy on the wheel.

Micah turned the word over in his mind. *Love.* They'd been dating for three months, and not a day went by without them at least talking, spending the nights together more often than not. It was entirely possible Devon thought he was in love with Micah. But Devon was too good to love someone as messed up as Micah, and Micah wouldn't allow Devon to be dragged down to his level.

Lost in his thoughts, it took Micah a minute to realize Devon had slid his hand across the seat and up onto Micah's thigh. He gulped as Devon moved farther to investigate his crotch. He squeezed and rubbed until Micah was half-hard and gasping.

"Not fair if I can't reciprocate," he managed.

"Lucky for you we're home," Devon said and parked the truck.

"Race you," Micah said, and he was out of the cab and up the stairs before Devon managed to get both feet on the ground. Devon caught up quickly, though, and crowded him against the door as Micah unlocked it. He rubbed his groin against Micah's backside until Micah tilted his head back and glared at him.

"Kind of can't concentrate on motor function when you're doing that," he pointed out.

"Hurry up or I'll tear your clothes off and take you right here in the hallway," Devon growled.

"Mrs.... Rothschild next door would... *love* that," Micah panted and shoved the door open to stumble inside. He kicked off his shoes and dropped them onto the shelf with little regard for their neatness. Then Devon's hands were on him, and Micah's brain shut down.

Devon kicked the door shut behind them and pulled Micah around to face him. He picked him up so Micah was straddling his waist and gazing down at his upturned face.

"Hey," Devon murmured.

"Hey back," Micah said. He ground his hard length slowly, deliciously, against Devon's flat abdomen.

Devon's eyes fluttered shut for a moment, and he took a step, then another, with his hands out to keep from running into anything in Micah's kitchen.

They reached the bedroom without incident, and Devon deposited Micah on the bed, dropped a kiss on his nose, and stretched up to reach the neatly wrapped box sitting on the nightstand. Micah sat up, crossed his legs, and turned the box over in his hands.

Devon rolled his eyes. "Just open it, dude."

"Shh," Micah retorted. "I'm savoring. I never get gifts. I'm enjoying the anticipation."

Devon's eyes softened. "I'll buy you more presents, then, love. Now come on. Open it."

There it was again—that word. But Micah was too keyed up, too turned on and jittery to address it at that moment. He tore into the paper and revealed a sleek maple-wood box. Micah lifted the lid, and his eyes widened at the sight of the vibrator inside.

"Oh," he breathed.

"You said you wanted toys," Devon said and kissed him over the top of the box. "This is the first we're going to play with, but very definitely not the last." He picked up a small square piece of plastic from beside the vibrator. "It even has a remote. Look." He flipped the switch, and the toy buzzed to life. Devon's eyes were blown dark, and he licked his lips and took a steadying breath. "You're not going to touch your cock at all tonight."

Micah jerked his head up. "At *all?*"

"At all," Devon repeated. "You touch it even once and it's game over, we're done for the night. I'm not going to spank you, because you'd enjoy that too much. I'm just going to... stop."

Micah bit back a groan as Devon lifted his collar out of the drawer and snapped it into place around Micah's neck. Micah took a deep breath, and the worries and tensions of the day dissipated. Devon was in charge. Devon would take care of him. Micah could trust Devon, turn his brain off, and just *feel* with him.

"There's my angel," Devon murmured. He kissed him again, then drew away and stood up. "Get naked," he commanded, and Micah hurried to obey.

Goose bumps rose on his skin when he was completely bare, and Micah rubbed his arms, suddenly unsure of what to do.

"On the bed, on your back, arms and legs outspread," Devon directed. When Micah was in position, Devon stripped swiftly and then picked up a velvet rope from another box beside the bed. He tied it around Micah's wrist, lashed it to the bedpost, and laid the end in Micah's palm.

"This is a quick-release knot," he said. "You need out, yank on it."

Micah nodded, and his throat worked as he swallowed. He was already fully erect from sheer anticipation and leaking in slow drops onto his belly. Devon skimmed a palm over the head of his shaft and then tied Micah's other hand to the bed. Micah whimpered deep in his throat, but Devon just laughed, took the vibrator from its box, and held it up for inspection.

"I've already sterilized it," he said, and Micah sagged in relief. That had been the question on the tip of his tongue.

Devon climbed onto the bed and knelt between Micah's splayed legs. Micah lay still, unable to see much of him from his position flat on his back, and waited, trembling. Devon smoothed a warm hand over his thigh.

"Relax, baby," he murmured. "You're gonna like this."

Micah heard the click of a bottle cap, and then something hard and cold nudged at his entrance. Micah spread his legs wider, consciously relaxed, and gasped as the tip slid inside, slick with lube.

Devon inched the toy farther in, in what felt like slow motion as Micah panted through the stretch and burn.

"Look at you taking it," Devon whispered, his voice heavy with awe. "My God. You're amazing, angel."

Micah couldn't remember how to talk. He was too focused on the sensations in his ass that were rapidly going from uncomfortable to fucking amazing. His breathing was unsteady, shallow, and rapid by the time the vibrator was fully seated. Devon lifted his head and looked up Micah's body.

"What's your safeword?"

"Manta ray," Micah said instantly. "C'mon, Devon, *please.*"

Devon pressed a button. The vibrator whirred to life, and Micah arched off the bed with a choked-off cry as it rubbed against the bundle of nerves at his center and sent lightning rippling through him. He couldn't breathe, couldn't *think.* His entire world was the amazing feeling radiating through his body.

And then Devon turned the speed up. Micah thrashed in his bonds and cried out, so hard it hurt. He already needed to come, and they'd barely even *started.*

Devon brought his hands down on Micah's hips and pinned him to the bed, and Micah had an awful feeling that he was going to come, untouched, before he'd had a chance to enjoy this at all.

"Gonna…. Devon… please… not yet—"

Devon locked his hand around the base of Micah's erection, throttling back the orgasm and making Micah writhe and sob as he bucked helplessly against Devon's unyielding grip.

Devon didn't release him until Micah sagged back onto the bed and drew a ragged breath. Only then did Devon let him go and press a kiss to Micah's inner thigh.

"I seem to remember you saying you wanted to be marked," he murmured.

Micah nodded, unable to speak. Sweat was already springing up on his skin with the effort of holding back. That damn vibrator was still buzzing mercilessly away inside him.

Devon nosed along Micah's thigh, inching closer to his groin and the soft skin there. Without warning he latched on and sucked.

Micah moaned as Devon's mouth worked, sucking a bruise into the sensitive skin. He nipped lightly and laved the sting of his teeth with his tongue. Then he moved to the next spot, fastened on, and sucked hard, and Micah thought it entirely likely that he wasn't going to make it out alive.

This went on longer than Micah had thought possible, until he was a shaking, whimpering mess on the bed. His skin felt too tight for his body. He was so desperate to come he couldn't *think*, and still Devon placed mark after mark, up and down Micah's inner thighs as he brought Micah to the edge over and over again with devastating precision but didn't allow him to come.

"You're gonna feel this for a week," Devon growled and lifted his head. "Every time you sit down, every time you close your legs, you're gonna feel what I did to you, and you're going to *remember*. You're going to remember how I marked you, how I claimed you. How I made you *mine*." He sank his teeth into the meat of Micah's upper thigh, and Micah came on a strangled scream, his cock jerking and spasming, and bliss overwhelmed him.

Dimly he heard Devon swear above him with horror in his voice. "Oh Jesus *fuck*. Halo, halo, fuck, fuck, fuck. *Halo!*"

Micah slammed back into his body with jarring force to Devon, panting and panicky, trying frantically to untie him. Devon swore again, almost sobbing, and yanked on the rope until Micah's wrist fell free.

"Devon, *what*—" Micah grabbed at the other rope and freed himself. He jerked the vibrator out and threw it off to the side as he sat up. Devon looked on the verge of tears as Micah grabbed his face and forced him to meet his eyes. "What is it, Devon? What *happened*?"

Devon swallowed hard and took a shaky breath. "You're bleeding," he managed, his voice wobbling. "I... made you bleed."

Micah looked down at his legs, which were littered with rapidly darkening marks, and his eyes widened at the sight of the teeth marks on his right thigh and blood dripping in a slow ooze.

"Oh," he said. "That would explain why I came so hard." He swayed as the shock of being yanked out of sub space so abruptly made itself known. But he pushed it away. Devon needed him. "Come here," he said and wrapped his arms around Devon's neck to pull him close. Devon obeyed, his cheek pressed to Micah's belly and his arms around his waist, seemingly uncaring about the mess of come and sweat all over Micah's skin. Devon trembled and Micah bent over him as a rush of tenderness swamped him.

"I'm sorry," Devon mumbled into Micah's stomach. "So sorry, Dosa. Went too far. Didn't mean to hurt you."

"Oh, sweetheart," Micah said as he stroked his hair back. "Devon, *look* at me." Devon rolled his head and looked up into Micah's face, his blue eyes wet with tears. Micah smiled down at him. "That was probably the most intense orgasm I've ever had," he said gently.

Devon blinked. "You're *bleeding*," he protested.

"Yeah, and I'll feel it for a week, just like you wanted," Micah said. "Every time I so much as *move*, I'll think of you marking me, claiming me, and I'm probably going to have a permanent boner until it heals." He cupped Devon's face. "If it was too much, I would've safeworded. It was… *amazing*."

Devon squeezed his eyes shut and took a shuddering breath. "I saw blood and… I freaked," he whispered. "Wasn't… wasn't ready for that. 'M sorry, Micah. I fucked up the scene. Shouldn't have panicked like that. I ruined—" Micah silenced him with a hand over his mouth, and Devon took another shaky breath.

"You didn't ruin anything, baby. Now come on. I think it's bath time." Micah helped him upright, and they made their way into the bathroom.

"You shouldn't bathe with an open wound," Devon said when Micah tried to step into the tub. "Let me bandage it for you, and then you can…. Would you sit with me?"

So Micah took the fastest shower he'd ever had as Devon hovered in the stall beside him and made sure Micah didn't collapse. He let Devon clean and bandage the bite, though his big, gentle hands were a little wobbly. Then Micah put his feet in the tub as Devon sat down in the warm water and leaned back between Micah's legs with a sigh, careful to avoid the wound on his thigh.

"These things happen," Micah murmured as he combed Devon's hair back from his face. "The important thing is that we talked through it. We can try again tomorrow, if you like."

"Okay," Devon whispered. He turned his head and pressed his cheek to Micah's stomach. "Thank you."

CHAPTER ELEVEN

WHEN MICAH woke up the next morning, Devon wasn't in bed with him. Micah sat bolt upright and looked around. Devon's watch was still on the bedside table, his street clothes neatly folded next to it, so he couldn't have gone far.

Micah pulled on a pair of soft pants and padded into the living room. Devon was on the sofa in his pajamas with his long arms wrapped around his knees and his eyes fixed on the far wall.

"Devon?" Micah came closer, and Devon turned away, but not before Micah saw the tears in his eyes. "Dev, what is it?" Micah climbed onto the sofa and knelt next to him. Devon took a shaky breath and swiped at his eyes with his sleeve.

Worry swamped Micah. "I can't help if you won't talk to me, baby."

Devon pressed his face to his knees and tightened his arms. "I... hurt you," he said in a muffled voice.

"Is that all?" Micah said, relieved. "Devon, we've been over this."

"It's not that," Devon whispered. "Micah... I... *liked* it." He covered his mouth and tears slid down his face. "I'm twisted," he managed. "I hurt you, and I liked it, and I'm—"

Micah reached out and pulled Devon into his arms. Devon didn't fight. He fell against him as his frame was wracked with sobs.

"What if I go too far?" he choked out. "What if I hurt you permanently—*really* hurt you? You shouldn't trust me, Micah, you—"

Micah smoothed his hair and rocked him back and forth. "This is a drop, Dev. That's all this is. Breathe, baby, and listen to me. You've been telling me that I'm not worthless or sick. Is that still true?"

Devon nodded and hiccupped.

"Then why wouldn't it be true of you too?" Micah asked. He pressed his cheek to Devon's brown hair, and the silky strands tickled his nose. "Devon, if I can enjoy being hurt and it doesn't make me perverted or awful, then why can't you like the opposite?"

"That's different," Devon protested.

"How?" Micah countered. "Dev, it goes both ways. You would never hurt me in any way I didn't ask for. No. Don't argue with me. I know you wouldn't. You *couldn't*."

Devon tightened his arms around Micah's waist. "But what if I did?"

"Look at me," Micah said gently. He pushed on Devon's shoulder until Devon sat up and wiped his face. Micah took his hands and met his eyes. "I trust you, Devon. I was with Barrett for over a year, and I never trusted him the way I trust you. I'm safe with you. I know that. You are good. You are *kind*. You are amazing, and I lo—" He snapped his mouth shut before he said the words. Instead he leaned forward and gently kissed Devon's lips. "What do you need from me?"

Devon closed his eyes and took a shuddering breath. "I... hold me?"

Micah scooted until his back was against the arm of the couch. He beckoned, and Devon crawled between his legs and collapsed on Micah's chest, facedown. Micah wrapped his arms around Devon's shoulders and just held on with his cheek pressed to his soft hair. They stayed that way, until Devon slowly relaxed into sleep as Micah held him.

Micah picked up the remote and turned the TV on with the volume muted on one of his favorite cooking shows.

When Devon finally stirred and woke, Micah set the remote down and smoothed Devon's tousled hair from his eyes.

"Hey," he murmured. "Sleep well?"

Devon yawned and nodded. He pressed his face against Micah's chest again. "Sorry for freaking out," he mumbled.

"Don't be stupid," Micah said gently. "You had a drop. You weren't 'freaking out.' You were dealing with legitimate emotional issues."

"Is that what you go through every time?" Devon asked, pushing himself upright.

Micah nodded. "More or less."

"Jesus," Devon muttered. "How do you *do* it? *Why* do you do it? The subbing, I mean, when you know the drop's going to hit you so hard?"

Micah lifted a shoulder. "It's not really something I have a choice in. Subbing is like an itch under my skin, the need to shut my brain off, just... be." He twined their fingers together and smoothed a thumb over Devon's knuckles. "Besides, once the drop's over, especially if I'm helped through it in the right way, I feel... clean. Empty. Washed out. Light and... free." He smiled ruefully. "I guess it's worth it. With the right person."

"I hope I can live up to the trust you put in me," Devon said, and Micah laughed.

"Oh, you already have. Several times over. Now, are you hungry? Shall I cook something for us?"

"I can do it," Devon said, but Micah caught his arm as he tried to stand up.

"Oh no. It's my turn to take care of you, for a change, and I intend to enjoy this. You can sit at the table and keep me company, but I'm making the meal. I have some dosa batter, if you'd like me to make those. The potato curry I tried last week was kind of shitty, though, so I don't recommend we eat that unless you *want* me to be accused of your murder."

Devon smiled, slow and sweet, and leaned in to kiss him. "Death by potato curry," he murmured when he pulled back. "I *like* your cooking."

Micah laughed and stood up. "As long as you understand I'm not actively trying to poison you."

"Oh, hey," Devon said as he followed him to the kitchen, "I have a game tomorrow. Do you think you could come?"

Micah tensed. "A… game?"

Devon came up behind him and kissed his shoulder. "Yes, Dosa. A game. Of baseball. You know, with the sticks and the balls and the running of the bases?" He ran his hands up and down Micah's arms, and Micah leaned back against his chest and deliberated. Part of him was delighted to see that Devon was clearly feeling steadier, but the rest of him was fixated on the problem at hand.

"But you'll be playing," he said.

Devon kissed his neck. "That's the general idea, yes."

"But… if you're playing," Micah said, shivering at the feel of Devon's warm mouth, "I'll be… alone. In the bleachers."

"Mmm-hmm." Devon was apparently intent on entirely mapping out Micah's neck with his lips, and Micah reached up and cupped his head. He tangled his fingers in Devon's soft hair and reveled in the undemanding contact, the sheer joy of simply being held and cherished.

"I don't—" Micah swallowed and decided on raw honesty. "I'm not sure I can do it, Dev."

Devon lifted his head and turned Micah so they were facing. Micah gazed up at him, and Devon bent to kiss him.

"I think you can," he murmured. "You can handle so much more than you think, and I really, really want to look up in the stands and see my boyfriend sitting there, cheering me on."

Micah sighed. "You don't play fair."

Devon's lips quirked, and he kissed him again. "Never said I did. So you'll be there?"

"Do I have to wear a huge foam finger?" Micah countered.

Devon laughed outright. "Not unless you feel like looking ridiculous." His eyes softened, and he pulled Micah into a hug. "Thank you," he said into Micah's throat. "If it helps, I'll be wearing teeny tiny shorts to warm up in and then really tight pants for the game itself."

Micah let go of him and smacked his shoulder as Devon laughed and pretended to cower. "Maybe next time don't bury the lede, dumbass!"

DEVON DIDN'T stay over that night. He warned Micah that it was an early game and he had to be there and ready to start before the sun was even up, so Micah spent the night alone. He missed Devon more than he wanted to admit, rolling over to reach for him in his sleep several times, and woke up to an empty bed. He ended up hugging his stuffed manta ray instead, which at least smelled like Devon, but wasn't nearly as warm and cuddly.

The alarm woke him at six, and Micah shuffled out to make breakfast. He leaned against the counter, and took his first sip of steaming coffee as he wondered what the hell he thought he was doing. Going to a baseball game, outside, with all the dirt and the germs and the *people*? It was insane. It was asking too much of him. He couldn't do it.

He reached for the phone to tell Devon he was canceling, and it buzzed. Micah read the text with an internal sigh.

Looking forward to seeing you.

Micah chewed on the inside of his cheek. Devon would understand. And he wouldn't push or nag or guilt-trip Micah in any way. But he would be so disappointed. Micah closed his eyes briefly and then tapped out a quick text.

What are you wearing?

The reply was quick. *Teeny tiny shorts, as advertised.*

Micah's lips twitched. *But how can I be sure? I think I need proof.*

This time the reply took longer, and when it came through, Micah forgot how to breathe. It was a picture of Devon, midstretch in the famous shorts, one endlessly long leg out to the side and the other folded beneath him. He wasn't looking at the camera, and his hair fell over his brow as he leaned forward to touch his toes.

Micah stared at the picture, spellbound, until the phone buzzed and startled him.

Sean took that for me, and now she's teasing me about my Tyra Banks pose. I better get some kind of reward for putting up with this.

It took Micah a minute to remember how to compose a reply, but he finally managed to fumble one out. *You'll be lucky if I don't jump you in the parking lot, Mallory.*

Hurry up and get here so you can!

Micah headed for the shower, smiling. He glanced out the living room window as he passed it and hesitated as a flash of dark red in the parking lot caught his eye. He turned back and got up against the window to peer down into the lot. Nothing except the cars that were supposed to be there.

"You're imagining things, Ellis," he said out loud.

SHOWERED, SHAVED, wearing a faded pair of jeans and a dark green, long-sleeved T-shirt that he knew Devon liked and with a packet of wet wipes in his pocket, Micah pulled into traffic and drummed on the steering wheel in a desperate attempt to calm his nerves.

It was a relatively short drive, which meant Micah didn't have time to come up with another reason to cancel before he found the park where the game was being held and turned in to the gravel parking lot. He bumped slowly over the tiny rocks, holding his breath, and found Devon's truck with a sigh of relief. The bleachers stood off to the side, with a scattering of spectators in clumps here and there. There were a few players on the field warming up and throwing a ball back and forth. Micah didn't see Devon anywhere, but he had to be in there somewhere.

Micah took a deep breath and headed down the gentle slope toward the dugouts and the players. He threaded his way between people and craned his neck for a glimpse of shaggy brown hair or a set of familiar shoulders. There was dirt *everywhere*. So many germs, so many possible infectious diseases. Anyone could just brush up against him, get him filthy, make him sick—

His breathing shortened, and his throat closed up as he searched. *Devon, where are you. I can't do this alone—*

Someone jostled his arm and murmured an apology, and Micah flinched as panic spiked through his chest. He turned, keeping his arms close to his sides, and desperately scanned faces. He was inches from bolting, but he summoned up a mental image of the manta ray, swimming in its tank, floating through the water in serene silence.

"Micah!" Devon's voice was delighted, and it cut through the din in Micah's mind. Micah nearly wept with relief as he spun.

Devon scooped him into a hug, and Micah melted into it, wrapping his arms around Devon's neck as he hung on for dear life.

"You okay?" Devon murmured in his ear.

"Just… need a minute," Micah managed.

Devon tightened his grip and just held on as Micah's breathing steadied and his heart rate slowed. Finally he relaxed as a wolf whistle ripped the cool morning air.

"Get a room!" Sean shouted.

Devon gave her the finger without looking and peered into Micah's face. "Okay?"

Micah nodded and summoned a smile.

"Why didn't you text me when you got here?" Devon asked. "I would have met you at the car."

Micah blinked. "It… didn't occur to me."

Devon laughed and stepped back a pace, and Micah got his first look at what Devon was wearing—tight-fitting pants and a jersey proudly proclaiming that he was a Blue Devil. A tiny indigo imp leered at Micah from the letter *E*, brandishing a pitchfork.

Micah marshaled his thoughts. "What—where are the shorts? I was promised shorts, Mallory!"

Devon grimaced. "We finished warm-ups, and Coach wants us on the field, so I had to change. I'm sorry?"

Micah glared up at him and realized with a surge of carefully hidden amusement that teasing Devon was steadying him, helping him find solid footing again. "I consider this a breach of contract, just so you know."

Devon's lips quirked up. "Yeah? What kind of penalty am I looking at?"

Micah couldn't help but smile. "I'm not sure yet, but I do know a *stiff* fine will be levied."

Devon burst out laughing and tugged Micah in for a kiss. "So very awful," he said against Micah's lips, and Micah laughed with him. "Go sit with Fallon in the stands, okay? I'll see you after the game, but you won't want to hug me then. I'll be all sweaty and gross."

Micah turned to look where Devon pointed and spied Fallon's neat figure perched on the bleachers near the top. "What am I supposed to say before a game?" he asked. "Break a leg?"

"Pretty sure that's just for theater," Devon said. "'Good luck' will work."

"Good luck," Micah said. "Kick their asses."

Devon winked and jogged off, and Micah watched him go and admired the view. Then he shook himself and headed for the bleachers.

Fallon rose and greeted Micah with a smile, but didn't offer to shake his hand. Instead she gestured for Micah to sit beside her.

Micah inspected the stainless-steel bench, and his chest eased when he saw that it was spotless and gleaming. Still he pulled out a wet wipe and cleaned it thoroughly. Then he settled next to Fallon and gazed out over the field, his hands in his lap.

"Do you come to every game?" he asked.

Fallon nodded. "Every one that I can, at least. Sometimes the hospital schedules me for clinic hours over the weekends, but most of the time I'm here."

"That's right. You're a doctor," Micah said. "What's your specialty?"

"Cardiothoracic surgeon, actually," Fallon said as she waved to Sean on the field. She slanted a smile at Micah. "Devon was so excited that you were coming. He couldn't stop talking about it over breakfast."

Guilt sliced through Micah as he remembered how he'd nearly canceled, but he managed to return the smile. "I'm glad I did," he said, surprised to realize he was being honest.

"Look. They're about to start," Fallon said, and Micah turned to pay attention.

AFTER THE game, Micah would have been hard-pressed to remember details. There were bouts of sporadic, frantic activity between long stretches of nothing much happening at all. But Micah cheered every time Devon took the field, and he stood and applauded wildly each time Devon scored a point for his team.

When the opposing team was soundly routed, Micah discovered his throat was sore from all the shouting and his face ached from his grin. He dashed out of the bleachers to meet Devon, leaving Fallon to follow laughing in his wake, and he fetched up outside the dugout as Devon emerged, sweaty and disheveled, carrying a sack of bats over his shoulder.

Devon's face lit up when he saw Micah, and Micah grinned back, wanting to hug him but deterred by all the dirt and sweat.

Devon handed the sack off to a teammate and turned to Micah but kept several feet between them. "What'd you think?"

Micah bounced on his toes. "It was awesome," he said, and delighted in the way Devon glowed at the simple words. "I can't wait to come to the next game."

Devon's smile stretched from ear to ear. "So," he said, taking one small step forward, "do you mind if I give Sean my truck keys and you drive my sweaty self back to your place? I was thinking of showering and then maybe doing a private showing of the tiny shorts."

Micah hesitated only briefly. He still had the wet wipes. He could clean the seat once they got back to his place. "Why are we still talking?" he demanded. "Get your sweaty ass in my car."

Devon laughed. "Give me a minute to find Sean. I'll be right there."

Micah climbed the hill back to his car, smiling to himself. But his smile slipped as he neared it and realized there was something under the wiper.

A sprig of dark pink-red flowers with round petals and a small button-like stamen had been carefully tucked into place on the windshield, neatly waiting for Micah.

He spun in place and looked wildly around even though he knew he wouldn't see anyone who shouldn't be there. Micah yanked the flowers out from under the wiper and slung them under the vehicle next to him as Devon jogged up the slope to join him.

"Everything okay?" Devon asked.

Micah straightened and forced a smile. "Yep. Let's get home and check out those shorts."

He made a determined effort to listen to Devon's lighthearted chatter as he drove, and respond properly when necessary. *It was nothing.*

Someone leaving a gift for their girlfriend and they got the wrong car. He shoved the fear down deep and stomped on it as he listened to the story Devon was telling, and eventually it began to lessen and he was able to breathe easier.

Just a simple mistake. It happens all the time.

Chapter Twelve

Micah went to work Monday to discover a bouquet of marigolds on Norma's desk.

"Got an admirer?" he teased.

Norma held up the card. "They're for you, actually."

Micah accepted the card and blinked. "Mine," it read in bold, unfamiliar script.

"Are they from Devon?" Norma asked.

Micah shook his head as a chill skittered down his spine. "No," he said flatly. "They were misaddressed. Throw them away."

"Shouldn't we send them back?" Norma protested as he brushed by her desk toward his office.

"*Throw them away*," Micah hissed. But then he stopped himself and pinched the bridge of his nose. "I'm sorry, Norma. It's not your fault, I'm—it's nothing."

"It's not my place, but it doesn't seem like nothing," Norma said carefully.

Micah took a deep breath. "Did you... send Devon flowers for me before our first date?"

Norma shook her head. "Of course not."

"Are you *sure*?" Micah pressed. "Did I maybe ask you to do it for me?"

"No," Norma said as she flipped through her appointment book. "Look, I always put what you ask me to do in here. See? The day you had me send Mallory Auto $250—that's in here. If you'd told me to send flowers, I'd have written it down, and if *I'd* done it for you, I'd remember. I didn't, Mr. Ellis. I promise—"

"Okay," Micah said, touching her hand and cutting her off. "It's okay, Norma. I believe you. I just had to ask."

He patted her hand and turned to unlock his office. "Throw those away, please," he said over his shoulder.

The day passed in a bit of a blur, and it took Micah a while to drag himself together and focus on work. Finally, though, he managed to shake off the morning's events when Norma informed him that the details for the office retreat had been finalized.

Just another coincidence. They happen all the time. He knew he was lying to himself, that something was going on, but he shoved the tiny thought down deep and sat on it. He'd deal with it later.

Devon met Micah at his place after work, and they spent the afternoon in the condo, lazing on the couch, watching movies and eating junk food. Finally Micah stretched and glanced at his watch.

"Oh shit, I forgot to tell you!"

Devon rolled his head on Micah's thigh and looked up at him. "Tell me what?" he inquired. He sounded lazily happy, and Micah cupped his face in one hand and smiled down at him.

"I'm going out of town week after next."

Devon sat bolt upright and his blue eyes filled with dismay. "You're *what?*"

"I'm… leaving," Micah said, suddenly cautious. Was Devon angry with him for not telling him sooner? Or was he upset at not being invited? "For work," he added. "It's just a week."

"You're going to be gone for a whole *week*, and you didn't tell me?" Devon demanded.

Micah shrank in on himself. "I just found out this morning and I… didn't think you'd really care," he said. "I'll have my phone. We can still text plenty, and I guess I just figured it wouldn't make much difference."

Devon went to his knees and took Micah's hands. "Of *course* I care, Dosa. Why would you even think—where are you going?"

"Umm…. Tahiti?" Micah said.

"Seriously?" Devon said, his eyes widening. "Your job is sending you to Tahiti? And they only gave you two weeks' notice?"

"Well, they've been talking about it for a while. It's just that there was apparently some debate about where we were going," Micah said. "We all cleared our calendars and were just waiting for the official word. I forgot about it, to be honest, because I really don't want to go. It's some sort of team-building exercise—conferences and games and stuff. I'm probably going to hide in my room the entire time. I'm not a fan of… sand."

Devon smiled at him. "Still. Tahiti. I've always wanted to go there."

Would you come with me? The words were on the tip of Micah's tongue, and he only just kept his mouth shut. Devon had work obligations. His shop was struggling financially. There was no way he'd be able to go, and he'd never accept Micah paying for his plane ticket, even if he could get the time off.

Instead Micah leaned in and kissed him. "Well, we'd better make the most of it until I leave. Would you like to go out to eat tonight?"

Devon kissed back willingly. He brought a hand up and threaded his fingers through Micah's hair. Then he sighed and broke away to nibble along Micah's jaw, making him shiver.

"We never did go to Madeleine's," he murmured. "Would you like to?"

Micah gripped Devon's upper arms to steady himself as Devon moved down his throat, nipping gently. "I, uh… oh *God*…." He gasped as Devon pulled his T-shirt aside and sucked a mark over his collarbone. "That… sounds good…. Jesus, Devon—"

"Make the reservation, then," Devon growled. He lifted his head. His pupils were blown, his eyes hooded and predatory, and Micah's skin prickled with anticipation. He scrambled to find his phone and make the call as Devon went back to Micah's collarbone and made an identical mark on the other side.

Micah was distantly proud of how he managed to keep his voice mostly steady as he placed the reservation, his eyes tightly closed as he spoke so he didn't have to see the way Devon had slipped a hand inside his own pants and was stroking himself in a slow, leisurely fashion as he sucked bruises to the surface of Micah's skin.

When Micah hung up, he was trembling, hard and needy. "Eight… ah, God… o'clock," he managed.

"Plenty of time, then," Devon murmured into his skin and pressed him back against the couch. "Now be still and don't touch yourself. I'll be right back."

Micah lay against the armrest and watched as Devon headed for the bedroom. When he came back, he was carrying Micah's collar, and Micah swallowed hard as a rush of relief swamped him. He'd been worried, deep in the back of his mind, that Devon had been scared off Domming after his drop over the weekend. He leaned into Devon's hands as they snapped the collar into place, and he briefly closed his eyes.

Devon brushed a thumb over Micah's cheekbone. "Get naked."

Micah hurried to obey as Devon disrobed more leisurely and settled… at the far end of the sofa? Micah stared, confused, as Devon let his long legs fall open and wrapped a hand around himself. Devon gestured with his chin.

"Back where I put you, angel," he said, and Micah sat down on the other end of the sofa, which was so big that the only thing within Micah's reach was one of Devon's feet, the other flat on the floor.

Disappointment and self-consciousness welled within Micah in equal measure. Was he not even going to be allowed to touch? His erection wilted a little, and he started to pull his knees to his chest, but Devon shook his head, still stroking.

"Legs apart," he commanded. "Spread 'em for me, baby. I want to see."

Micah obeyed reluctantly. He splayed his legs and bit his lip when Devon moaned.

"Jesus, you're so gorgeous," Devon whispered and tightened his fist. "Touch yourself."

Micah hesitated. Devon was two hundred and twenty pounds of muscles and golden skin, all long, toned limbs and tousled brown hair, utterly unselfconscious and accepting of his own attractiveness, and Micah felt like an unruly sack of potatoes next to him—lumpy and unprepossessing, no matter how many times Devon said he liked what he saw.

Devon tilted his head, and his eyes narrowed. "Is there a problem?"

"No," Micah said hurriedly. He made a loose fist around his half-hard length, and his eyes fluttered briefly closed at the sensation.

"God yes," Devon said and he jacked himself faster. "Here's what we're going… to do." He took a steadying breath, and Micah waited and hardened under his own hand as Devon gathered his thoughts.

"You're going to play with yourself," Devon continued. "You're going… to tell me… what you do to get yourself off. And then you're… going to do it while I watch. If I come first, then you can choose the scenes for the next week. If you come first, then you're mine, and I'm going to—" His breath caught as Micah whimpered in spite of himself. "Oh yes. Now," Devon managed once he composed himself. "Start talking, angel."

Micah struggled to focus. "I like to… oh *God*… I start with slow strokes with my right hand. With… my left I play with my nipples a bit. Can I…?"

Devon nodded. "Show me."

Micah slid a hand up his chest, pinched his right nipple into a peak, and rolled it between his fingers. Devon watched, his eyes dark and hungry, as Micah repeated the process on the other side. When he let his hand fall back to his side, Devon smiled.

"Beautiful," he whispered. "Now what?"

"I… can't *think*," Micah protested. Devon laughed, his head falling back as his body shook.

"Then I'm going to win," he said when he sobered. His eyes gleamed with amusement, but he never stopped his easy strokes, his hand steady on his cock. "Keep going."

"I like to feel the marks you put on me," Micah said, and Devon sucked in a startled breath. Micah touched the red mark on his collarbone. Devon followed the movement of his fingers, and his rhythm faltered.

Micah hid his smile, pressed against the bruise, and moaned for effect. Devon couldn't seem to take his eyes from Micah's hand. His tongue was caught between his teeth, and sweat beaded on his skin. It was heady, that much power, and suddenly Micah was determined to win, his self-consciousness all but forgotten.

He skimmed his hand back down his chest, over his stomach, and lower, between his legs. "I play with my balls some then," he said. He tugged lightly on his sac, stretching the skin, and sighed. Devon seemed to have forgotten how to speak. His hand moved faster, his cock flushed a deep red as a steady trickle of precome slid from the tip.

Micah rolled his balls back and forth in his palm and groaned at the feeling. His stomach tightened and fire coiled in his gut, but he wasn't going to lose this game.

"If I have lube, I'll finger myself," he gasped out and pressed a finger against his hole. His muscles seized, and he tightened his hand around his cock as he throttled the orgasm back by sheer force of will. When he looked up, Devon's mouth was slightly open, and his eyes were fixed on Micah's hands.

"If I don't," Micah managed, "then I find the best bruise or mark—" He pulled his hand away from his opening and up across his right thigh to the fresh bandage that Devon had applied that morning. He rolled his thumb against it and groaned. "Oh *God*. It feels so good, Devon. Want you to do it again. Want you to mark me, bruise me, *hurt me*—"

A choked moan ripped from Devon's chest and his back arched as he climaxed and long jets covered his chest and stomach. Micah drove upward into his fist and followed on a shaky exhale, striping his own stomach with hot come and then collapsing against the arm of the sofa. His head fell backward.

"*Jesus*," he whispered.

Devon panted for air, his breath ragged, and he stared at the ceiling. They lay like that for several minutes, slowly getting their pulses back under control, and then Devon rolled to his feet with a groan and held out a hand for Micah to take.

Micah accepted it and made it upright, wavering. His legs felt like overcooked spaghetti, and he clung to Devon's arm to keep himself on his feet.

Devon pulled him close, and Micah wrapped his arms around Devon's waist. They stood that way for a minute before Devon sighed and pulled away.

"Come on, champ," he said as he ran a thumbnail along Micah's jaw and leaned in to kiss him. "Let's go take a bath, and you can tell me all about your plans for me this week."

Micah smiled and followed him to the bathroom.

Chapter Thirteen

Micah packed and repacked his bags obsessively, until Devon tackled him onto the bed and kissed him breathless. He raised himself above Micah's prone form, braced himself with an elbow on either side of Micah's head, and smiled down at him.

"You're going to be fine," he breathed and lowered his head to kiss Micah again, slow and sweet.

Micah braced his hands on Devon's ribs and clung to him. "I don't... I don't want to go," he admitted.

"I don't particularly want you to go either," Devon said and pressed their foreheads together. "But it's just a week. You'll be back before you know it. You're gonna have so much fun you'll forget all about me."

Micah couldn't help but laugh. "Pretty sure that's not possible."

Devon smiled, and something around his eyes eased as he kissed him again. "Come on. I'll drive you to the airport."

"I was just going to take my car," Micah protested. "You don't have to do that."

Devon sat up and pulled Micah with him. "Sooner or later you're going to have to get used to people doing things for you, Dosa."

"People *don't* do things for me," Micah countered. "Not unless they want something."

Something like sorrow slid through Devon's eyes, but he tugged until Micah leaned against him. "I don't know what happened to you," he murmured as he smoothed Micah's hair back, "but I swear to God I'm going to hunt down every last fucker who hurt you and make them pay."

"No one hurt me," Micah said, confused. "It's just... life."

Devon tightened his arms around him. "Jesus, baby," he whispered and tipped Micah's chin up to kiss him. Then he let him go and stood up. "I'll make sure your bags are packed properly. You go make us some sandwiches so we can eat before we go. Okay?"

"Okay," Micah said and headed for the kitchen. He felt better with a clearly stated job to do, able to relax, and he loved that Devon knew that.

THE DRIVE to the airport went quickly, and if Devon seemed distracted, drumming the steering wheel and gazing absently out over the traffic ahead of them, Micah pretended not to notice.

He checked his bags with the agent, and Devon walked him as far as he could. Micah turned to face him in the wide, carpeted hallway, and Devon smiled and ran his hands up and down Micah's arms.

"I'll see you soon," he said gently.

Micah sighed and rested his forehead against Devon's chest. "I'll call you when I land."

"Good." Devon leaned down and kissed Micah gently. "I'll miss you every second."

"You big sap," Micah said, but his heart wasn't in it. He could feel the anxiety closing his throat, making him twitchy, and he closed his eyes, took a steadying breath, and stepped back.

"Go," Devon said. He touched Micah's cheek, and Micah nodded.

"Bye, Devon," he said and handed the attendant his ticket. He glanced over his shoulder at the door, but Devon had turned away, lifting his phone to his ear. That was that, then. Devon was already getting back to his life. With his heart sinking, Micah headed down the hall to his gate.

THE FLIGHT was a multitude of horrors, even in first class. There was a suspicious stain on the seat beside Micah, which thankfully was empty, but that was as far as his luck went. There was a small child kicking his seat. The flight attendant stifled a sneeze and offered Micah a flute of champagne with the same hand she'd used to cover her mouth, and Micah recoiled in horror. And when, halfway through the flight, he got up to use the bathroom, he was forced to wait outside the cubicle for several minutes until a disheveled couple emerged, rumpled and giggling.

Micah's mouth fell open, and he blinked several times. Holding it until Tahiti it was, then. He headed back to his seat and sat down, where he crossed his legs and prayed for a swift death.

Time crawled, and Micah kept his eyes closed until they touched down on the tarmac. He stayed in his seat until everyone had filed out and the pretty brunette attendant came back and cleared her throat discreetly.

"Sir, would you like some help with your bags?"

"No," Micah said. He offered her a small smile and stood up. "Just… waiting for the crowds to clear out a bit." He pulled his carry-on bag out of the overhead compartment and made his way off the empty plane, up the gangplank, and into the airport.

It took him a minute to orient himself. The sun was shining and smiling people in brightly colored clothes surrounded him, cheerfully jostling each other, laughing and talking, but Micah was not heartened.

He rode the escalator to the ground floor, lost in his thoughts, and made his way toward the baggage-claim area. He stopped dead at the sight of Devon fucking Mallory standing beside the luggage carousel with a box of chocolates in one hand, a sign that said MICAH ELLIS in the other, and a wide grin on his face.

"*Devon*…." Micah couldn't breathe through the roar of relief and joy that swamped him. Devon dropped the chocolates and the sign as Micah threw his arms around him and clung desperately.

"Hey, baby." Devon laughed and bent to pick him up, and Micah wrapped his legs around his waist, burying his face in Devon's throat, and held on as hard as he could. He was dimly aware that he was trembling but he didn't care. Suddenly the week ahead looked much less daunting.

"So I was thinking," Devon said as he rubbed Micah's back. "A walk on the beach before dinner sounds really nice, wouldn't you say?"

Micah lifted his head and punched Devon's shoulder. "You sneaky little *shit*," he said, and Devon laughed again as Micah loosened his grip and slid to the ground. "What… how? And why? And *how*?"

Devon grinned down at him and took his hand. "I'll explain everything, I promise. But let's get your bags and find a taxi. Okay?"

"Yeah, okay," Micah said, dazed. He couldn't stop smiling. Devon was *there*, his big hand warm and solid around Micah's, his dimples flashing as he smiled, and Micah suddenly laughed outright. Devon squeezed his hand, and they waited for the bags in peaceful silence.

TRUE TO his word, once they were in the taxi and on the way to the hotel, Devon explained.

"I had the idea after you told me you were going. I've always wanted to visit Tahiti or Hawaii or *somewhere* tropical, and I thought it would be fun to surprise you."

Micah pretended to glare at him. "Consider me surprised," he said tartly.

Devon rubbed a thumb across Micah's knuckles, their hands in Micah's lap with their fingers still intertwined. "I packed my stuff in with yours," he continued. "That's why I sent you to the kitchen to make food for us."

"Unbelievable," Micah said, shaking his head. "How'd you get the time off work?"

"Told Sean I needed a week to help you through a really stressful situation," Devon said and shrugged. He snorted a laugh suddenly. "'Course, I didn't tell her the situation involved *Tahiti*. She probably wouldn't have said yes if she'd known."

A delighted laugh bubbled up, and Micah squeezed Devon's hand. "She's going to kick your *ass*."

"I can take her," Devon said, laughing with him.

"Did you catch a different flight?" Micah asked. "Or were you on the same damn plane as me?"

"Same plane," Devon said, his eyes sparkling. "I was seated in the tail section and counting on your hatred of cramped spaces to keep you in first class. Soon as we were stationary, I bailed and ran for the baggage claim as fast as I could. I got lucky and beat you there."

"But how did you afford the ticket? Dev, flights aren't cheap. You shouldn't have—"

"Hope's cousin works for the airline," Devon interrupted. "She had a crap-ton of miles, and I put the rest on my credit card. It wasn't that much, all things considered, and more than worth it."

"And the passport?"

"Irene, Jim, Sean, Fallon, and I went to Italy two years ago. My passport was still valid. No further paperwork required." Devon smiled and tightened his hand around Micah's.

"You are unbelievable," Micah repeated. "I should kick your ass, but I'm just too happy to see you."

Devon wrapped an arm around Micah's shoulders, pulled him close, and pressed a kiss to his hair. "So… walk on the beach before or after dinner?"

"After," Micah said. He closed his eyes and smiled. "After would be good."

THE HOTEL room was spacious and welcoming, and Devon offered to let Micah use the large shower first.

"Wanna use it with me?" Micah countered. "Conserve water and all that jazz?"

Devon closed his eyes and groaned. "Get thee behind me," he said. "And I don't mean that literally, so don't get any ideas."

Micah grinned at him. "Is that a yes?"

"That's an 'I have plans for you that shower sex would derail at this particular point,'" Devon countered. "So go get clean and dressed, and let's go have dinner. And believe me when I say that shower sex is *absolutely* on the agenda for later this week. Just not today."

Micah snickered and obeyed.

THEY ATE in the hotel restaurant, smiling at each other in the dim lighting over fresh sea bass and plantains. Micah nudged Devon's foot with his own to reassure himself that he wasn't hallucinating and Devon's dimples flashed again.

"So what's your schedule look like?"

Micah grimaced. "Conference in the morning and then lunch with everyone, which you can come to if you want. In the afternoon we have team-building exercises. I'm probably going to play hooky on those, though."

"I'd love to have lunch with you guys," Devon said as he bumped Micah's foot. "Meet your friends and all that."

Micah snorted and swallowed a bite of fish. "You're assuming any of them *are* my friends."

"None of them?" Devon said and frowned. "You've been working there how long now?"

"Five years," Micah said. He hunched his shoulders and looked at his plate.

"Five years," Devon repeated, "and you're not friends with *any* of them?"

Micah shrugged and set his fork down. "I'm not... I'm not friend material, really. I'm too neurotic, too mean when I get upset. I drive people away."

Devon gazed at him with sad eyes.

"It's not important," Micah said, eager to change the subject. "Want dessert or are you ready to take that walk?"

"Let's walk," Devon said. "We can order dessert in our room."

Micah followed Devon through the dining room and onto the stone patio that fronted the beach. There Devon stopped, took his shoes and socks off, and rolled his pant cuffs up.

"Going barefoot?" he asked, and Micah took a quick step back. Devon smiled and held out his hand. "Yeah, okay. Shoes on for you, then. Let's go."

"Sorry," Micah said and accepted his hand. They stepped onto the sand, and Devon squeezed his fingers.

"Don't apologize, babe."

It was a gorgeous night, clear and warm, and the sky was spangled with crystalline stars bright against a velvet backdrop. The sea lapped quietly against the shore, and Micah took a deep breath and let go of the worry and fear that had plagued him for days.

They walked in silence, hand in hand across the firm sand, and Micah felt peace steal into his soul.

"Thank you," he said quietly.

Devon brought Micah's hand to his lips and kissed it. "I'm just glad you were happy to see me," he admitted, his voice a little muffled against Micah's skin.

"Are you serious?" Micah demanded.

Devon shrugged. His eyes gleamed in the starlight. "I basically invited myself along on your vacation," he said. "I had a couple of self-doubt moments, I guess."

"It wasn't a vacation until I saw you. Before that it was just work." Micah pulled Devon around to face him and stepped close to wrap his arms around Devon's waist. "Besides, I've never been happier to see someone in my *life*," he said into his shirt, and he could feel Devon's chest vibrate as he laughed.

"Come on," Devon said, "I want to get some dessert."

"Race you," Micah said and started running. Behind him Devon swore and laughed. Then footsteps pounded on the sand as he caught up.

Micah didn't have a chance in hell of winning, not with Devon's long legs. So when Devon drew abreast and inched ahead, Micah had absolutely no compunction about tripping him.

Devon went down in an uncoordinated sprawl with a startled grunt, and Micah grinned and ran harder, up the steps and across the patio. He slowed to a brisk walk for the benefit of the patrons still in the restaurant, but as soon as he was in the hotel proper, he burst into a run again and pelted down the hall. He opted for the stairs and pounded up them, knowing Devon wasn't far behind. Then he nearly fell out the door onto his floor and sprinted for his room.

Devon caught up as Micah shoved the door open and staggered inside, and he grabbed Micah around the waist and tackled him onto the bed.

Micah yelped as the air was driven out of him by Devon's weight. He burst out laughing and shoved weakly at Devon's shoulder.

"Micah Bartholomew Ellis, you *cheated*, you little shit," Devon gasped.

"Get used to it," Micah managed through his giggles. "I fight *dirty*."

"Noted," Devon said as he braced an elbow on either side of his head. Micah sobered. Suddenly aware of Devon's weight pressing him into the mattress and how close his mouth was to Micah's, he swallowed hard.

"Wait," he said as a thought struck him. "Did you call me *Bartholomew*?"

"Maybe," Devon said and kissed Micah's jaw.

"That's not my middle name," Micah pointed out. "I don't *have* a middle name." Devon's mouth made it hard for him to think, his breath hot against Micah's skin.

Devon lifted his head and smiled. "You do now," he said and dropped his head to kiss him.

Micah wrapped his arms around Devon's neck, and their tongues met and slid together in easy, familiar sweeps. When Devon lifted his head, his pupils were blown, his lips swollen, and he looked dazed.

"Strip," he said. "There's something I've been wanting to try."

He rolled off and rummaged in the bag as Micah obeyed. When he straightened, Micah was naked and sitting cross-legged on the bed.

Devon lifted Micah's collar with a quirk of his eyebrow. Micah squared his shoulders and nodded. A smile flickered over Devon's lips, and he pulled his clothes off, knelt next to Micah, and gently snapped the collar into place.

Micah sighed as he slid into a more docile headspace, and Devon tipped his chin up and kissed him again.

"What's your safeword?" he asked when he pulled away.

"Manta ray," Micah said and he swayed after him. Devon steadied him with a hand on his shoulder, and Micah blinked, already more at peace.

"Elbows and knees. Facedown against the mattress," Devon said.

Micah moved to obey, and his mind drifted. When he was settled, his face resting on the comforter and his ass in the air, Devon knelt between his spread legs. He gently skimmed across Micah's buttocks and flanks, and Micah pressed his face a little harder to the bed.

Devon gripped the globes of Micah's ass and pulled gently until he was spread open and exposed. Holding him like that, Devon leaned forward and blew across Micah's twitching hole. Micah jerked.

"What—"

"Trust me," Devon murmured and blew again.

Micah clutched the blanket in both hands and sucked in air. Devon's breath was warm as it ghosted across his skin, and Micah's mind spun. Was Devon going to…? Surely he wasn't.

Devon kissed the curve of Micah's left buttock. His lips were soft and gentle as he trailed kisses up along his spine and then lower, his nose brushing the skin.

Micah tensed and began to tremble, and when Devon touched his tongue to his asshole, he jerked up and away so fast he nearly fell off the bed. "Manta ray. Fuck, *fuck*. Manta ray! Oh Jesus, please, Devon—"

He scrambled up the mattress until his back pressed against the headboard and wrapped his arms around his knees as he struggled in vain to stop the panic.

Devon didn't move at first. He waited for Micah to be still, and only then did he move slowly up the bed, keeping his eyes fixed on Micah's.

"Micah?" he said.

Micah squeezed his eyes shut and shook his head.

"It's *dirty*, Devon. You can't—"

"May I touch you?" Devon asked quietly.

Micah opened his eyes. Devon was cross-legged a foot away from him, watching him with concern all over his face. Micah let go of his knees and crawled into Devon's lap to wrap his arms around Devon's neck and bury his face in Devon's throat.

Devon rubbed his back and gently rocked him back and forth.

"'M sorry," Micah mumbled.

Devon tightened his grip. "*I'm* sorry, baby. I should've talked to you first. I didn't even *think*."

"It's just—you could get sick, Devon," Micah managed. His stomach roiled, and he thought he might throw up. "It's... filthy."

"It's not that dirty," Devon said gently. "I'll use mouthwash and brush my teeth after. You're clean. I'm clean. We're in a monogamous relationship. People do it all the time, sweetheart. And it feels *amazing*."

"But—"

"Have you ever had it done?" Devon asked.

Micah shook his head, but still clung to Devon's shoulders and kept his face hidden. "Barrett...." He didn't miss the way Devon tensed, but he said nothing. "Barrett made me do it to him once. I... threw up. Ruined the mood." Micah smiled a little in spite of himself, and Devon snorted quietly.

"I'm not asking you to do it to me," Devon said, rubbing Micah's spine. "But... will you let me? I promise the mouthwash is on standby, and I won't kiss you during."

Micah was silent. Did he trust Devon enough? Devon waited quietly, continuing to gently sweep a hand up and down Micah's back. Micah knew if he said no, Devon wouldn't punish him. He would simply accept his decision and move on, and there would be no consequences— no angry silences or passive-aggressive comments. And truth be told, Micah *was* curious. Barrett had waxed rapturous about how it felt, how intense the orgasm could be, and he'd been angry with Micah for a solid week for ruining it for him.

Finally he swallowed hard and nodded. Devon hugged him, and his smile was blinding when he pulled away. Micah managed to smile back, but he was already trembling again.

"Breathe, baby," Devon murmured. "Elbows and knees again."

Micah slid out of Devon's lap, resumed his previous position, spread his legs, and sank into the pose. He took a deep breath as the collar shifted against his throat and he let the movement soothe him. Devon was in control. Devon would take care of him.

He pressed his face against the comforter and smelled laundry detergent and fabric softener as Devon settled between his legs again. *I am relaxed. I am calm. I can do this.*

Still he nearly jumped out of his skin when Devon touched his ass, and Devon caught his hips and quelled Micah's abortive escape attempt with a huff of stifled laughter.

When he spoke, though, his voice was serious. "I'm going to eat you out now, Micah. Don't move."

And then he went to work, and Micah forgot how to think, how to breathe, how to do *anything* that didn't involve begging for more. Please, God, please, *Devon.*

First Devon flattened his tongue against Micah's opening and wet the area thoroughly with broad swipes. His licks were firm and sure, and Micah gasped against his forearm as his erection sprang to life. Devon spread Micah's asscheeks wide and kneaded and pulled gently to give himself the best access possible.

Micah moaned as Devon pointed his tongue and dipped inside, working slowly to give the muscles time to relax before he pressed deeper and *hummed.* The vibrations shot through Micah, and he choked on a whimper.

"Devon, Dev, oh *God….*"

Devon's hums took on a distinctly satisfied edge, and he pushed farther in, his breath hot against Micah's skin and his stubble scraping Micah's ass. Micah writhed, his cock hard and full between his legs. The need to come already made his skin hot and tight as lightning coiled at the base of his spine.

Devon pulled back. "Don't come yet," he ordered. "I'm nowhere near done with you."

Then a finger probed his spit-slick entrance and pressed deep. Micah suppressed another moan with effort.

"I like your noises," Devon growled. He added another finger and curled them sharply against Micah's prostate. "Don't hide them."

Micah bucked hard and sobbed for breath as fireworks exploded behind his eyes and Devon moved his fingers hard and fast over the bundle of nerves at Micah's center.

Devon drove him right to the edge, caught Micah's cock in one big hand, and gripped it tightly just before the orgasm burst free. Micah twisted, and a hot tear fell onto the bedspread between his hands.

"*Please*," he begged.

But Devon didn't answer. He was too busy spreading Micah's ass again and diving back in.

This was it. This was how Micah died—of Devon's fingers spreading him wide so his tongue could flick inside and explore as far as it could reach—of the sensations that gathered throughout his body, threatening to shatter him. Micah bit down hard on his forearm and prayed the pain would center and ground him as Devon worked. His fears were forgotten, lost in the heat and the pressure and the way Devon's tongue felt as he ate him out with smooth, devastating movements.

Devon pulled away, and Micah didn't try to stop the disappointed whine that fell from his lips at the lack of contact. He turned his head and forced his eyes open.

Devon leaned over the bed and rummaged in the bag with an intent look on his face. Micah pressed back against him, and Devon caught his hip with his free hand and steadied him.

"Patience," he murmured.

A bottle cap clicked open. Lube landed on Micah's skin, cold and wet against his opening, and he stifled a shout as Devon drove three fingers in without warning.

"Yes," Micah gasped. "*God* yes. More, Devon, now, *please*...." He rocked back against Devon's hand, delighting in the ache and burn.

"Pushy," Devon said, and he pulled his fingers out. Micah whined sharply to protest their loss.

"I'm sorry," he said, stumbling over the words in his haste to get them out. "So sorry, Devon. Please. I'll be good. Please Dev, *please*—"

Devon didn't answer at first, and Micah pushed up onto his hands and craned his neck to look over his shoulder. Devon was back on his heels as he held on to his own cock with a death grip and hunched over as he struggled to keep from coming. His shaft was flushed a dark, angry red, and he breathed in short, sharp gasps.

"You beg so pretty," he managed to say as he looked up and into Micah's eyes. His own were almost black, the pupils blown so wide with lust. His lips were bitten red, his chin shiny with saliva, and Micah had never seen anything more beautiful in his life.

"Please," Micah whispered, his throat suddenly tight. "Please, Devon, will you fuck me?"

Devon went to his knees and curved forward to drop a kiss to Micah's spine between his shoulder blades. Then his slicked-up cock was at Micah's entrance, pressing inside, and Micah dropped to his forearms again with a sob of relief as his body stretched to let Devon in.

"Yes, baby, yes," he babbled. "Need you. Fuck me. Yes. More, Devon, *please.*" Some dim part of him was aware that he wasn't making sense, but he didn't care. He couldn't think, couldn't focus. His world was Devon's cock stretching him wide, *impaling* him, and he rocked back onto it and sobbed for air.

Devon didn't stop until he was fully sheathed. Then he ran his hands restlessly over Micah's sides, and his breath sounded ragged and harsh in the quiet room.

"*Micah,*" he whispered as he pulled out and slid back in, slowly at first but picking up speed as he moved harder and faster until Micah had to reach out and catch himself against the headboard to stop his forward motion. That allowed him to brace against Devon's thrusts, and a groan ripped from Devon's throat.

"Y'wanna...." Devon sucked in a breath and moved his hips relentlessly. "Wanna come, baby? Gonna come for me?"

Micah couldn't remember how to form words. Devon tilted forward and changed his angle of entry just enough to make the head of his cock drag over Micah's prostate, and Micah cried out again.

"Ask me," Devon gritted out as he slammed home again. "Ask me to come."

"I—"

Devon pistoned his hips, and Micah forgot how to speak.

"*Ask me,*" Devon growled. His hands bit into Micah's hips, hard enough to bruise. "Ask me or you don't get to come, Micah."

Micah struggled to form words. His body was an aching mess of need and want, his skin tight, and his cock painfully hard between his spread legs.

Devon thrust deep again as he leaned forward and nosed at where Micah's shoulder joined his neck. "Say the words," he ordered. His hips still worked, scattering Micah's brain cells.

Words. Devon wanted him to say something. What did he want Micah to say? He struggled to focus. His thoughts were slippery and slid away as he reached for them. Rational thought was subsumed by his need to—

"*Come*," he gasped out. "Please, Devon, let me come, *please*—"

"*Now*," Devon growled, and fastened his teeth in Micah's shoulder.

Micah's orgasm roared over him like a freight train, and every muscle in his body locked up tight as he spilled untouched all over the bedspread. He was vaguely aware of Devon emptying deep within him in hard jerks, groaning desperately against Micah's skin.

Micah passed out right there, facedown on the bed with Devon still buried to the hilt inside him.

CHAPTER FOURTEEN

MICAH WOKE up clean and dry, facedown on Devon's supine form. Devon's hands rested on Micah's waist, ready, even in sleep, to catch him if he moved, so Micah lay still and studied Devon's face.

Devon's nose tipped up just a bit at the end. His lips were soft and curved, and silky brown hair spread out on the pillow. His eyes moved under their lids as he dreamed, and Micah was swamped with a rush of love so dizzying he had to close his eyes and take a steadying breath.

He couldn't deny it anymore. He *loved* Devon Mallory. Loved everything about him, from his laugh to the way he touched Micah with reverent wonder, the way he knew what Micah needed before Micah did, the way he teased and laughed and *lived* with that openhearted kindness that bled into everything he did.

And that was a problem.

Devon was too good for Micah. Micah dirtied everything he touched, sullied it with his neuroses and his asshole tendencies, his selfish ways, his ugly thoughts. Devon would leave. He *had* to leave, and he would find someone who matched him, someone good enough for him, who gave to charity and helped old ladies across the road.

Devon couldn't know how Micah felt. He'd feel obligated to stay, to try to love Micah back even though he *couldn't*. So Micah would hold on to him for as long as he could, and then he'd cut Devon free before things got too hopelessly tangled. It was the right thing to do, and Devon would thank him for it eventually.

When Devon opened his eyes, a few minutes later, Micah had his arms crossed on Devon's chest, chin on top of them.

Devon blinked and awareness rushed into his face. "Subdrop? Are you okay? What do you need?"

"I'm okay," Micah said hastily, and Devon relaxed and took a relieved breath. "It hasn't hit me. Dunno if that means it won't or if it just hasn't yet, but I'm okay right now."

"Good," Devon said. He yawned and stretched with one hand absently on Micah's waist. "Time 'zit?"

"Early," Micah said. "You can sleep a little more."

"M'kay." Devon ran a thumb along Micah's cheekbone, and Micah leaned into it and sighed. "Sure you're okay?" Devon asked.

Micah nodded and turned his head to press a kiss to the inside of Devon's wrist. "I'm fine. Go back to sleep."

Devon bit his lip. "I want to... tell you something," he said, and Micah froze.

Don't, Devon, please don't. You don't know what you're doing, what you're saying. He said nothing, though. He was unable to form the words.

"I just... this is going to sound weird," Devon continued "But I've wanted to tell you for a while. You're my best friend, Micah. I'm just so glad I have you."

Relief hit Micah like a hammer, and he took a deep breath. Devon still cupped his cheek. His eyes looked nervous, and Micah brought his hand up to twine their fingers together.

"Same," he murmured and scooted forward enough to press a kiss to Devon's mouth. He tasted toothpaste. "I mean, you're kind of my *only* friend, but I didn't really expect friendship from you at all. And instead I got... you."

Devon's lips curved. "We're going to work on finding you more friends," he promised. "As long as I stay your *best* friend, of course."

"Of course," Micah agreed gravely and kissed him again. "Go back to sleep. I'll let you know if the subdrop hits me."

"Okay," Devon said. He was asleep again almost immediately, and Micah put his chin back on his forearm and watched him.

MICAH SLIPPED out of the room for his conferences that morning without waking Devon. He headed down the hall for the meeting room, but trepidation slowed his steps, and he slipped in the door and made straight for the coffee-and-pastries table.

A familiar-looking redheaded girl stood there, bopping her head to internal music. She glanced up and smiled at him. "Morning," she said cheerfully. "How was your flight?"

"Fine," Micah said cautiously as he tried to remember her name. "Yours?"

She rolled bright green eyes. "Boring as hell. This gross, sweaty guy was sitting next to me, and he hit on me the entire fucking time. I finally told him he lacked the necessary genital equipment for me to be interested, but that just made it worse. He started asking if he could watch. Shit like that."

Micah winced. "That's awful." He leaned past her for the carafe and got a glimpse of her nametag. *Celeste Milton.* Of course. He'd met her briefly two years before at another conference. She worked two floors down, and they almost never ran into each other. "So what'd you do?" He took a bite of croissant and poured his coffee.

"Oh, I spit in his coffee when he went to the bathroom," Celeste said happily, and Micah choked on his pastry.

Celeste pounded him on the back as he sputtered.

"Sorry. Could've timed that better," she said, laughing.

Micah wiped his streaming eyes. "If you were going for comedic effect," he managed through coughs, "then I'd say you timed it *perfectly.*"

"Sit with me," Celeste said. "This is going to be boring as hell, and I can practice my comedic timing on you."

Micah followed her to a table, and they settled in as a portly older man tapped on the microphone.

True to her word, Celeste kept Micah entertained throughout the presentation with a stream of running commentary, and Micah found himself laughing too hard to take his usual notes. Not that it mattered. From what little he caught of the speaker's words, it was the same basic script that had been rolled out the last year *and* the year before.

Halfway through, the door behind them opened and Barrett sauntered in. Micah froze midlaugh and ducked down behind Celeste's slim frame.

"Micah?" she asked as worry formed a line on her forehead. "What's wrong?"

"I... nothing," Micah said as he straightened and picked up a pen. He stared at the speaker, but every fiber of his being was focused on

Barrett, behind him at the coffee urns. *What is he doing here?* It was a retreat for Adler Headhunting employees. Barrett should *not* be there.

"It's definitely not nothing," Celeste said. She glanced behind them at Barrett, who scanned the room for a place to sit. He headed for them, and Micah stiffened and sent up a silent prayer.

No one seemed to be listening, though, because Barrett leaned over the empty chair beside Micah and flashed his most charming smile. "Good morning," he said. "Mind if I sit here?"

"Sorry," Celeste said, matching his smile. "That seat's actually reserved. He'll be here any minute."

Barrett narrowed his eyes and looked at Micah, who stared at the tablecloth. Celeste smiled brilliantly and waggled her fingers at him, and Barrett scowled and moved to the next table over.

"I *hate* him," Celeste hissed as soon as he was out of earshot.

Micah glanced at her, startled. "You know him?"

"He dated my best friend a few years ago," Celeste said and glared in Barrett's direction. "Broke his heart and left him nearly suicidal."

"Jesus," Micah said and swallowed hard.

"I'm guessing there's history there," Celeste said as she watched Micah's face.

Micah lifted a shoulder. "You could say that."

"Not over him yet?" Celeste asked.

"*God* no. It's not that," Micah said, startled into a laugh. "No, it's safe to say I am *very* over him. There's just… yeah. History."

"I'll run interference," Celeste said, patting his shoulder.

"Thank you," Micah said, surprised at the relief that flooded him. Maybe this wouldn't be so bad after all.

THE MORNING dragged. Celeste kept him entertained by doodling caricatures of everyone within their field of view. She showed a startling aptitude for it and made Micah struggle to keep his laughter contained between surreptitious glances at the table where Barrett sat.

When lunchtime rolled around, Micah was on his feet immediately, gathering his notes. Celeste looked disappointed as he took a step toward the door, and he hesitated.

"Would you…?" He gnawed on his lip a second. "Would you like to eat lunch with my boyfriend and me?"

Celeste's face lit up as she agreed, and Micah smiled all the way to the elevator, even as he cast backward glances for Barrett, who thankfully never appeared.

DEVON WAS emerging from the shower when Micah pushed open the door.

"Hey, babe," he called. "Give me just a minute, and I'll be ready to go."

Micah dropped his notebook and pens on the dresser, headed for the bathroom, and walked right into Devon's still-damp embrace.

Devon wrapped his arms around him and held on tightly. "You okay?" he murmured.

Micah nodded with his eyes closed. "Should warn you... Barrett's here."

"What the hell is *he* doing here?" Devon demanded.

Micah shrugged helplessly. "I didn't exactly stop to ask."

"Awesome," Devon muttered and tightened his grip. "Don't worry, love. I'll run interference."

The echo of Celeste's words made Micah smile, and he tilted his head back so Devon could kiss him.

"I think I made a friend," he said, and Devon's eyes lit up.

"Tell me while I get dressed," he said, and Micah obeyed as Devon finished drying off and pulled his clothes on.

They made their way downstairs while Micah described how Celeste had successfully deflected Barrett's attempt to sit beside them, and Devon grinned.

"I like her already."

They found the dining room without difficulty. It was a long, welcoming space with a wall of windows that looked onto the crystal blue waves that lapped the beach. Devon sighed happily.

"I could get used to this," he said as he headed for the buffet table.

He heaped his plate with food while Micah scanned the half-full room and fought his nerves. Devon seemed completely at ease, focused on the table with its contents, but Micah found it hard to breathe.

"Relax," Devon said quietly as he piled several ham steaks on top of his mashed potatoes. "It's going to be fine. Fill your plate."

Micah obeyed and stuck close as they moved down the buffet line. Celeste's bright hair caught his eye as she waved, and Micah nudged Devon's arm.

"Do you see Barrett?" Devon asked from the corner of his mouth as they moved in her direction.

"Not yet," Micah said. He smiled at Celeste, who was sitting by a scrawny young man with the kindest brown eyes Micah had ever seen.

"Micah, this is Alan," Celeste said. "And you must be Devon. Holy *shit*."

Micah stifled a snort and shook Alan's hand.

"Nice to meet you," Alan said amiably. "Have a seat."

Micah and Devon sat down, and Celeste leaned forward. Her eyes sparkled. "Dude, are you as excited as I am about the team-building exercises this afternoon?"

"Probably not," Micah said, spearing a chunk of pineapple. "What are they?"

"Paintball," Celeste exclaimed.

Micah dropped his fork and stared at her in dismay. Beside him, Devon cleared his throat.

"Micah's, ah… allergic to the latex in paintballs," he said.

Celeste grimaced. "Oh no," she said. "I was hoping you guys would be on our team."

"Sorry." Devon smiled. "I was actually thinking I'd take Micah out on the water for the afternoon, anyway."

Micah sat up straighter, and Devon winked at him.

"Eat," he told him. "It's going to be a long day."

THE MEAL was going smoothly when Barrett pulled out the chair beside Micah, dropped into it, and slung an arm around Micah's shoulders.

"I didn't get to say hello to you this morning, Mike," he said as he shot a tight smile at Celeste, who bared her teeth at him. "How've you been? Sorry you've been missing my calls lately. It's getting to the point that I'll have to schedule an appointment with Norma just to get some face time with you." He laughed, and Micah forced a frozen smile.

"What are you doing here?" he managed. "This is an Adler employee retreat."

"Oh, I know," Barrett said. "I'm just here on vacation. Happy coincidence that I saw the sign for your conference in the lobby when I got here."

Happy coincidence. As if. Barrett had engineered this down to the last detail. Micah would bet his bottom dollar on it.

Devon leaned around Micah, holding out a hand. "We haven't met. I'm Devon."

Smiling widely, Barrett removed his arm from Micah's shoulders and shook Devon's hand. "Barrett. The one who got away. I'm sure Micah's told you all about me."

"Barrett," Devon said thoughtfully. He tugged Micah's chair closer and wrapped an arm around Micah's waist so he was tucked firmly against Devon's side. "Doesn't ring a bell… wait, no. Micah, I think you did mention him once. He's the one responsible for the hole in your ceiling, isn't he?"

Micah nodded as he fought the nausea that wanted to well up.

Barrett's eyes were tight with anger, but he smiled. "Making yourself at home in Mike's life, I see. Does he make you bathe before you touch him?"

"Oh no," Devon said, his eyes wide with innocence. "I do that anyway. I'm a mechanic—didn't he tell you? Covered in grease and sweat and dirt by the end of any given workday, so it'd be pretty shitty of me *not* to clean up before I kissed him hello."

"He's lucky to have found you," Barrett said, and Micah flinched at the venom in his voice. Celeste stared at Alan, who was studying the tablecloth, and Micah thought he might throw up.

Devon dropped a kiss to the top of Micah's head. "I'm the lucky one," he said fondly. "In any case, I have to thank you."

"What for?" Barrett asked.

"Oh, for breaking up with Micah so I had a chance with him," Devon said.

An awkward, heavy silence fell, and Micah turned his head and pressed his cheek to Devon's chest, closing his eyes. "If we're going out on the water, we should probably get moving," he managed to say.

"You're right," Devon said. He stood up and nodded at everyone. "Nice to meet you all. I'm sure I'll see you again before the week's out. But right now, I have to go spoil my boyfriend rotten."

Micah stole a look at Barrett as he followed Devon out of the room. Barrett sat stock-still and watched them leave, his knuckles white on the tablecloth. Micah's stomach lurched, and he gripped Devon's hand harder.

Instead of leaving the hotel, though, Devon pulled him around a corner and into an alcove. He tipped Micah's chin up with one long finger and peered into his eyes.

"Are you okay?" he murmured.

"Why did you do that?" Micah asked.

"I don't like him," Devon said simply. "And he's the type who needs to be thrown off guard or he'll think he's 'won' or some shit like that."

"You made him angry," Micah whispered. "You don't know… what he's like when he's angry."

Devon's lips twitched. "He's nowhere near as hot as Bruce Banner. Besides, you've got me with you. He can't do anything to you. Okay? You're safe. And if he *does* try anything, I'll pop him in the nose."

Micah closed his eyes as the nausea began to recede. "Okay," he said. "You're the lucky one, huh?"

Devon cradled his face in both warm hands and smiled down at him. "I *am*," he said and kissed him.

Chapter Fifteen

Devon kept Micah out on the water until the sun was just above the horizon and they were both sunburned and pleasantly exhausted, salt drying on their skin. Micah was surprised, at first, by how well Devon handled the small boat they rented, but Devon just laughed.

"Jim owns a cabin on the edge of a national preserve in South Dakota," he said. He was at the tiller, his eyes squinted against the sun, and somehow managed to be sexy even with the ridiculous lifejacket hanging off his frame. "Sean and I used to take his boat out on the lake all the time. Sean threatened to dump me in the water and leave me more than once when I was being especially obnoxious, but she never actually did."

Micah snorted a laugh from his position flat on his back in the prow of the boat, soaking up the sun with his eyes closed and his hands behind his head. "Older siblings are a plague upon this world," he said lazily.

"Do you have any?" Devon asked.

Micah opened one eye a crack and looked at him. Devon looked back with honest curiosity on his face.

"We've never talked about your family," Devon said. "I just… wondered."

"Nothing to wonder about," Micah said. "I was a foster kid. No idea who my parents are. My mom gave me up for adoption when I was a few hours old. They found me outside a firehouse—in a cardboard box, of all the fucking clichés. My mom was Indian. There was a letter in the box. No names—it just said that she was married, and she'd gotten pregnant by a white man, and her husband had insisted she get rid of me. Guess I came out a little too pale for him."

He snorted humorlessly and closed his eyes again, and Devon killed the engine and let them drift. The boat rocked as he made his way forward, dropped to his knees beside Micah's still form, and took his hand.

"I'm over it," Micah said without opening his eyes.

Devon squeezed his hand. "Not sure anyone ever really gets over something like that," he said quietly. "It's the kind of shit that haunts you."

"If you say so," Micah said, still not looking at him.

"So you stayed in the system?" Devon asked. "No one adopted you?"

"Came close once," Micah said. He sighed and opened his eyes. Devon blocked the sun with his shoulders, concern and curiosity on his face. "Turns out no one wants a germaphobe with more baggage than a cross-country traveler. My... issues got to be too much, and I was sent back to the group home. After that I was in and out of various foster homes until I was sixteen and just... left."

"God, Dosa," Devon breathed.

Micah shrugged and looked away. "It wasn't that bad a life, all things considered," he said. "I was never molested, never abused. Caught a hand across the face in a few homes if I stepped out of line, but that's normal."

"No. No, it's *not*," Devon said with horror in his voice. "Micah, did *anyone* love you? Take care of you? *Nurture* you?"

Micah propped himself up on his elbows and searched Devon's face. "Not everyone had the apple-pie life, Mallory," he said. "I turned out okay." He stopped and considered. "Mostly okay, I guess."

"You turned out *more* than okay," Devon said fiercely and leaned in to kiss him.

Micah kissed back willingly, and when Devon pulled away, he blinked. "What... why'd you stop?"

"I actually wanted to talk about some stuff," Devon said, and Micah tensed. "It's nothing bad," Devon said hastily. "Just... I had some questions."

"Okay," Micah said warily.

"You said you wanted to experiment, try a few different things," Devon said. "Other than what we've done, what else did you want to do?"

Oh. Micah sat up and crossed his legs. "Um... cock rings."

"Yeah?" Devon said. A smile flickered across his lips. "You *do* seem to come untouched a fair amount."

"Not my fault you know how to push my buttons," Micah countered. "Umm... I've never done sensory deprivation, and I've always been kind of interested in trying that."

"Blindfold, gag, maybe earplugs?" Devon said.

Micah shifted. His cock had stirred and taken an interest in the discussion. From the way Devon's eyes creased, he didn't miss it.

"Yeah, uh… yeah," Micah said. "That sounds… good."

"Still want to try whipping?"

Micah closed his eyes and took a deep breath. "You're going to *kill* me."

"I'm not even touching you," Devon protested, but there was a smile in his voice. "Is that a yes?"

Micah opened his eyes, glared at him, and shifted his weight again. "*Yes*. That's a yes, and you know it."

"What else?"

"Hard limits would be knife or blood play, sounding, fecal play, and watersports," Micah said. "Breath play is more of a soft limit, but if it's something you're really into, I guess we can talk about it."

Devon shook his head. "I don't know enough about it, and I don't want to risk it. We're in agreement on the other stuff. What about role play?"

Micah considered. "I've never done it before. I guess I'm willing to give it a try."

"Semipublic sex?"

Micah swallowed a moan, and Devon's eyes darkened.

"Oh, you like that idea, don't you? Like the idea of me getting you off in public, with people all around you, no clue that I'm driving you insane. Maybe I'll put the vibrator in and take you out, see how much you can take before you make a mess of yourself."

Micah doubled over, fisting his hands in the towel under him, and willed himself not to come. He breathed in short, sharp gusts through his nose as Devon waited. Finally he managed to straighten and meet Devon's eyes.

"You're so good," Devon murmured. "Now. Take your shorts off."

"*Here?*" Micah said, not sure he'd heard right. "Devon, we're—"

"We're the only boat out here," Devon said. "And no one on the beach can see us, especially if we're lying down. Did we not *just* have a discussion about this? We're easing into it slowly."

Micah stared at him and tried to figure out if he was joking. Panic began to prickle his skin. The sun beat down, the boat rocked, and Micah swallowed hard.

Devon arched an eyebrow. "Take. Your shorts. Off."

"*Manta ray*," Micah burst out and covered his face with both hands as shame washed over him.

Devon pulled him into his lap, wrapped him in his warmth, and rocked him back and forth gently. Micah twined his fingers in the placket of Devon's shirt and held on, burying his face in Devon's chest.

"I'm sorry," he whispered after a few minutes.

Devon smoothed the hair off his forehead. "Shh. So now we know that the *idea* of public sex is hot, but actually doing it is a no-go. We can work with that."

Micah leaned back enough to see his face. "I wanted—"

Devon bent to kiss him. "I know. And when we get back to the room, I'm going to suck you off so hard your toes will curl. It's okay, baby. This is part of figuring out what we want."

Micah took a deep breath, closed his eyes, and buried his face in Devon's shirt again. Sometimes, in moments like this, he could almost believe they were going to work. He could almost let himself imagine a future together.

CHAPTER SIXTEEN

MICAH WOKE up early the next morning as the sun barely peeked through the curtains. Devon was wrapped around him like a living blanket, and his warm breath stirred the curls on the back of Micah's neck.

Micah lay quietly for a minute, enjoying the easy intimacy, but finally the needs of his bladder and empty stomach were too much to ignore, and he squirmed out from under Devon's arm, holding his breath.

Devon mumbled something and pulled a pillow against his front as Micah tiptoed into the bathroom.

He dressed quickly, stepped into his shoes, and headed for the door. "Dosa?"

Devon still sounded mostly asleep, but he was propped on his elbow, blinking drowsily. His hair was in his face, the blanket falling to his waist, and Micah had to fight the urge to crawl back into bed with him.

"Just going to get breakfast," he said. "Go back to sleep."

"M'kay," Devon murmured. He was asleep again before Micah left the room.

DOWNSTAIRS, MICAH filled two plates in the mostly empty dining room. He didn't see anyone he knew, so he kept his head down and moved through the line quickly, which was probably why he didn't see Barrett until his hand was on his waist and he was leaning in close to press a kiss to Micah's cheek.

Micah stiffened, and Barrett pulled away enough to smile at him.

"Good morning," he said.

"Ah… hi," Micah said. He added some fruit to his plate and focused on the food in front of him, but Barrett didn't take the hint.

"So your boyfriend seems nice," Barrett said and shoved his hands in his pockets. "And… sickeningly perfect."

"Oh, he is," Micah said. He smiled at the memory of Devon giving him a brain-melting blowjob after their discussion on the boat.

Barrett's eyes tightened. "Does he know your dirty little secret, pet? Does he know how you beg for it like a whore? How long do you think he'll stick around once he knows how perverted you are, hmm?"

Micah was frozen in place.

"Maybe I'll tell him," Barrett purred.

"He already knows," Micah managed around the fear that choked him.

Barrett leaned a little closer. "But does he know just how sick you are? I think I'll tell him. Tell him how you've begged me to hurt you, *thanked* me for it, crawled for me like a—"

Micah dropped the plates, uncaring of the mess they made, and broke for the door. Barrett was right behind him, though, and Micah barely made it through the double doors of the dining room before Barrett caught his arm, dragged him into a shadowy corner, and shoved him up against the wall.

It was the same alcove Devon had kissed him in, some tiny part of Micah's brain noted. The rest of him was focused on Barrett's arm across his collarbones and the fingers of his left hand digging into Micah's arm so hard he knew there'd be bruises there.

Micah rolled his head sideways against the marble and gasped for air as Barrett leaned in. His handsome face was twisted with fury.

"You don't walk away from me," he hissed. "You don't leave until *I* say you leave. I trained you better than that, you disobedient little—"

"Let me *go*," Micah choked. He was helpless against Barrett's larger bulk, his hands scrabbling against Barrett's forearm.

"You need a reminder of your manners," Barrett growled. "Your *boyfriend* will thank me. Maybe I should show him how obedient you can be, how *good*. You've forgotten everything I taught you, haven't you?"

Nausea roiled in Micah's stomach and acid burned the back of his throat. He squeezed his eyes shut as Barrett leaned even closer, his breath hot on Micah's cheek.

"How fast will *Devon* run when he learns how perverted you really are?" he murmured as he rubbed his nose along Micah's jaw. "He'll leave you, just like everyone does. No one wants you, Micah. No one cares about you. You know why?"

Micah couldn't speak, couldn't breathe. Devon was asleep upstairs. No help was magically going to appear. The guests who had witnessed their discussion in the dining room had clearly decided to keep their noses out of it.

"*You're not worth it*," Barrett whispered in Micah's ear, and then he was gone, and Micah thudded to his knees, coughing for air and struggling to keep from throwing up.

He stayed that way for several long minutes and finally managed to drag himself to his feet as a hotel employee came into view, clearly concerned.

"Sir?" she said. "Sir, someone in the dining room said there'd been an altercation…. Are you all right? Do you need help? Is there someone I can call?"

Micah shook his head. "I'm fine," he whispered. The young woman watched, her eyes worried as he limped for the stairs with his arms wrapped around his middle. He climbed the flights to his room, his thoughts a dull buzz.

It wasn't until he was at the door that he realized Devon couldn't see him like this. Micah knew Devon, knew he wouldn't hesitate to confront Barrett and probably beat the shit out of him for hurting Micah, and that would mean Devon would end up in jail. Devon couldn't know what had happened.

Micah took a deep breath and rubbed his face. He wasn't going to be able to hide it. Devon was too sharp-eyed. He'd know something was wrong the second Micah walked in.

So maybe Micah could disguise it.

He pushed the door open. Devon was still in bed with his back to him. Micah went straight for the bathroom and was washing his face when Devon found him. His eyes were sleepy, and his hair stood on end.

"Hey, you okay?"

Micah looked up. He knew he was pale and trembling.

"I think… I think I'm sick," he whispered. "Like I might… throw up."

Devon's eyes filled with concern, and his brow furrowed. "Oh shit, baby. Come on. Come to bed and let me take care of you." He took Micah's arm, helped him to the bed, and felt his forehead. "You don't have a fever. Was it something you ate, do you think?"

"Don't know," Micah mumbled as he burrowed into his pillow. He caught Devon's wrist. "Devon... I wanna go home. Please... can we just go home?"

Devon's eyes softened, and he bent to stroke Micah's hair back from his forehead. "Of course. Let me call the airline and get our tickets changed."

Micah let go of him and closed his eyes. "Sorry, Devon... didn't get you breakfast...."

"Shh," Devon said gently. "It's okay, baby. Hold tight, and we'll get you back to your own bed."

SEVERAL HOURS later they were on an airplane. Micah plastered himself to Devon's side and kept his eyes closed throughout the entire flight. He was barely aware of Devon talking to the stewardess in low tones when she offered them drinks.

He followed Devon out to the truck, climbed into the cab, and leaned against the door. Devon slid into the driver's seat and touched his hand.

"You don't look as pale and sweaty," he said. "Still feel like you're going to throw up?"

Micah shook his head against the window, the glass cool on his cheek, but he said nothing.

"Micah... did something happen?" Devon asked.

Micah jerked his head around and met Devon's worried gaze.

"You... something's really wrong, and I don't think you're that sick," Devon said. "Can you tell me what happened?"

"I...." Micah opened and closed his mouth several times, and finally Devon squeezed his hand.

"Was it something to do with Barrett?"

Micah nodded, biting his lip, and Devon's grip tightened.

"Did he hurt you?" he asked sharply.

Micah shook his head, unable to speak.

Devon waited until it was obvious the words weren't coming. "Tell me when you're ready," he said. "Let's get you home."

"Devon—"

Devon lifted his eyebrows and waited.

"Can we... can we go to the aquarium instead?" Micah asked.

"Of course," Devon said instantly and started the engine. He drove without speaking, intent on the road and traffic, and Micah stayed silent and watched his profile.

When they arrived at the aquarium, Micah made straight for the manta ray's tank with Devon close behind him. Micah got as close as possible without touching the glass and peered through the murky depths for a glimpse of the big black fish.

"There." Devon pointed.

Micah leaned back against Devon's chest and let peace wash over him as he watched the ray slowly undulate through the water. Devon wrapped his coat around him and pressed their cheeks together, and Micah found his favorite button and absently slid his thumb across the ridges.

"Did you know that mantas don't have noses?" Devon murmured.

Micah blinked, startled. He *hadn't* known that.

"They can get up to twenty-five feet in length and weigh as much as three thousand pounds," Devon continued. "A lot of people are afraid of them because they look like stingrays, but they don't even have a stinger, and they're very gentle."

Micah sighed and relaxed into Devon's arms. The manta ray floated toward them. It filled Micah's vision and hung suspended in the water on the other side of the glass as they watched it. Micah could feel the poison leaving his soul, draining from him as the enormous fish floated gracefully away, toward the other side of the tank.

"What do they eat?" Micah asked.

"Plankton, tiny fish, crustaceans like shrimp," Devon said into his ear. "They're closely related to sharks, and they have a lot of teeth, but they don't use them to eat. They have a... a filtering system, sort of like whales."

Micah smiled. He turned in Devon's embrace and went up on his tiptoes to wrap his arms around Devon's neck. "Did you learn all those facts for me?"

"Maybe I just find manta rays fascinating," Devon teased.

"Thank you," Micah whispered. He leaned back and looked into Devon's affectionate, worried eyes. "Take me home, Devon. I need to make love to you."

Devon swallowed hard. "Yeah, okay," he murmured and pulled Micah away from the tank, toward the door.

They passed by the mantas' public tank and the small crowd gathered around it who were petting the rays in it, and Micah hesitated.

Devon stopped and glanced at the little girl who was giggling manically and leaning into the shallow tank to pet the ray as it swam past. He looked back at Micah, who met his eyes, and Devon grinned and tugged Micah toward the tank.

Micah leaned over, careful not to touch the glass with bare skin, and watched the closest ray, which was currently on the other side of the tank.

"Two or three fingers. Just pet it as it swims by," the mother told her little girl.

The ray floated closer, and Micah swallowed. He couldn't—quite—make himself put his hand in the water.

Devon took his hand, squeezed it, and reached into the tank with Micah's fingers tangled between his. The water rushed cool over Micah's skin as the ray swam right up under their joined hands and then past them.

Micah sucked in a delighted breath.

"How was it?" Devon asked, watching him closely.

"So slippery," Micah said. "And... softer than I expected, somehow." He shook the excess water off his hand, and Devon leaned down to quickly kiss him.

"I've got wet wipes in the truck," he said. "Let's get you cleaned up."

"Okay," Micah said. He smiled as Devon towed him out of the aquarium and into the sunlight.

THEY HOLED up in Micah's condo, and Devon devoted himself to making sure Micah wanted for nothing. He made them breakfast, lunch, and dinner, and did the shopping while Micah rested or before he woke up in the mornings so he was never alone with his own thoughts.

He let Micah choose what they did, and Micah almost always opted to stay home and allow Devon to educate him in all the movies that Micah had missed.

They didn't scene for the rest of the week. Micah wasn't feeling up to it, and Devon clearly sensed that, because he spent his time worshiping Micah in every way possible and let him take the lead and decide what they did both in the bedroom and out of it.

ON MONDAY Micah went back to work. Devon hadn't spent the night but he'd promised he'd be waiting when Micah got home that evening, so Micah got ready for the day alone as he tried not to let his nerves overwhelm him.

His phone buzzed on his way out the door.

Breathe. Just tell them you had food poisoning.

Micah closed his eyes and finally texted back.

Key's under the mat. See you tonight.

THE DAY was a disaster. *Everyone* wanted to know why he'd left early, and even Celeste's bright face at his door wasn't enough to make Micah feel better, especially since she seemed to sense that food poisoning was the least of Micah's worries. Thankfully she didn't push, but her visit left Micah off-balance, and when Norma forgot to tell him that he'd missed a very important client meeting, he only just managed to keep the anger locked behind his teeth.

When she informed him, an hour later, that Barrett was on hold and did he want to take the call, he'd had enough. His fury left her in tears, and Micah stalked out, seething, and drove home hating the world. He felt sick, full of self-loathing and disgust, and he shoved his door open hard enough to make it bounce off the far wall. Devon startled awake from his doze on the couch as Micah kicked his shoes off, hurled them at the shelf, and stalked past him, unbuttoning his shirt.

"Dosa? Micah, what the hell?"

He could hear Devon scrambling to catch up to him, but Micah didn't slow until he reached the bedroom. He yanked off his shirt in quick, angry movements, shoved his pants down, grabbed the collar from the nightstand, snapped it into place, and knelt at the end of the bed as Devon skidded into the room.

Micah kept his eyes fixed on the floor. In his peripheral vision, he could see Devon's bare feet moving closer to him, and Micah laced his hands behind his back.

"What happened?" Devon asked.

Micah squeezed his eyes shut. "I... lost a client. I shouted at Norma. I was... bad. I—" He couldn't make the words come, couldn't explain how angry and hurt and sick he was, so he closed his mouth and prayed Devon would understand what he couldn't say.

There was silence for a moment, and then a warm hand trailed across his back.

"Take it from me," Micah whispered, almost choking on the words. "Please."

Devon rested his hand briefly on Micah's hair. "On the bed," he said. "Facedown."

Micah stood up, climbed onto the mattress, and stretched out on his stomach.

"Arms by your sides," Devon said, and a drawer opened somewhere out of sight.

Micah didn't look. He kept his face pressed against the comforter, and he trembled but stayed as still as possible.

The bed dipped, and then Devon was there, his hand solid and comforting against Micah's lower back.

"Count them," he ordered.

Without further warning he struck the first blow, and Micah cried out as pain exploded across his buttocks.

"One," he gasped.

The next blow fell, and Micah writhed. The pain was sharp and immediate.

"Two," he managed.

The hits that followed were quick enough Micah couldn't count between them.

"Three, four, five," he groaned into the bed as he clutched handfuls of the blanket.

His ass was already burning, stinging sharply, and Micah let go. He let go of the self-hatred, the terror of losing Devon—the only truly good thing in his life—the sick nausea that had plagued him since Barrett's phone call that afternoon, and the disgust he felt for shouting at Norma, and let himself float free of it all.

Blows rained down, and Micah had lost count after the seventh or eighth. He sobbed in deep, desperate heaves, his entire body shaking, and still Devon spanked him until there wasn't an inch of skin from midthigh to the top of his buttocks that wasn't covered in welts.

Only then did Devon stop and throw the riding crop to the side. He rolled Micah over, wiped his tears away with a thumb, and pressed a soft kiss to the corner of his mouth.

"You're going to come for me now," he informed him, and Micah shook his head and choked back another sob.

"No, Devon, no. I don't... don't deserve it."

"Yes, you do," Devon said. He sounded implacable. "I've taken this from you, just like you asked. And now you're going to come, because you need to. And you trust me, don't you?"

Micah gulped back more tears and managed a nod.

"Say it," Devon ordered.

"I... trust you," Micah whispered. And he did. He knew he could safeword, but he also knew Devon had only his best interests in mind.

He looked into Devon's beautiful face, blurred through the tears in his eyes, and Devon's mouth curved as he helped Micah to a sitting position and then pulled him into his lap. Micah lay unresisting in his arms, his head lolling on Devon's shoulder, as Devon closed one hand around Micah's half-hard cock.

Micah gasped. The rough texture of Devon's jeans was almost unbearable against his tender skin, and the pain only served to make him harder as he suddenly ached for release.

Devon wrapped his other arm around Micah's waist and pinned him in position.

"It doesn't matter what happened," he growled in Micah's ear. "Because I took it, okay?" He swiped his thumb over the tip of Micah's cock, never losing his rhythm, and Micah sobbed out loud. "It's mine now," Devon continued. "And you're going to give me this too."

Micah writhed. His groin tightened and balls drew up, and Devon sped up his movements but kept the strokes sure and firm.

"Now," he commanded. "Come for me now, Micah," and Micah was helpless to do anything but obey, and his mouth fell open as his body locked up tight and bliss seized him.

When he came back to himself, he was still in Devon's arms, but they were in the bathroom, sitting on the edge of the tub. Devon was rocking him back and forth with tiny movements he seemed unaware of as he waited for the water to fill the huge tub, and Micah looked up at him with hazy vision.

Devon didn't notice. His eyes were fixed on the water, and Micah stared at his perfect jawline and long throat for a while. Devon had *known*, somehow. He'd understood and given Micah what he'd needed. He'd taken the ugliness and left Micah feeling clean and purified, and Micah didn't understand why, or how he'd gotten so lucky.

But his thoughts were too fuzzy to tease out the puzzle just then. Devon stood up and stepped into the tub—he'd taken his clothes off at some point, Micah realized—and settled down in the water.

Micah jerked when the steaming water hit his abused skin. He whined and curled in on himself.

"Breathe through it," Devon said gently as he caressed his thigh. "It'll fade in a minute."

Micah took sharp, jerky breaths, and slowly the stinging burn eased and he was able to relax. He pressed his face against Devon's chest and closed his eyes again.

Devon dropped a featherlight kiss on his hair. "Rest," he said. "We'll talk when you wake up."

Micah sighed, let the sub space pull him back out, and sank gratefully into oblivion.

CHAPTER SEVENTEEN

MICAH WOKE up the next morning to Devon inches away from his nose. He held his breath to keep from waking him, but Devon's eyes slid open and awareness filled them.

"You okay?" he whispered.

Micah nodded. He was lying on his stomach, warm and comfortable. He tried to move and gasped as nerve endings flared to life and his ass and upper thighs set up an angry throbbing. Devon sat up, looking worried.

"Don't move," he said. "I'll get the arnica."

He was back in under a minute to spread the cool cream across Micah's skin. Micah took a relieved breath as the stinging faded into a gentle heat. Finally Devon sat back on his heels and put the lid on the jar.

"What time is it?" Micah mumbled.

"Six," Devon said and settled back down on the bed until they were nose to nose again. "You can go back to sleep. I want you to call in sick today."

Micah tried to sit up but Devon caught his shoulder and gently pressed him back against the pillow.

"Devon, I have *work*. I can't just play hooky because I had a bad day."

"You had a *horrible* day," Devon corrected. "So bad you needed an intense scene to rid yourself of the worst of it. You need to recover. I've already called in, and I'm going to stay here with you and spoil you all day long. I'll make you breakfast in bed, and then we'll cuddle on the couch and watch *MasterChef* and *Kitchen Nightmares* and just… recuperate together. Okay?"

Micah searched his face. Devon's eyes looked earnest, vulnerable… and worried as they looked into Micah's.

"I'm not going to order you to," Devon said quietly. "But… will you? Please?"

Micah sighed. "Okay," he whispered.

Devon's face lit up, and he leaned forward to press a kiss to Micah's mouth. "Thank you," he murmured. "Now what would you like for breakfast?"

The day passed smoothly. Micah curled on his side on the couch with his head resting on Devon's thigh for most of it. His phone buzzed from the bedroom around noon, and Micah looked up, but Devon was already on his feet.

"Stay there." He was back in a few seconds, handed Micah the phone, and sat down again beside him.

Micah looked at the sender and sighed.

"Everything okay?" Devon asked.

"Fine," Micah muttered as he deleted the message, which was just more gibberish. "My phone's been acting up. I need to get a new one, I think. Maybe I can do that tomorrow."

MICAH DROVE to the store first thing the next morning. He sat on the edge of the seat as gingerly as possible and grinned to himself as he parked and stepped out. He pulled his phone from his pocket and sent Devon a text.

Something tells me I'm going to be on my feet all day.

He got a reply as he was pushing open the door of the business.

I can freshen those up when you get home if you want.

Micah laughed out loud and earned a strange look from a technician.

You do that, and I'll never get any work done. Be too busy thinking about my boner and all the ways you can help with it.

Devon's reply was almost immediate.

I see no problem.

Micah grinned to himself.

Of course you don't, you horny beast.

Jays game next week, Devon sent instead. *Go w/me?*

Micah hesitated. Going to Devon's games was one thing. Going to the actual Rogers Centre was something else entirely, with all the sticky shit on the floors and unwashed masses in close proximity.

His phone went off again, startling him, and he glanced down at it.

I bought stock in Purell. ;)

Micah huffed a quiet laugh and thumbed a quick reply. *Fine, but we're both bathing in the stuff after.*

He turned to the employee who approached with a smile on her face.

"My phone's been acting up," he told her. "Getting weird, random calls and texts from unknown numbers. I was wondering if that's a problem with this model or if it's specific to my phone and whether I need a new one."

"Let me just take a look at it," the girl said. Her nametag said AMY on it in reassuringly professional block letters, and her fingers were quick and deft on the phone's screen. But after a few minutes, she looked up and shook her head. "Sir, nothing appears to be wrong with this phone. I'll run a few more tests, but it seems to be in perfect working order."

"What about the weird texts?" Micah asked.

Amy grimaced. "I don't know. Someone pranking you, maybe?"

Micah accepted the phone back after she finished running the rest of the diagnostic scans and shook her head in defeat.

"I'm sorry," she said. "Would you like to change your number?"

"I don't know," Micah admitted. "Let me think about it, and I'll get back to you."

HE DROVE to work, gnawing on the problem in his head, but he set it aside as he rode the elevator to his floor. He needed to apologize to Norma properly, and he couldn't do that if he was distracted.

Norma ducked her head and focused on her computer when Micah stepped out of the elevator, and Micah bit the inside of his cheek as he tried to figure out what to say.

In the end he settled for stepping around the side of her curved desk, holding out the enormous bouquet and not moving until Norma turned to face him.

Her soft brown eyes were wary, and Micah swallowed another surge of self-hatred.

"I'm sorry," he said quietly. "I'm an asshole, and I took it out on you, and you didn't deserve it, and I'm so sorry, Norma. Can you possibly forgive me?"

Norma sighed and took the lilies—her favorite flower, Micah knew—and stroked one velvety petal. "This must have cost an absolute fortune," she finally said as she glanced up and smiled at him.

Relief swamped Micah. "I'd have paid twice as much for them if I had to. You're the best assistant I've ever had, and I'm an idiot."

"Yes, you are," Norma agreed, her lips twitching. "But I suppose you're forgiven. Only if I get a proper hug from you, though."

Micah stiffened briefly. *Don't be stupid.* He moved into her arms. Norma smelled like gardenias, and she didn't hold on to him long, but patted his back and released him with a smile almost immediately.

"I'd better put these in some water," she said and headed for the break room as Micah unlocked his office door with a relieved sigh.

CELESTE POKED her head in just as he was getting ready for lunch. "Hey," she said brightly. "Feeling better?"

"Ah…," Micah said intelligently from where he stood next to the window. "Yes. Thanks. How are you?"

Celeste came into the room, collapsed into the chair in front of his desk, and slung her dainty feet up onto the mahogany. Micah winced but said nothing.

"Hungry?" she said. "Wanna eat with me?"

"Sure," Micah said, surprising himself. "I mean, if you don't mind doing it in here. I'm not a fan of the cafeteria food."

Celeste shuddered delicately. "Who is?"

They spent the lunch hour trading stories of their coworkers, and Micah couldn't remember ever having that much fun at work before.

He ate standing up, and eventually Celeste sighed. "Okay, dude. Spill."

"About what?" Micah said, feigning innocence.

"Why aren't you sitting?" she demanded.

"Umm… hemorrhoids," Micah improvised hastily, and Celeste's eyes narrowed, but she let it pass.

When he opened the door for her to go back to work, though, she swatted him on the butt, and he couldn't keep the yelp in. Celeste winked as she sashayed past.

"Get one of those donut pillows," she advised. "I hear they work wonders."

Micah shut the door behind her, gingerly rubbed his sore ass, and muttered under his breath. But he couldn't help the smile that spread across his face.

THE NEXT week passed surprisingly easily. Celeste fell into the habit of having lunch with him most days and gossiping about their colleagues, and Micah began to look forward to seeing her every day.

Devon was at Micah's place almost every night, and one day Micah got a text from him as he was leaving work.

Straight to the bedroom, Mr. Ellis.

Micah stared at the phone for a minute but finally shrugged and shoved it into his pocket. The condo was quiet when he pushed the door open, and he headed for the bedroom, wondering what the hell Devon was up to.

He stopped dead on the threshold and stared at Devon, who was leaning against the wall, holding a ruler and wearing khakis, an honest-to-God *sweater vest*, and… heavy-framed glasses? *He looks like an English professor.*

Devon gestured to the child's desk Micah hadn't even noticed at first. "Have a seat, Mr. Ellis," he said.

"I—" Micah floundered for words.

Devon arched an eyebrow. "Have. A. Seat," he said clearly. "Or would you prefer detention?"

Oh. The pieces clicked into place, and Micah shut his mouth with a snap. They were role-playing.

He set his bag down, sat down at the desk, and tucked his feet behind the legs of the seat.

Devon pushed off the wall and circled the desk. "I asked you to see me after class because we need to talk about your grades."

Micah kept his face straight with an effort. Devon was very drool-worthy in that getup, it was true, but the entire situation just felt ridiculous.

Devon brought the ruler down on the desk with a crack, and Micah jumped and jerked his gaze up. Devon looked back at him mildly.

"Pay attention, please," he said. "Your grades. They're abysmal. What do you think we should do about that?"

"I, uh…." Micah couldn't think of anything to say. "You could… tutor me?" he suggested.

Devon's lips twitched and he turned away briefly before facing him again with a serious expression. "What makes you think I have time to do that?" he growled. "I'm a busy man. A lot on my plate. I'd need a pretty compelling reason to keep you after school and work with you one-on-one."

Laughter welled inside Micah but he fought it back and gripped the desk hard. "I... could make it worth your time," he managed.

"How exactly would you do that?" Devon asked. Mirth danced in his eyes, and he rubbed his mouth, clearly fighting another smile.

"I could clean the chalkboards?" Micah offered.

Devon snorted a laugh and then sobered. "That's not what I meant, and you know it. Now, Mr. Ellis." He bent down and placed his hands on the desk to look Micah in the eye. "I'm sure I can be persuaded to give you an A on this paper, but first, you're going to have to let me give you the *D*."

Micah couldn't hold it in any longer. "Oh my *God*!" He burst out laughing, slid sideways out of the desk, and ended up on the floor in a heap. He wrapped his arms around his stomach and howled helplessly as Devon landed on his knees next to him, laughing just as hard. Every time one of them made eye contact, it set the other off again, until they were both flat on their backs on the floor, staring up at the ceiling and hiccupping occasionally.

"That was the *worst line ever*," Micah finally gasped, and Devon chortled again.

"I thought of it last week," he sputtered. "I couldn't resist."

Micah wiped the tears from his face and rolled over to drape himself across Devon's chest, still giggling sporadically. "Hey there, Professor," he managed.

Devon snorted and pulled Micah down for a kiss. "Well, that was an abysmal failure."

"I don't know," Micah protested. "Personally I think that was a resounding success. I needed that laugh."

Devon grinned up at him. "Happy to help," he said. "So I guess it's safe to say that role-play is not for us."

"Probably not," Micah agreed. "But damn, it was fun figuring that out."

Devon laughed quietly and kissed him again.

MICAH WOKE up the next morning with an idea brewing. He wriggled out from under Devon's sleep-heavy arm and made them breakfast while he thought about it. He liked the notion more and more and didn't bother fighting the grin as he whipped eggs for the omelet and decided how exactly he would carry out his plan.

Once he was at work, he sent Devon a text.

We need to talk. My place tonight.

His phone buzzed immediately.

Something wrong?

Micah replied just as quickly.

Just need to discuss something.

He was distracted all day and dodged Norma when she tried to detain him for conversation. Instead he made one quick stop and then hurried home to his condo.

Devon was waiting in the parking lot, looking anxious.

Micah kept his mouth tight, gave him a quick nod, and climbed the steps with Devon on his heels. He didn't speak until they were inside and he'd put his shoes away and hung up his and Devon's jackets.

"Couch," he finally said.

"You're really freaking me out," Devon said as Micah led the way to the couch and settled on it on his knees. Devon sank down next to him.

"Something's been bothering me a while," Micah said. "It's not personal. It's definitely not you, but… this isn't working."

Devon took a sharp breath. "Micah, no. *No.* Don't… please don't do this. Whatever it is, we can—"

Micah held up a hand, and Devon stopped.

"I hate seeing you waiting in the parking lot for me," Micah said. "So I want you to have this." He reached in his pocket and pulled out the spare key he'd had made that afternoon.

Devon's mouth fell open, and he stared at the key and back up at Micah, who grinned at him with a hint of nerves.

"You *asshole,*" Devon breathed and tackled Micah backward onto the cushions.

Micah landed with a thud, the air driven out of him, and he laughed helplessly as Devon propped himself above him and glared down.

"You little *shit.* I thought you were breaking up with me," he growled.

"I know," Micah gasped as he squirmed underneath him. "That's what made it so funny. Your *face.*"

Devon narrowed his eyes. "You will pay, Ellis. You will *beg* for forgiveness."

"Is that a promise?" Micah asked.

Devon dipped his head and kissed him slowly. Then he pulled him upright and sat back against the cushions with a sigh. "God, this has been the *worst* day, and then you go and pull this shit…. It's a good thing for you you weren't serious."

"What happened?" Micah asked. He lifted Devon's arm and curled up against his side.

Devon pulled him close and sighed again. "Sean says we may have to close the shop."

"What?" Micah said as he sat up straight. "You *love* that shop. You can't close it!"

Devon tugged him back down. "Love doesn't pay the rent. We're tucked away on a side street, and no one knows about us. It's kind of hard to run a business with no customers, and we've been in the red for too long. We've already let go everyone we possibly can, but we're still not clearing a profit."

Shit. Micah rested a hand on Devon's thigh. "Can I help?" he asked.

"No, but thanks for listening," Devon said. He dropped a kiss on Micah's hair. "Thank you for the key," he murmured. "Even if you had to give me a heart attack first."

Micah patted his leg absently while his mind worked. He had to help. He didn't know how, or what he could do, but he had to do *something*.

CHAPTER EIGHTEEN

THE NEXT day was the Jays game. Micah had put it from his mind and opted to pretend it wasn't fast approaching, but Devon was up bright and early that morning.

He slid out of bed and hurried to the bathroom but was back in record time to bounce on the mattress beside Micah's determinedly still-asleep form.

"Time to wake uu-up," he singsonged and tugged on the blanket Micah had wrapped around his shoulders.

Micah moaned, rolled to his stomach, and pulled his pillow over his face. A second later a heavy weight landed on top of him, and Micah wheezed as the air was driven out of him and Devon kissed the back of his neck.

"I'll make it worth your while," he whispered, his breath hot on Micah's skin.

Micah freed one arm from where it was pinned beneath him and reached up and back. The angle was awkward, but his aim was true as he poked Devon square in the ribs and made him yelp and squirm to get away.

He rolled off Micah's prone form, and Micah lunged upright, landed on top of him, and tickled him mercilessly as Devon begged for mercy, laughing too hard to get the words out.

Micah only stopped when Devon flipped them again, straddled Micah's waist, and pinned his wrists above his head.

Devon grinned triumphantly and bent to kiss him. He took his time about it as Micah melted into the shape and feel of Devon's mouth, sweet and warm on his. He sighed as Devon broke the kiss and nipped the curve of Micah's jaw.

"You little shit," Devon murmured, and Micah smiled at the ceiling as Devon moved lower and his breath tickled Micah's skin. But Micah's half-formed idea that he could distract Devon with sex was dashed when

Devon looked up at the clock and growled. "Go shower," he ordered as he sat up on his heels and pulled Micah upright. "We have a long day ahead."

Micah wrapped his arms around Devon's waist as Devon still straddled his thighs. He held on for a minute with his eyes closed. Devon ran his hand up and down Micah's back.

"Hey," he murmured. He slid a finger under Micah's chin and tipped his head up. "Remember how well you did at the barbecue? And my first game—you came to that by yourself, which still just amazes me, and you did so well. You're going to be fine. I'll be with you the entire time. Okay?"

Micah nodded fractionally and tightened his grip. He could do it. He *could*.

Devon made breakfast, and they headed out the door, hand in hand, after their showers, as Devon talked a mile a minute.

"Do you want to go to the aquarium again since it's right next door?" he asked as they reached the parking lot.

Micah perked up and dug for his keys. "Yeah, I'd like that." He smiled at Devon across the roof of the car, and the smile slipped as a dark red Porsche drove past the condos, moving too quickly for Micah to see who was driving.

"You okay?" Devon asked.

Micah fumbled the keys and nearly dropped them, but finally managed to press the button to unlock the car. "Fine," he said brightly. "Let's get going."

Even with the heavy traffic that clogged Toronto's downtown streets, the drive to the stadium took less time than Micah had hoped, and far too quickly they pulled into one of the parking garages.

Micah set the brake and took a deep breath as Devon's warm hand covered his. He glanced up and Devon smiled at him.

"This is supposed to be fun," he said gently. "Try to relax. Okay?"

Micah nodded and squared his shoulders. They got out and walked hand in hand out of the parking garage toward the stadium. The day was crisp and cool, with a brisk wind that nipped at Micah's cheeks and made him shiver.

They found their seats without problem, and Devon pulled out a packet of wet wipes with a cheeky grin that made Micah laugh in spite of his nerves. Devon cleaned off the plastic seats thoroughly and then ushered Micah to them and made a show of settling him in.

"You're such a nerd," Micah said, smiling up at him.

Devon just chortled and flopped down next to him. "You want a beer?"

"It's not even noon," Micah said.

"And you're at a baseball game," Devon pointed out. "It's tradition."

"Maybe later," Micah said and leaned into Devon's warm side. Devon freed his arm and wrapped it around Micah's shoulders as the opening pitch was thrown and the game began.

AN HOUR in, Micah had to admit that he preferred Devon's games. Knowing the people on the field seemed to make the difference in rooting for them, but watching Devon cheer for his favorites made the entire expedition worthwhile.

Devon's blue eyes sparkled, the tip of his nose was pink with cold, and he kept letting go of Micah to applaud wildly.

He pulled Micah against him again and dropped a quick kiss on his hair. "Doing okay?" he murmured.

"Fine," Micah said, surprised to realize it was true. "Need to go to the bathroom, though."

"I'll go with you," Devon said instantly.

"I think I can manage to pee on my own, but I appreciate your concern," Micah said. His lips twitched as he stood up and stepped over Devon's long legs to get to the aisle.

He found the public bathrooms without difficulty and used his shoulder to push the door open so he wouldn't have to touch the handle.

The room was empty except for a heavyset man at the far end of the urinals, and Micah took care of business quickly without touching anything and turned to wash his hands, anxious to get back to Devon.

"Fancy meeting you here, stranger," Barrett said from behind him. Micah spun and drops of water flew from his hands.

Barrett stood by the door, hands in his pockets, smiling at him.

"What—" Micah cleared his throat. "What are you doing here?"

"Attending a baseball game, as I assume you are," Barrett said, arching a sardonic brow.

"You don't like sports," Micah said, off-balance. He reached for a paper towel and dried his hands without taking his eyes off Barrett's slim form.

"It's become more interesting to me of late," Barrett said as a wicked smile curved his mouth. His chestnut hair had tumbled free of the gel that he used to sweep it back, falling forward over his high brow.

Micah floundered and looked for words. To get out, he was going to have to approach Barrett, who was blocking the door, and he'd sooner set himself on fire.

"So is the perfect Devon here too?" Barrett asked as he rocked back onto his heels. "I'd love to see him again." His tone was light, but a frisson skittered down Micah's spine anyway.

The portly man at the far end finished washing his hands and glanced between Micah and Barrett. "Everything okay, son?" he asked Micah.

Micah glanced at him. The stranger had a kind, open face and keen brown eyes that were narrowed.

Micah seized the opportunity. "I don't remember where my seat is," he said, flashing a winning smile at the stranger. "I think it's in the *J* section, but I'm so turned around, I don't even know where to start."

"Why don't I show you?" the man said and smiled back at him. "I'm William."

"Micah," Micah said, and he followed him toward the door and kept William between him and Barrett as Barrett took a step back, his gray eyes dark with fury. "Thank you so much, William. I'd probably have starved to death in this rabbit's warren without you."

William's laugh was easy and open and shook his whole body, and Micah decided he liked him. He led Micah through the concrete halls to the *J* section, and Micah spotted the back of Devon's head, several rows below. He turned and smiled at William.

"Thank you."

William smiled back. "You take it easy, son. And if you don't mind me saying so, maybe you should consider avoiding the hell out of your friend from the bathroom. He strikes me as a nasty piece of work."

"You couldn't be more right, sir," Micah said. Devon turned and waved, and Micah waved back and hurried down the steps toward him.

He settled into his seat next to Devon, who wrapped his arm around Micah's shoulders and pulled him close again.

"Everything okay?" Devon asked. "You feel… tense."

Micah leaned into Devon's warmth. "Yeah," he said. "Everything's fine. Did I miss anything?"

MONDAY, MICAH woke up to Devon's mouth on his cock, and he arched up into it with a shaky moan and slid his hand into Devon's hair.

Devon hummed happily around his mouthful and pushed Micah's thighs apart to rub a slick finger against his entrance. Micah let his legs splay wide as Devon swallowed him down and worked him open with quick, rough shoves at the same time.

When Micah's stomach tightened and his thighs started to tremble, his orgasm imminent, Devon only redoubled his efforts and pushed three fingers deep inside Micah's body. In no time at all, Micah came down Devon's throat with a soft groan.

Devon gentled him through it, eased his fingers out, and got to his knees. He looked a question at Micah, who nodded, still dopey on endorphins.

"Do it," he whispered.

Devon lined up and pressed forward. Micah was so loose and open that Devon slid right in with almost no resistance, making Micah gasp.

"God, yes," he managed. "*Harder*, Devon."

Devon obeyed. He lifted Micah's legs and slung them over his arms so he could slam home with greater accuracy as Micah writhed.

He was still blissed out, easy and relaxed, and he dug his heels into Devon's lower back to command him to go harder, faster. *Come on, Devon.*

It wasn't long before Devon stiffened above him and shuddered through his orgasm as his eyes fell shut. Micah ran his hands up and down Devon's arms, loving him silently and wishing he could say the actual words.

When Devon slid out, he didn't collapse on Micah immediately like he usually did. Instead he reached for something in the sheets Micah hadn't noticed before, and then hard plastic slid into Micah's hole and settled into place.

Micah gasped. "Devon… what—"

"You're going to wear this to work," Devon growled, and Micah gulped. "It stays in all day, and I'll know if you take it out."

Oh God.

"You're also going to wear these," Devon said and held up a pair of blue satin panties.

Micah whimpered.

HE GOT precisely no work done. It was almost impossible to sit with the plug rubbing against his prostate every time he shifted position. He was in a state of near-painful arousal, made worse by the satiny slide of the fabric against the sensitive head of his cock when he moved.

He wasn't going to be able to do it. He was going to come in his pants like a teenager and spend the rest of his day in wet, sticky clothes, hiding from everyone.

Micah bit his lip and made a decision.

DEVON KNEW the second Micah walked through the door. His eyes narrowed, and he stood up from his comfortable sprawl on the couch and closed the gap between them in a few long strides.

Micah couldn't meet his eyes, and Devon caught his chin and pulled his head around.

"You took it out."

"Just for ten minutes," Micah said. "I needed... I couldn't.... Devon, it was *torture*. I—" He fell silent and swallowed hard.

"Bedroom," Devon said flatly.

Micah gulped and obeyed. He stopped dead inside the door, and his mouth fell open. The punching bag was gone, and where it had hung was, instead, a restraint system made of black nylon rope. There were *pulleys*, Micah realized, and he swung back to stare at Devon, who was right behind him.

Devon just arched an eyebrow. "Strip."

Micah yanked his clothes off, but when he reached for the waistband of the panties, Devon stopped him.

"Not those." He maneuvered Micah into position and snapped the soft cuffs into place. "Comfortable?" he asked.

Micah nodded wordlessly. His cock strained against the satin as another damp patch formed. His powers of speech had deserted him.

Devon fastened the cuffs to the rope and pulled until Micah's arms were stretched above his head. Then he turned to the bedside table and retrieved Micah's collar. He snapped it in place, and the anxious knot under Micah's breastbone eased as Devon knelt and reached for something Micah hadn't even noticed and pushed his feet apart.

A spreader bar. Micah gritted his teeth to keep the whimper back as Devon locked the bar in place and fastened Micah's ankles about shoulder width apart.

Micah teetered there with his arms pulled taut above his head and his feet spread. He could feel himself already sliding into sub space, relaxing, and letting go.

Devon stood up and inspected his work. He brushed a hand over the front of the underwear, and Micah's hips rocked forward.

"Easy, tiger," Devon said, his voice deep with arousal. "We'll get there."

Micah closed his eyes and drifted as Devon took his own clothes off and circled him. There was a rustling noise as he rummaged in a drawer, and then he returned and pulled the underwear down. Micah gasped and opened his eyes as cool metal closed over his shaft and locked tight.

"Devon," he whispered.

"You disobeyed," Devon said as he pulled the satin fabric back up over Micah's straining erection. "And you have to be punished for that." Despite the words, his tone was full of affection. "You're not going to come until I say you can, and I'm going to discipline you now." Leather popped somewhere out of sight, and Micah tensed.

"Relax," Devon ordered. "What's your safeword?"

"Manta ray," Micah said and he closed his eyes again. Devon would take care of him.

The first crack of the leather flogger made him cry out with shock and twist as the skin on his ass ignited. The next blows landed quickly, and Micah's head fell back as he tumbled ever deeper into sub space and floated free in the dark, only vaguely aware of Devon counting off the stripes as they landed.

Devon stopped soon, though, and stepped in close to run a hand over Micah's backside.

Micah moaned as Devon brushed across the welts, and then Devon slipped a hand inside the underwear, caressed the curve of Micah's ass, and slid lower. He found the plug where it was firmly in place and hooked a finger in the small ring at the end.

He didn't pull it out. He just tugged it gently, but Micah whined as the movement scraped his abused rim and made nerve endings fire.

"You disobeyed me," Devon murmured. "You took it out when I told you not to."

"I was… going to come," Micah moaned. "Couldn't—"

"So maybe next time, you'll have to wear the cock ring as well," Devon mused.

Micah whimpered again.

"Oh, you like that idea, don't you?" Devon asked. "Wearing the satin panties, feeling them rubbing against your flushed and leaking cock, but unable to come. But can I trust you? What's to stop you from just taking the cock ring off and coming whenever you feel like it?"

"You can. You can trust me," Micah panted. Devon was still behind him. Micah couldn't see his face, but he wasn't moving, and one finger was still hooked through the plug end. "I'll be… good. I swear," Micah continued. "I'm sorry, Devon. I'm sorry. Please can I come, please, it hurts—"

Devon reached one hand around, pulled the panties down, clasped Micah's shaft, and gave it several rough strokes. "Not yet," he said, and Micah sobbed out loud and twisted in his restraints.

"*Please.*"

Devon let go and went to his knees behind Micah. He gripped the plug and pulled it out in a slow, easy slide, and Micah sighed at the sense of loss, the sudden emptiness. But Devon wasn't finished. The plug clattered on the floor, and then Devon pulled Micah's asscheeks apart to blow lightly on his tender hole.

Micah moaned, almost insensible. His knees were weak—giving out on him—and his arms in their restraints were the only things supporting his weight. His shoulders ached, and the starbursts of pain only served to send him spiraling deeper into ecstasy as Devon ate him out.

His breath was hot against Micah's skin as he delved as deep as he could until tears flowed down Micah's cheeks in a hot, steady slide and he begged in a thick voice he barely recognized.

Only then did Devon reach back around, his tongue still busy, to open the ring. He barely had it off before Micah came helplessly, bucking in his bonds as his come splattered on the hardwood floor.

Devon unbuckled the spreader bar and stood up, supporting Micah with one arm around his waist as he undid the wrist cuffs in quick, jerky movements. Micah sagged against him, and his arms fell free as Devon picked him up and carried him to the bed. Devon laid him facedown on the mattress and straddled his thighs.

Micah was only vaguely aware of Devon beginning to stroke himself, the slick sound of his hand on his shaft the only sound in the room, and it was less than a minute before Devon's breathing sped up and he hissed.

"Micah, shit, shit, *Micah*." Then wet heat splattered Micah's ass. It felt like melted candle wax on his abused skin and made him writhe and whimper.

Devon fell forward. He caught himself with a hand on either side of Micah's prone form, his softening cock nestled between Micah's cheeks. He leaned down, pressed his chest to Micah's back, and kissed the shell of his ear.

Micah smiled and fell asleep.

HE WOKE up in the bathtub, cradled in Devon's arms. He stretched, and Devon smiled down at him.

"Welcome back," he murmured. "How are you feeling?"

"Like misbehaving more often," Micah slurred.

Devon laughed deep in his chest. "Come on. Let's get you out and dry so I can put arnica cream on you."

Micah obeyed placidly, still at peace with the world.

"I love you like this," Devon said into his hair as he carried him to the bed. "So docile, so sweet. You make me want to wrap you in a blanket and put you in my pocket. Keep you there forever."

Micah hummed agreement, barely aware of Devon's words. Devon set him on the mattress, and Micah obediently rolled to his stomach so Devon could work the cream into the welts as he drifted.

HE CAME fully back to himself on the couch, as delicious smells wafted from the kitchen.

"Dev?" he called.

"Making dinner, love," Devon said. "I hope you're hungry."

Micah stood up and padded into the kitchen to wrap his arms around Devon's waist. He took a deep breath of Devon's T-shirt—cotton and fabric softener and *Devon*, motor oil and pine and mountains.

Devon pressed his cheek to Micah's hair. "Hey, you," he murmured. "Doing okay?"

"No subdrop yet," Micah said as he released him to dig in the fridge for a drink. "Sorry about... you know." He waved a hand vaguely, and Devon's eyes creased.

"Sure you are," he said.

"I am," Micah protested. "Well... sort of." He grinned back, sat down at the table, and drew his knees to his chest. His ass was sore from the flogging, but it was a pleasant ache, nowhere near the intensity of the first time they'd tried spanking.

"So have you figured anything out about the shop?" he asked.

Devon shook his head and poured cream into the saucepan. "Not yet. We have to get the word out, up our visibility, but we can't afford to take out a billboard or a huge ad in every newspaper in town. And really what we need is a better location. I'm still not sure how *you* found us."

"It was a series of accidents," Micah admitted. "I took what I thought was a shortcut, and I got completely lost, and then the belt snapped, and there you were."

"Exactly," Devon said. He sighed, shoved his hair out of his face, and smiled at Micah. "Let's talk about something else. Doing anything this weekend?"

"Other than you?" Micah said, and surprised Devon into an undignified snort. "Nope. My schedule's clear."

"Sean and Fallon have something they want to tell us," Devon said. "They're cooking dinner, and everyone's coming over. You're invited. It'll be an indoor thing. No barbecue outside, I promise."

"I'd like that," Micah said. "Also there's something I meant to talk to you about."

"What's that?" Devon asked as he stirred what smelled like Alfredo sauce.

"Have you talked to any Doms since we started scening?" Micah said.

"No," Devon said. "Should I?"

Micah lifted a shoulder. "Not unless you *want* to, because you've been doing a great job on your own, but I thought... if you're interested, you could talk to Kali."

"Who's Kali?"

"My ex," Micah said. "And actually my best friend, at least until you came along."

Devon's smile lit up the room.

"Anyway, we fooled around a bit, started experimenting with Dom and sub. We were never serious—it was just some fun for both of us. But then she got a promotion and moved back to India, and I met Barrett. We still keep in touch some. She's gone a lot further with the Domming, and she's pretty damn good at it. She can be kind of an asshole, but she means well. She might be able to give you some hints, if you're... interested."

Devon nodded and poured sauce over the pasta already arranged on plates. "I'd like that, yeah. I have a few questions. After we eat?"

Micah checked his watch. "Yeah. It's midafternoon there. Sounds good."

COMFORTABLY FULL, they curled up on the couch, and Micah dialed Kali's number.

"Micah," Kali's cool voice greeted him. "I thought you'd forgotten about me. How are you?"

"I'm well," Micah said. "It's good to hear your voice, Kali. I'm sorry it's been so long. How's work treating you? Running the company yet?"

They talked for several minutes as Devon listened quietly with his arm around Micah's waist.

"So listen," Micah finally said. "I was actually wondering if you'd be willing to talk to my boyfriend. He's new to Domming, and I thought maybe you could give him some pointers. Allay any fears he might have."

"Of course," Kali said. "What's his name?"

"Devon," Micah said.

"Give him the phone," Kali said, and Micah obeyed.

He turned so his chest was pressed to Devon's abdomen and listened to the steady thump of Devon's heart. Before long he drifted off as Devon's breathing lulled him to sleep.

HE WOKE up slowly and floated to awareness in the same position.

"I know," Devon said. "I just... I worry, you know?"

There was silence as Kali spoke too quietly for Micah to hear.

"Yeah," Devon said as he rubbed Micah's shoulder. "When we're scening, I... it's hard to describe, but it's like everything is sharper, more focused somehow. Like I know what he needs before he does, and I'm going to give it to him. I'll give him everything he needs. It's... an incredible feeling, but it scares me a bit too."

Micah kept his breathing steady as Devon listened to Kali.

"I just want to keep him safe," Devon whispered. "Take away the bad and protect him from everything. I know he's a grown man. I'm trying to stay out of his life unless he asks, but you have no idea how much I want to smash Barrett's face in." There was a pause, and Devon huffed a humorless breath. "Yeah," he said. "Yeah, I know. You've got my number. I'll probably call you again, if you don't mind. Thanks for listening, Kali. You've helped me a lot."

He hung up and kissed Micah's hair.

"Hey," he murmured. "I'm done. Want to move to an actual bed?"

Micah nodded, and they climbed to their feet and headed for the bedroom with their arms around each other.

CHAPTER NINETEEN

MICAH WAS in a good mood when he left for work. He and Devon had experimented with sensory deprivation the night before, and it had resulted in truly spectacular orgasms for both of them. Then they'd had a long, luxurious bath, and Devon insisted on giving Micah a massage that left him a boneless lump of pleasure.

They were going to Sean and Fallon's party that weekend to hear their news, and Micah was apprehensive, but still looking forward to it.

Micah pulled into the drive-thru to get coffee for Norma and himself. He parked and made it through the parking garage, balancing the hot coffee somewhat precariously on his briefcase, and caught the elevator just as it was about to close.

His smile slipped when he realized Barrett was the one holding the door for him.

Micah swallowed hard, stepped into the elevator, and kept his head down.

The steel doors closed, trapping him in the small space, and Micah focused on his breathing. *In, out. Steady and slow.*

He summoned Devon's face to mind, contorted in helpless giggles as they lay on the floor and laughed after their failed role-playing attempt and the way Devon's eyes had caught the light and sparkled vividly. Micah's breath hitched in his chest, and he couldn't help the smile that crept across his face.

"What's so funny?" Barrett asked.

Micah stiffened. "I… nothing."

"Did you find your seat again?" Barrett said, leaning in closer. His heavy aftershave clogged Micah's nostrils, and a cough caught in the back of his throat. Barrett's bright gray eyes gleamed with malicious curiosity, and Micah gritted his teeth.

"Yes, thank you," he said tightly.

"I'm glad," Barrett said, all false solicitude. "I'm even gladder to see that you seem to be overcoming some of those awful hang-ups you had when we were dating."

Micah stiffened as Barrett smiled at him.

"Anyway, I have a meeting with your boss," Barrett said. "It's long past time for us to start working more closely together, don't you think? My firm needs an infusion of fresh blood, and you are just the man for the job."

Horror flooded Micah, and he froze.

The door dinged before he could formulate a response, and Barrett stepped out and dropped him a wink.

And thus it began.

Zachary was more than happy to assign Barrett's account to Micah. Barrett took this as his opportunity to send Micah constant texts throughout the days that followed.

At first they were fairly innocuous.

Need to talk to you about a new employee. The one you got for us last month. Don't think he's working out. Gonna need a replacement.

Micah stifled a groan. He was a professional. He could handle this. *Lunch, 12:30,* he sent back.

The meal was awkward, but Micah kept his desk between them, and Barrett mostly stayed on his side.

He got another text as he was pulling into his parking lot.

Was nice to see you today. Like old times.

Micah didn't answer, nor did he tell Devon the news.

Several days went by with Barrett mostly behaving himself—other than giving him the occasional heated look and letting his fingers brush against Micah's skin if he got too close. The texts stayed professional, with the occasional smiley face or joke thrown in.

Micah relaxed a little. Maybe it would be okay. Maybe Barrett had accepted that Micah was with Devon and wasn't interested in Barrett anymore.

Lunch? Barrett texted as if on cue.

Micah sighed. *In the office. Too much work to go out.*

Barrett knocked on the door as the clock ticked noon. He held cartons from Madeleine's, and Micah's stomach growled. Barrett's smile widened and he set the food out on the desk.

"I got your favorite," he said as he settled into the chair across from Micah. "I *have* missed you."

Micah applied himself to his food as Barrett launched into a story.

He found himself laughing in spite of himself. Barrett's eyes sparkled as he talked. He waved his hands animatedly as he described the situation he'd been in, and Micah couldn't help being amused.

"And then the woman says, 'Well, *I* think'—"

A tentative rap on the open door interrupted him, and Micah looked up. His mouth fell open when he saw Devon standing in the doorway, looking tense and unhappy.

"Hey," Micah said as he rose to hurry to him. Devon was covered in engine grease and motor oil, but his face was clean, so Micah went up on tiptoe and kissed him lightly on the mouth, careful not to touch him anywhere else.

Devon smiled down at him. "I had to make a delivery for a client in the area," he said, "and I thought I'd surprise you, maybe take you out for lunch, but I guess I wasn't fast enough."

"Oh God, I'm sorry," Micah said. He glanced behind him. "I was just... we were...."

Barrett leaned back in his chair, his arm draped across its backrest and legs stretched out in front of him. He flipped a lazy hand at Devon.

"How's the automobile industry?" he asked.

Devon's eyes tightened. "It's fine," he said, his tone clipped. "Micah, I'll see you later. Have a good lunch." And with that he was gone, leaving Micah gaping helplessly after him.

Micah sat back down at the desk, and Barrett grimaced.

"Jealous type, huh?" he commented as he leaned forward and took a bite of crepe.

"Devon? No, of course not," Micah said automatically. "He's not.... Devon's not jealous. He knows he has nothing to be jealous *about*."

Barrett looked at him silently for a minute and then shrugged. "You know him better than I do," he said. "God, Mike, how do you stand all that *dirt*?" He shuddered. "It must get everywhere, and I *know* you're not keeping your opinions to yourself on that score. I remember how you bitched me out every time I so much as left a dirty dish in the sink for more than five minutes at a time."

"Devon's very good about doing dishes," Micah said, his voice low.

"Well, I'm sure he's getting tired of hearing you nag," Barrett said. "But I imagine you make it up to him in other ways, right? And anyway, he strikes me as way too polite to actually complain. Does he care you're picking up that spare tire around your middle?"

Micah shot to his feet. "I have a lot of work to do," he said, "and I really need to get it done, so I'll talk to you later."

Barrett stared at him, but clearly decided not to argue. Instead he shrugged and closed his carton of food.

"See you for lunch tomorrow," he said over his shoulder as he left the room.

Micah waited until the door was shut and then sat down hard in his chair and covered his face.

God, he was so stupid. Of *course* Devon was sick of Micah's hang-ups. He was too kind to say anything, too polite to point them out, but he had to be thoroughly fed up with the way Micah insisted he bathe and wash his hands constantly and not leave anything lying around.

It wasn't like Micah really had anything to offer Devon, anyway. He was short, plain, chubby, and a neurotic mess. He brought nothing to the relationship except mental hang-ups and emotional baggage. He didn't have any talents, any skills. He was the most boring man alive.

Micah took a shaky breath just as his phone buzzed.

It was Devon. *Sorry we couldn't have lunch. Need to talk when you get home.*

Micah gnawed on his lower lip for a minute. *See you soon,* he finally replied.

DEVON WAS freshly showered and waiting on the couch when Micah walked in. "Hey," he said softly. Devon's blue eyes looked worried, and Micah swallowed more nerves.

He bought himself time by setting his shoes on the shelf, arranging them neatly, and hanging up his coat. But finally he couldn't put it off any longer, and he moved slowly into the living room and sat down on the far end of the couch from Devon.

"I'm sorry," he said quietly.

"About what?" Devon asked. He was sitting very still, as though afraid to move.

"Barrett," Micah said. "Eating lunch with him."

Devon scooted closer. "You have every right to have lunch with anyone you want, Dosa. Did you think I was mad at you?"

"Thought crossed my mind," Micah admitted. He stared at his hands.

Devon leaned in and rested a palm on Micah's knee. "I'm not mad at you," he said gently. "Very much the opposite, actually. I was going to take you out to eat because I was working at the garage today, and I just—how long have we been dating?"

"Seven months and four days," Micah said immediately.

Devon laughed and took Micah's hand. "I love your methodical brain. Nothing escapes you."

"Why do you ask?" Micah said.

Instead of answering, Devon changed the subject. "Do you remember that woman who made my life a living hell the day we met?"

Micah nodded.

"She came in again today," Devon said. "Had a problem with her alternator. It's a common issue on that particular model of car, but she *insisted* it was my fault, that it was something I did to the car last time I worked on it, and she demanded I fix it immediately. For free, of course."

He stopped and shook his head. "Sean sweet-talked her around. She's got some serious charm when she wants to. I ended up working on the alternator, but at least the woman agreed to pay."

"What's... are you going somewhere with this?" Micah asked.

Devon looked taken aback, but he smiled again and rubbed Micah's knuckles. "It's nothing big," he said. "And it sounds really stupid, but... the whole time, I was wishing I could talk to you. You make everything better. You listen when I complain, even when there's nothing you can say to make things right. You calm my mind."

Dread welled inside Micah's throat. *No, no, Devon. Don't say it. Please don't.*

Devon scooted closer and took both Micah's hands in his. "Micah."

Micah stared at his lap, at Devon's huge hands that enveloped his.

"Look at me?" Devon asked gently.

Micah looked up into Devon's eyes.

Devon's lips curved up. "There you are," he whispered. "Micah, I just want you to know... I love you."

There was hope in the depths of Devon's eyes—hope and fear and, of all things, *joy*—and Micah wanted to curl in on himself and weep. He'd left it too late.

"Say something," Devon said.

"You have to go," Micah whispered. His lips were numb.

Devon pulled back and a wrinkle formed on his brow. "I what?"

"You have to go," Micah repeated.

"That's not funny," Devon said. "Dosa, now's not the time for jokes. Don't do this to me again." His smile wavered, and it made Micah's chest ache to see it.

He jerked his hands back and stood up. "You can't love me," he said flatly.

Devon followed him to his feet. "Micah, what are you talking about? I *do* love you. I've loved you for a while."

"You *can't*," Micah said desperately. He twisted away when Devon reached for him. "Don't touch me," he hissed, and the ache in his chest spread.

Devon stared at him. "Micah, this isn't *funny*," he said. There was a thread of desperation in his voice. "Why are you doing this?"

"You need to go," Micah said, and pointed at the door. "I'm sorry, Devon. I was hoping it wouldn't come to this, but I don't—" He stopped to clear his throat. He thought he might be choking on something. "I don't love you," he said in a rush. He was going to throw up.

"No," Devon managed. He shook his head hard, as if to negate the words Micah had just said. "Tell me this is another one of your jokes."

"We had fun," Micah said. He couldn't meet Devon's eyes, so he turned away and climbed up the steps to the kitchen. "I never wanted to get this involved," he said over his shoulder. "This was just supposed to be some fun, a way to pass the time. You sure as hell weren't supposed to fall in love with me."

Devon still stood in the middle of the living room, staring at him. Micah wanted to hunch forward around the hollow feeling that wound through his sternum, but he forced his shoulders back and his head up.

You're doing this for *Devon. You'll only drag him down if he stays. He* can't *stay with you. Not if you want him to stay the decent man he is.*

"Please just go," he said around the lump in his throat.

"No," Devon said.

Micah jerked his eyes up.

Devon stood stock-still with his fists clenched. Frustration and fury and grief flickered in rapid succession across his face, and Micah swallowed hard.

"I'm not going to just walk out without a fight," Devon said. "I opened my heart to you. I don't—" He stopped to take a shaky breath. "I don't believe you don't love me too."

Micah abruptly lost his patience. "For fuck's *sake*, Devon," he snapped. "I don't love you. I never have. I don't *want* to love you, I don't *want* to spend the rest of my life with you, what do I need to do to get this through to you? *Just fucking leave.* Get out! I don't want to see you again!"

How does such a large man manage to look exactly like a kicked puppy?

Devon's shoulders were bunched and his eyes were wounded. He wrapped his arms around himself as though trying to hold in the hurt, and Micah wanted to weep. He wanted to rush over and hold him, tell him he'd never loved anyone more, please, *please* don't look like that, Devon.

But he said nothing, and finally Devon nodded. He walked into the kitchen as though his bones hurt and picked up his shoes from the shelf. Then he lifted his keys off the hook by the light switch and turned back.

"I meant it," he said, his voice thick with unshed tears. "I still mean it." He pulled his coat off the hook and something fell with a tinkle. Devon wrenched the door open, stumbled through, and it shut behind him with a bang that shook Micah to his core.

Only when Micah was sure he was alone did he allow his knees to weaken and deposit him on the floor. He ended up in a heap, curled on his side, his knees drawn to his chest.

I'm so sorry. I'm so sorry, Devon. I love you so much, but I'm not good enough for you. Please forgive me.

IT FELT like hours before Micah was able to lift his head, but the sun was still up when he slowly climbed to his feet. His joints ached, and he hugged his ribs as he stood in the middle of his kitchen, unsure what to do.

Devon hadn't officially moved into Micah's condo, but he'd made his presence felt in myriad tiny ways. There on the couch, they'd made love so many times. The empty spot on the shelf above the couch reminded Micah of how he'd been giving Devon a blowjob and Devon had accidentally knocked a vase off and shattered it when Micah found a good rhythm.

The restraint system was still in place in the bedroom, the arnica cream in the bathroom. Micah knew he wouldn't be able to look at the tub without thinking of all the baths they'd taken together.

Devon saturated the walls. He'd soaked into the atmosphere, permeated every room with his laugh, his vibrant energy, and his vivid, loving spirit.

Micah had to get out of there. He shuffled to the door and slowly, painfully dragged his shoes on. He left his jacket on the hook, lifted his keys from the nail, and stopped with his hand on the doorknob as his eye caught on a brass button lying on the floor. *It must have fallen off Devon's coat*, he realized, and he bent to pick it up before he thought about it.

In his car Micah sat for a minute and stared straight ahead as he absently rubbed his thumb over the ridges of the button. He was drifting, aimless and lost, unable to find his bearings. Finally he managed to start the car and pulled out onto the highway, but he drove without really knowing where he was going. All he knew was he had to get away.

He didn't realize he was at the aquarium until the car was in Park. Moving on autopilot, he paid the entrance fee and stumbled down the ramp into the building.

The room was blessedly empty, and Micah headed straight for the manta ray's tank.

He couldn't *see* it. Where was it? Micah pressed himself right up against the glass, flattened his palms against the cool surface, and peered into the depths.

Please, where are you, please.... Tears slid down his cheeks, but Micah didn't bother to wipe them away.

There. The manta ray appeared and undulated slowly through the water. Micah took a shaky breath and gulped back a sob. *Devon, I'm so sorry. I love you.* The ray swam closer, and Micah kept his eyes fixed on it.

Maybe I just find manta rays fascinating. Devon's voice in Micah's head was light and teasing, and Micah couldn't help the sob that tore through him.

His legs gave out, and he landed on his knees on the hard concrete floor, weeping in desperate, gasping heaves.

You're not worth it. Barrett's voice was hard, and Micah squeezed his eyes shut and shook his head to block it out. *You're not enough.*

I can't do this.

He had to get away, out of this city with all its memories. He dug his phone out of his pocket and dialed Kali's number with shaking fingers.

CHAPTER TWENTY

SOME TWENTY-FOUR hours later, Micah touched down in Mumbai and walked into Kali's arms.

He clutched the back of her sensible business suit and buried his face in the crook of her neck, smelling her sweet jasmine perfume as he fought back a fresh wave of tears.

"Micah," Kali said, patting his back. "Micah, you're going to wrinkle my suit."

Micah couldn't help his watery laugh, and he let go of her and wiped his eyes with his sleeve. Kali cocked her head and looked him up and down.

"You look terrible," she observed.

"Yeah, well… you look amazing," Micah said. It was true. Kali's air of cool elegance was as understated and undeniable as ever. Her black hair was swept up into a sleek chignon, and her dark eyes were calm as she surveyed him, but Micah knew her well enough to see the sympathy that lurked in their depths.

"Come on," Kali said. "We're not doing anyone any good by standing around the airport."

She led him through the terminal, and Micah dodged travelers and looked around him in wonder. The latticed-concrete canopy that vaulted high above him gave the huge space an open, airy sense and made Micah suddenly feel small and insignificant. But instead of making him shrink further into himself, it was an oddly reassuring sensation. It didn't matter that he'd fucked his life up or that everything had gone as wrong as it possibly could. The universe would spin on.

Micah took a deep breath and caught up to Kali, who was striding toward the baggage terminal.

"I don't actually have any luggage," he said.

Kali stopped dead and stared at him. "You're joking."

Micah held up his carry-on bag and smiled apologetically. "I shoved some clothes in this, grabbed my toothbrush and my passport, and took off. I couldn't...."

Kali sighed and changed direction. The heat hit Micah like a slap in the face as they stepped outside and he gasped. Kali lifted an eyebrow. "Didn't think that far ahead, did you?"

She bundled Micah into a taxi, settled opposite him, and fixed him with a gimlet eye.

"Let's get one thing straight," she said. "I'm not sleeping with you."

"Dear God," Micah sputtered. "I just broke up with the man I love, Kali. I don't *want* you to sleep with me!"

"As long as we're clear," Kali said, and she leaned forward to give the taxi driver the address. As the car moved into the whirlpool of traffic, Kali sat back and turned to Micah again. "Probably best not to look too closely at the traffic," she advised, "unless you want to give yourself heartburn or a panic attack."

Micah nodded. He turned his back to the window and focused on Kali's face.

"You're staying with me, of course," she said. "My mother will appreciate the company while I'm at work. All you have to do is eat her cooking and maybe wash some dishes, and she'll love you. She and my father had a restaurant together in the city when he was alive. She still runs it three days a week, and you'll be more than welcome to join her there any day that she goes."

"Will it just be me and her at the house?" Micah asked.

"And Ladli, our housekeeper," Kali said. "She's sweet, but very shy. Don't flirt with her."

Micah rested his head against the glass and closed his eyes. He was so tired. "I'm not going to flirt with anyone," he whispered.

Kali took his hand and held it silently for the rest of the drive. Somewhere in there, Micah dozed off. When Kali gently shook him awake, he blinked sleep from his eyes. "We're here," she said.

Micah climbed out of the taxi and looked around as she paid the driver. They were standing on a narrow street shaded by towering trees. Most of the houses on the street were hidden by high stone walls, many covered in creeping ivy. Kali unlatched a gate in the wall directly behind him, and it swung open with an ominous creaking noise. "Need to get that oiled," she muttered and waved Micah inside.

He stepped into a shaded garden and took a deep breath of fragrant air. There were flowers everywhere—splashing the walls with riotous color, carpeting beds under the trees, and flourishing in the few sunny spots of the garden. Lilies, irises, a big yellow flower he didn't recognize, and several huge magnolia trees dominated the area, and Micah stood still and let the peace of the place fill his bruised soul.

Kali plucked one of the yellow blossoms from the branch closest to her and handed it to him. "It's a *champa*," she said. "They're related to jasmine."

Micah turned it in his fingers, brought it to his nose, and drew its sweet scent into his lungs. "Thank you for having me, Kali," he said abruptly.

"I'm glad you called," Kali said. "My mother will be waiting to meet you. Come on."

A tiny Indian woman was at the counter in the kitchen, rolling out circles of dough and putting each round between floured towels. She looked up. Her dark eyes were sharp amid the wrinkles of her face, and a smile transformed her dour expression into breathtaking beauty.

Kali took her hand and raised it to her forehead. "Amma, *yeh hai* Micah. Micah, this is my mother, Manya Krishnan. Call her Manya or Mrs. Krishnan."

Micah stepped forward, blinked in the sunlight from the window, and took the dainty hand Kali's mother held out. He held it for a moment, unsure whether he was supposed to raise it to his forehead like Kali had done or just shake it.

Manya's eyes creased in amusement, and she said something in rapid-fire Hindi to Kali, who laughed.

"Amma doesn't speak English," she told Micah. "So I'll translate for you."

"Thank you for having me, Mrs. Krishnan," Micah said, hoping the diminutive woman would read the sincerity in his tone.

Kali translated, and Manya smiled and reached up to cup Micah's face in cool, dry hands.

"*Farishta*," she said.

"Micah, Amma. *Micah*," Kali said, clearly amused.

"Farishta," Manya repeated, and her smile widened.

Kali rolled her eyes, and Micah blinked as Manya patted his cheek and turned back to her counter.

"Come with me, Micah," Kali said. "I'll show you to your room."

Micah followed her into a huge living room with ceilings easily thirty feet high. He glanced around and took in the comfortable furniture and marble floors, but Kali didn't give him time to sightsee.

"You're in this wing of the house," she said. "We live on the other side, but Amma likes to cook over here. She prefers this kitchen's layout."

There was a short flight of steps at one end of the living room and a door to what looked like a courtyard on the other side. Kali waited impatiently at the top of the steps while Micah looked around the room.

"Ladli lives off the kitchen. I offered her one of these rooms," Kali said as Micah joined her, "but she didn't like how big they are. So you have this end of the house to yourself."

She led the way down the hall and pointed to two doors on her right. "Bathroom here, shower here. And this is your bedroom." She pushed open the door at the end of the hall, and Micah squinted in the sunlight that flooded the enormous room. It was empty except for a huge four-poster bed at one end, hung with mosquito netting.

"Keep the windows open at night," Kali said over her shoulder. "It's cooler that way. You'll want to maximize on the times when it's not hot as balls out there."

Micah stood in the middle of the room and suddenly felt lost. The flight, the exhaustion of his travels, and the bustle of Mumbai had distracted him for a while, but the events of the past two days crashed in on him. Kali's eyes softened.

"You need to rest," she said. "We'll talk later."

Micah nodded, unable to move, and Kali took his arm and pulled him toward the bed. He sat down on the edge and Kali gently pushed him over on his side. Micah curled up on the soft mattress and pressed his face into the sweet-smelling pillow as Kali pulled the blanket over him.

"I'll check on you in a few hours," Kali said.

Micah just closed his eyes, and after a minute, Kali left the room.

Devon. A sob clawed at the back of his throat. *Devon, I miss you so much.* Micah rolled over, pulled the pillow to his chest, and clutched it tightly.

He'd done the right thing. Devon was free to live a full life with someone who matched him, who was good enough for him. Micah hadn't been able to give him that. He'd had nothing to offer him.

But oh God, it hurts so much.

Micah wept until he was wrung dry and finally fell asleep with his arms still wrapped around the pillow.

HE WOKE up to early morning sunlight streaming through the windows. He'd slept all the way through the night without waking once. He sat up, stretched and yawned, and then padded down the hall to the bathroom, which was a simple concrete cell with a toilet, sink, mirror, and nothing else.

Micah took care of business and inspected himself critically in the small mirror over the sink. There were dark circles under his eyes and lines of grief etched into his forehead. He scowled at his reflection, ran a hand through the black hair that insisted on flopping forward into his eyes, and stomped back out into the hall, where he nearly mowed down a slim girl who was carrying a stack of towels.

"Oh God," Micah gasped as she stumbled backward. "I'm so sorry. I didn't see you. Did I hurt you? I'm sorry."

The young woman hunched her shoulders and gave him a tentative smile. She had luminous black eyes, a straight nose over a delicate chin, and inky-black hair that fell nearly to her waist in a heavy braid. This must be Ladli.

She spoke rapidly in Hindi and Micah grimaced, spreading his hands.

"I'm sorry," he repeated. "I know I look Indian, but I'm an ignorant Westerner. I don't speak Hindi."

Ladli ducked her head and offered him a shy smile that he returned. Then she scurried past him with her armful of linens.

Micah headed back into his bedroom and sat down on the bed as he pulled out his phone. Startled, he swore as he realized he'd missed half a dozen phone calls from Celeste, several from his supervisor, and too many texts to count, including at least fifty from the blocked number that had been plaguing him. He took the easier route and called Celeste first.

"Are you okay?" she demanded.

"I'm fine," Micah said. "I'm sorry, Celeste. I didn't... I had to get out of town."

"What happened? Where *are* you?"

"Ah... India?" Micah said.

"*India?*" Celeste shrieked, and Micah winced. "What the fuck are you doing in *India*, and why didn't you *say* something?"

"Devon—" Micah stopped to clear his throat. "We broke up."

"Oh, Micah, *no*," Celeste said with shock in her voice. "What happened?"

"I can't... please don't ask me," Micah said desperately. "I can't talk about it, Celeste, please—"

"Of course," Celeste said instantly. "So what made you decide to go to India, you utter loon?"

Micah took a shaky breath. "My ex... umm, Kali. She lives here. We're still close, and I had to get away. I couldn't stay in Toronto. I'm sorry to freak you out, but I didn't think anyone would really even care, to be honest."

"Your self-esteem is impressively awful," Celeste informed him. "No one knew where you'd gone, and it's not like you to just not show up for work without at least calling in. I was really worried. So is Norma, by the way."

Micah winced again. *Time for more flowers for that poor woman.*

"Zachary wants to talk to you," Celeste said. "He's not happy that you missed a meeting with him and Barrett this morning. Apparently Barrett's pretty annoyed too."

"Barrett can shove it up his ass," Micah snapped and pinched the bridge of his nose. "Sorry, not upset with you. Didn't mean to lash out. Listen, Celeste. I'll talk to Zachary in a minute, but you should know I'm not coming back to work."

"At all?" Celeste asked. "Micah, *no*. Why not? Is it because of Barrett? I'm sure Zachary would reassign him if you just asked."

"He probably would," Micah agreed. "But I need to get out of there. I'm coasting. I have been for a while, and I'm going to take some time, live off my savings, and try and figure out what I want to actually *do* with my life. I don't know how long I'm going to stay in Mumbai, but... a while, I think."

"God, Micah. What am I going to do without you?" Celeste asked. "Hanging out with you was the only thing I had to look forward to. I've really missed you the past week while you've been eating with Barrett."

"I'm sorry," Micah said. "I really am, but I had to go. I'll e-mail you, okay? Or Skype or something. I have to call Zachary, but—" He stopped as an idea occurred to him. "Celeste, can you do me a favor?"

"Anything," Celeste said.

"You handle Myra's account, don't you?"

"Oh yeah," Celeste said. "She's such a sweetie."

"Here's what I need," Micah said, and he outlined his plan.

"Totally doable," Celeste said cheerfully.

"Tell her to send me the bill," Micah said. "Celeste... you're the best."

"Don't you forget it," Celeste said and hung up.

Micah smiled to himself despite the pain in his heart and dialed Zachary's number to formally give notice. Zachary wasn't happy about it, which wasn't a surprise to Micah.

"What if you just take a six-month leave?" Zachary suggested. "You're one of our top account managers, Micah. I really don't want to lose you. Take as much time as you need and come back when you're ready."

Micah closed his eyes. "Thank you," he said. "But I don't know when that will be. I just... I need to cut this tie, sir."

Zachary sighed heavily. "All right, son. I'll e-mail you the necessary paperwork. Good luck to you."

Micah hung up and made his way downstairs as the smell of frying bread found his nose. He sniffed deeply and followed it to the kitchen, where Manya smiled up at him.

"*Namaste*, farishta," she said.

Micah blinked, and Kali, who was sitting at the table looking at her phone, snorted. "Mi-cah, Amma. *Micah*."

"Farishta," Manya said, scowling.

Kali rolled her eyes and gestured for Micah to join her.

"Why does she call me that?" he asked as he sat down.

"Farishta means angel in Hindi," Kali said. "She thinks you're beautiful. Amma always did have a fanciful streak. Are you hungry?" She was as neat and polished as usual in a silver suit that highlighted the sheen of her dark curls.

Micah stared at her, and tears pricked at his eyes. *You're always my angel.* Devon's voice echoed through his head, and Micah took a shaky breath. *I can't do this.*

Kali looked at him with sharp eyes. Micah just shook his head, and Kali took the hint. "Are you hungry?" she repeated.

Micah nodded. "Can I... help?"

"Not today. Today you sit back and let Amma take care of you. She's worried about you, you know."

"What did you tell her?" Micah asked, alarmed.

Kali lifted an elegant shoulder and continued to type something on her phone. "That you had your heart broken, you're here to rest and heal emotionally, and she's not to badger you to do any work at the restaurant unless you offer."

Micah couldn't help his smile.

"Anyway," Kali continued, "I can't take off work just because you need your hand held, so you'll have to struggle through without me until I get home tonight."

"I've missed you," Micah told her. "Your particular brand of honesty is both horrifying and refreshing."

Kali set her phone down and grinned at him. "You wouldn't have me any other way."

Manya interrupted the discussion by setting several platters of savory-smelling dishes on the table between them. She swatted Kali's shoulder and scolded her in Hindi.

Kali snapped back, but stood up and sighed as she smoothed her clothes. She followed her mother to the kitchen to bring out the rest of the food but shook her head at Micah when he tried to help. Finally the table was full of platters, and Kali and Manya sat down again.

"It smells delicious," Micah told Manya, who looked confused.

"She absolutely *refuses* to learn English," Kali said and translated.

Manya dimpled at Micah and pushed a platter of fried, puffed bread in his direction. "*Poori*," she said.

Micah put one, still warm from the fryer, on his plate, and Manya handed him a bowl of what looked like chickpeas, tomatoes, and chilies.

"*Chana masala*," she said, and she held up a piece of poori and showed him how to scoop the chickpea concoction onto the flatbread.

Micah took a bite, and his eyes opened wide at the spicy, citrusy, tangy flavor that exploded in his mouth. He chewed and swallowed quickly so he could take another bite.

Manya watched him carefully for his reaction, and she smiled, clearly satisfied.

Kali laughed quietly and spoke to her mother in rapid syllables that Micah didn't bother trying to follow. "She's glad you like it," she told him.

Micah swallowed. "It's *amazing*. Do you think she'd teach me how to make it?"

Manya's face lit up when Kali relayed the question—all the answer Micah needed.

When he was done with his serving, Manya handed him another piece of poori and another bowl, with what looked like yogurt in it.

"What's this?" Micah asked Kali.

"It's *shrikhand*," Kali said as she added chana masala to her own flatbread. "I told Amma that you have a sweet tooth, so she prepared it for you. We don't usually have it for breakfast, but Amma's taken a liking to you."

Micah scooped some out onto his poori, remembering to use his right hand, and took a tentative bite. The shrikhand was sweet and tangy, with coarsely ground almonds and hints of saffron, and it paired perfectly with the bread. He might have whimpered as he chewed.

Manya was still smiling at him, and she said something to Kali, who nodded and turned to Micah.

"She wants you to know that if you actually do want to learn how to cook traditional Indian food, she will teach you all she can. Anyone with an appreciation for food like you have should know how to create it."

Micah swallowed and wiped his mouth. "I would really love that," he said. "How do you say thank you in Hindi?"

"*Shukriyaa*," Kali said and stood. "That's settled, then. And now I have to go. I'll be back tonight, and we'll go out, have some drinks." She dropped a kiss on her mother's hair and flipped a wave at Micah as she dashed out the door.

The room was quiet without her, and Micah applied himself to his food, suddenly self-conscious. Manya patted his hand but left him to eat in peace, and Micah helped her clear when they were done.

She wouldn't let him help her wash the dishes, though, pointing at Ladli, who had come in the door with laundry over her arm.

"Okay," Micah said, feeling stupid. "I think... I think I'm going to take a walk." He pointed to himself and out the door, and Manya nodded and flapped a hand in dismissal.

Micah let himself out of the garden gate and stood on the street. He felt lost again, but he picked a direction at random and set out.

The neighborhood was wealthy, mostly hidden behind high walls. The streets were clean and swept, and the people he saw were well dressed, clearly comfortable. Kali lived halfway up a hill, and Micah climbed to the top of it and turned to survey the view, panting.

Mumbai sprawled at his feet—soaring skyscrapers and slums right next to each other, and the sea in a glittering half-circle curve off to his left. A haze hung over the city, slowly lifting as the sun burned through the mist.

Micah took a deep breath and sat down with his back to a tree. He leaned against the trunk and reached into his pocket to touch the button that was always with him as he rubbed his chest absently with his other hand. Missing Devon was a nearly physical ache. It felt like he'd been cored—as though his heart had been scooped out and replaced with sawdust.

"I miss you, Devon," he said aloud. "I don't know what I'm doing. I don't know why I'm here or what I should be doing with my life. I just want to talk to you again."

He sighed and closed his eyes. It had to get better. It *had* to.

Chapter Twenty-One

HE SPENT the day wandering the neighborhood and didn't go back to Kali's house until the sun hovered just above the horizon. His stomach growled then, and he realized that he was famished, so he retraced his steps.

Kali stepped out of a gleaming Mercedes as he walked down the hill, and she blinked. "Have you been out all day?" she asked.

Micah shrugged. "I was exploring."

"Well, go take a shower and get dressed," Kali said as she held the gate open. "We're going out."

Micah obeyed, smiling at Manya as he hurried through the kitchen.

In a half hour, he met Kali in the living room, and he whistled in admiration at the sight of her. She wore a formfitting, sleeveless black dress that showed off her toned arms, her hair pulled up into a cascading riot of messy curls on the top of her head.

"Looking good," Micah said.

Kali grimaced as she looked him over. "I wish I could say the same."

Micah glanced down and tugged at the hem of his faded shirt. "Sorry," he said. "Like I said I didn't bring much. Left in a hurry."

"Well, we're going to fix that," Kali said decisively.

She bundled Micah into the car still waiting by the curb and gave directions to the driver.

Micah watched out the window as they rolled through the city. Traffic was heavy. Taxis and buses and motorcycles flew by with seemingly little regard for such irrelevant things as traffic laws, and after a minute, Micah squeezed his eyes shut, dizzy.

Beside him, Kali laughed. "It takes some getting used to."

"How do they not constantly crash?" Micah asked.

"It's less common than you might think," Kali said. They pulled up in front of a department store, and Micah followed her inside.

Kali took her time. She picked out linen and cotton shirts, held them against Micah's frame, and pursed her mouth as she deliberated. Micah followed as the pile in his arms grew ever higher.

"How many shirts do I actually *need*?" he finally protested as Kali tossed yet another on the heap.

"Whatever you brought, it's going to be unsuitable for Indian autumn," she informed him over her shoulder. "You'll thank me when you don't die of heatstroke. Now, pants." She headed in that direction, and Micah sighed and followed her.

After he paid for the clothes, Micah dressed in the bathroom of the department store and emerged feeling suddenly self-conscious as he smoothed down the soft tan cotton shirt over dark brown khakis. Kali smiled.

"Much better," she said. "Now. Let's get shitfaced."

THEY LEFT Micah's purchases in the car and ended up at a booth in a noisy club. Micah glanced around as Kali placed their drink order and then folded her hands on the table and looked at him.

"You don't seem nearly as twitchy about germs as you used to be," she observed.

Micah blinked, a little startled. "I... hadn't thought about it," he admitted. "I guess it just hasn't really been that high on my 'Things to Care About' list. What about you, though? How's your love life going?"

Kali lifted a shoulder. "Haven't found anyone worth settling down for," she said. "Right now I have two lovely boys begging to be spanked on a regular basis, but nothing serious. I have a very discreet club I go to about once a month. No attachments, no personal ties—it's perfect. But we're not here to talk about me. What the hell happened between you and Devon?"

Micah rubbed his sternum absently. "He... wasn't right for me. Or, more accurately, I wasn't right for *him*. So I ended it. That's all there is to it."

"You are the *stupidest* smart man I've ever met," Kali said as their drinks arrived.

Micah downed half of his sugary, fruity concoction in several quick gulps.

"I mean it," Kali said as she leaned forward. "You're so convinced that everyone's going to leave you that you end up pushing them away first. Hurts less, right?"

"Everyone *does* leave," Micah snapped, stung. "*Everyone*, Kali. Even you left me, remember?"

Kali met his eyes. "We were never... that, Micah."

"I know," Micah said, glancing down at his drink. "I didn't take it personally. But... it's true. No one stays, because there's nothing for them to stay *for*."

Kali sighed and took a sip of her margarita. "One of the first things we're going to do is work on your self-esteem. You are such a sad sack."

Micah glared at her. "Do you think we could go with a little less 'tough' and a little more 'love'?"

"Doubt it," Kali said. She shrugged and took another sip. "You didn't show up on my doorstep all puppy-dog eyes and drooping shoulders for me to pat you on the head and tell you that you did the right thing. You fucked up. You *know* you fucked up, and you don't know how to fix it."

Micah slumped in his seat. "There's nothing to fix," he said, almost inaudibly.

Kali snorted. "Agree to disagree. Devon's as head over heels for you as you are for him."

"You weren't there," Micah said, looking up. "I ripped his heart out, Kali. I told him I didn't love him, that I'd never loved him. I lied straight to his face, and he believed me. *There's nothing to fix*."

"Okay, so it'll take more than a straightforward 'I'm sorry,'" Kali said. "That was a given. You never do anything by halves, after all. But first we have to work on getting you back on your feet. Does your job know you're not coming back for a while?"

"I quit," Micah admitted.

Kali just sighed. "Nothing by halves. So you're free and clear for now. And you're also completely directionless. Even when we were together, you didn't have any hobbies—it was work and sex, sex and work. What do you like to *do*?"

"I... don't know," Micah said quietly and traced the rim of his glass with an absent finger. "I don't like hearing my brain, you know? So I fill it up with sex and work so I don't have to be with myself too much."

"I know," Kali said. "But you're going to *have* to learn to like yourself, Micah. Because, in the end, you're the only one you can count on. No one's going to save you but you. So what do you like?"

"Food," Micah said, and sighed.

Kali laughed. "Yeah. You've always liked food. What do you like about it?"

"How it makes me feel. Picking out the ingredients, preparing it, making the perfect dish, and then eating it. It's such a visceral satisfaction. It's more than just how good it tastes—it's the whole process."

"So we'll start there," Kali said. "Amma already said she's willing to teach you how to cook Indian food. Take a few months and learn everything she can teach you. Go to the restaurant with her and follow her around."

Micah drew back, alarmed, and Kali rolled her eyes.

"For one thing," she said, pointing a finger at him, "you *just* told me you're not as bothered by germs. For another, it'll be good for you. Push you out of that comfort zone of yours. Give you something to think about that's not neuroses or how much you miss Devon."

Micah gnawed on his lip.

Kali arched a brow at him. "But in the meantime, let's get drunk." She lifted a slim hand and signaled the waiter for another round.

SEVERAL HOURS later they stumbled out of the club with their arms around each other's shoulders as they tried to stay upright.

"I love you, Kal," Micah slurred.

"I don't love you," Kali retorted.

"You don't love *anyone*," Micah pointed out, unfazed. "An'way, I know... you *do* love me... somewhere. Deep down." He blinked and struggled to focus.

"Oh look," Kali said. She straightened and waved off the car as it crept toward them. "That's my favorite tattoo parlor. C'mon, Micah. You're getting a tattoo."

She dragged him toward the shop as he protested.

"Kali, no. I don't want a tattoo, I don't like needles!"

Kali ignored him and tugged him through the door. "Parvati," she greeted the pretty young woman behind the counter. "Micah here wants a tattoo."

"No, I don't."

Kali spun around and fixed Micah with a fierce glare. "You. Want. A. Tattoo," she said through her teeth, and Micah gulped and closed his mouth.

Parvati smiled and pulled out a book of sketches, and Micah sat down—the alcohol haze made it hard for him to see straight—to pore over them.

The shop was tiny but immaculately kept, which allayed Micah's worries a little, and he blinked again and refocused on the drawings in front of him. His fear of needles aside, the idea was growing on him.

Kali leaned over. "Oh, that one's pretty," she said, pointing at a unicorn.

"I'm not getting a unicorn," Micah said. He turned the page. "You may be able to bully me into doing this, but I'm getting what *I* want on my skin."

He flipped a few more pages and stopped on a page with detailed sketches of wings. *You're my angel.* Devon's voice echoed through Micah's head.

"You're rubbing your chest again," Kali observed.

Micah dropped his hand and glared at her. "I want this one," he told Parvati, pointing to a pair of stylized wings. "I want it in black with golden accents on the feathers, across my shoulder blades."

"That'll hurt," Kali pointed out. "Easier if you do it over muscle, rather than bone."

"Because I'm such a stranger to pain," Micah shot back. He followed Parvati to the table, pulled his shirt off, and closed his eyes.

DEVON'S PUPILS were blown, and he looked almost drugged. He pinned Micah's hands to the bed, thrusting deep inside his welcoming body as Micah's eyes rolled back with every slick shove. Devon dropped his head and took Micah's mouth in a desperate, hungry kiss, and Micah arched up into it with a helpless moan.

"I love you," Devon said as he lifted his head, and Micah came, untouched—safe and secure and loved—*as Devon fucked him through it.*

MICAH JERKED awake with a gasp. His pajama pants were a wet, clammy mess and stuck to his skin, and he didn't bother to stifle the sob that ripped free. He rolled over, clutched the pillow to his chest, and wept into it.

It felt like ages before he was able to lift his head and get his bearings. His shoulder blades itched, and he resisted the urge to scratch as he poked his head out the door, made sure neither Ladli nor Manya were around to see him, and dashed for the shower.

He bathed quickly, careful to keep the healing tattoo dry, and avoided looking at himself in the mirror as he toweled off and dressed.

Back in his room, he checked the time—early—and his phone. A message from Celeste to call immediately was foremost, so Micah lifted the phone to his ear and bit back the worry.

"Dude, I've been trying to reach you all damn day," Celeste snapped.

"I was out," Micah said. "I got back late, and I just woke up, and I'm sorry. I've… been busy. What's going on?"

"I wanted to let you know I talked to Myra and she's taking care of things," Celeste said, and her voice softened into concern. "Are you okay?"

Micah rubbed his face. "I've been better. Is that the only thing you wanted to tell me? You couldn't have texted me?"

"I saw Devon," Celeste blurted, and Micah froze. "Micah? Are you still there?"

Micah made a monumental effort and breathed again. "Yeah," he managed. "I'm… what'd he… why—" His throat closed up, and he shut his eyes.

"I went by the shop," Celeste was saying. "I'm sorry. I know you're going to think I was meddling, but I was so *worried*, Micah. I needed to find out what had happened, make sure he was okay, so I went by and talked to him. I kinda figured you probably hadn't told him you were taking off, and I don't care *how* bad a breakup you guys had, from everything you've told me about him, he's a worrier. He deserves to know you're okay."

She was right. Micah knew she was, but he couldn't speak, couldn't *move*. He was numb. He waited for Celeste to continue, pressing a hand to his chest.

"He looked awful," she said. "Dark circles under his eyes, he couldn't seem to focus, and he looked like he'd been crying."

Tears pricked Micah's eyes. *Please, stop.* He couldn't take this, couldn't hear Devon was doing poorly. He was supposed to bounce back quickly, find someone worthy of him, and live a long and happy life— not pine away after Micah, who could never give him what he needed. But Micah couldn't speak, and Celeste kept going.

"I asked him what had happened, and he said he couldn't talk about it, that it was between you and him. I asked him if he was okay, and he just… laughed. It was an awful sound. I've never heard anything like it before. And then he covered his face, and his sister grabbed me and hustled me out the door and told me not to come back."

The first hot tear slid down Micah's face, and he took a shaky breath.

"Micah?" Celeste sounded miserable. "I'm sorry, Micah, I just—"

"I have to go," Micah whispered and hung up as the tears fell faster. He curled up in a ball on the bed, and his shoulders shook through his sobs. *I did the right thing. I did what had to be done. So why does it hurt so much?*

IT WAS some time before Micah was able to gather himself enough to go out and face Kali, who was sitting at the breakfast table as Manya worked in the kitchen.

Kali took one look at him and straightened. "What happened?" she demanded.

Micah just shook his head as he sat down, and Kali took the hint, although her eyes narrowed in a way that Micah knew meant she wasn't dropping the subject entirely.

Manya bustled around the counter to take Micah's face in her hands and peer into his eyes.

Micah attempted a smile. "Namaste, Mrs. Krishnan," he said. He took one of her hands and pressed it to his forehead as Kali had done, and Manya smiled down at him.

"Namaste, farishta," she said. Her dark eyes were full of concern, and she said something rapid-fire to Kali.

"She says you can call her Manya-ji," Kali said.

"Oh, umm… okay," Micah said.

"Ji is a term of respect," Kali explained.

Manya tugged on Micah's hand until he took the hint and followed her back to the counter where she'd been rolling out circles of poori.

She took the wooden roller and applied it to the soft ball of dough waiting for her. Micah watched as she flattened the ball in quick, precise movements and lowered it into the hot oil on the stove beside her. Then she set the next dough ball on the counter and turned to Micah, who blinked.

"Oh, I—" He shot a panicky look at Kali, who looked back without sympathy.

"You said you wanted to learn. She's teaching you," Kali said. "Amma's a fan of the sink-or-swim method."

Manya held out the rolling pin with an impatient noise, and Micah took it and swallowed hard.

His hands were shaky and uncertain as he rolled out the dough, and he couldn't seem to get it round or flat enough, but Manya didn't seem perturbed, making approving noises as he labored over the floury board.

Finally she reached forward and lifted the lumpy, oblong piece of dough with a nod and dropped it into the oil.

"It's awful," Micah said. "I'm sorry—"

Manya didn't bother to respond. She just reached under the towel and set out another ball.

"Right," Micah said. He set to work and focused on keeping the rolling pin steady and flattening the dough in even increments.

This attempt was better, and Manya clicked her tongue approvingly as she scooped the finished poori out and added the next one. Micah smiled back at her, surprised at the flush of victory that swelled within him, and pulled out another dough ball.

He fell into a rhythm and quickly figured out what worked and what didn't. He realized, after one particularly disastrous result, that working the dough too much made it shrink in on itself and created a tough round that was barely edible.

Manya laughed and tossed that one in the trash as Micah cringed. She set another one on the board and gestured, and Micah took the hint and got back to work.

Before long he was turning out passable poori almost every time, although they were still lumpy and a little uneven. Manya patted his cheek as she passed a plate of the fried bread to Ladli, who set them on the table and came back for the various fillings. Micah barely noticed, focused on getting the next piece just right, and Manya laughed and said something to Kali.

"She says you can leave the rest and come eat while it's hot," Kali said, sounding amused.

Micah blinked and came back to himself. He'd worked his way through most of the pieces of poori, and he couldn't help but smile as he washed his hands and settled at the table to eat.

"Not bad," Kali said when she took a bite. "It's almost edible!"

Micah shot her the finger, forgetting the other women, and he flinched as he remembered he was in polite company. But Manya laughed and spoke to Kali in rapid-fire Hindi.

Kali snorted a laugh and turned to Micah. "She says I must have corrupted you."

"Oh yes," Micah said, his face straight. "I was pure as the driven snow before you came along."

That made Kali laugh out loud. Manya interrupted to say something, and Micah stiffened as he caught the word *dosa*.

"What... what's she saying?" he asked.

"She said she's going to teach you how to make dosa next," Kali said.

Micah closed his eyes briefly. It was a common word in India. He had to get used to hearing it. Finally he nodded. "I was starting to teach myself some of the basics, but I'll be happy to learn whatever she can show me."

Kali watched him with sharp eyes, but she nodded.

"I'll take you sightseeing this weekend," she told Micah as she got ready to leave for work. "Amma goes to the restaurant tomorrow, if you want to go with her."

"That's fine," Micah said. "I'll entertain myself today, help your mother if she doesn't mind, maybe explore some."

Kali gathered her purse and kissed her mother on the cheek. "See you tonight," she said over her shoulder, and then she stopped, with her hand on the door. "Oh, I almost forgot. You'll be staying at least two months, right?"

Micah nodded. "If... that's okay with you."

"Good," Kali said, smiling at him. "You'll be here for Diwali, then."

"Diwali? What's Diwali?" Micah asked, but Kali was already gone. He glanced at Manya, who just patted his hand and stood to clear the dishes, so Micah got up to help her.

CHAPTER TWENTY-TWO

MANYA TOOK Micah to the restaurant the next day. She talked in a quick, near-nonstop dialogue all through the streets and pointed out various sights to Micah, who nodded and craned his neck to see more.

The restaurant was bigger than Micah expected, and Manya bustled inside, flipped on lights, and gestured for Micah to follow her through the big dining room into a spacious kitchen.

Some of the tension eased from Micah's shoulders as he glanced around the room. It was clear that Manya was a stickler for cleanliness—every surface gleamed.

There were several people seated around a table at the back of the room. When Manya entered they made various noises of greeting.

Manya spoke rapidly and gestured to Micah, who squirmed at suddenly being the center of attention but lifted a hand in a quick wave.

One young woman stepped forward, her dark eyes limpid in her heart-shaped face and her sleek black hair pulled back from a high forehead. She smiled at Micah.

"I'm Sara," she said in a soft, lilting voice. "Manya's sous chef. Welcome to the Churchgate Café. Manya says I'm to look after you, show you what we do here, answer any questions you have."

Micah smiled back at her. "I have no idea what I'm doing," he confessed.

"Perhaps you'd like to julienne some carrots for me?" Sara asked. She gestured to a counter and showed him the knives and vegetables ready to be prepped.

Micah began to peel and slice, sinking into the work as his mind's buzz faded to a quiet hum. His chest ached, but he didn't have time to stop and deal with it. Instead he chopped and diced and did his best not to think about Devon.

As they worked, Sara told Micah about the restaurant's history.

"Manya-ji and her husband started it forty years ago," she said quietly, her hands a blur of motion as she showed Micah how exactly to dice the potatoes for the curry. "It is difficult for a woman to gain respect in this industry, but Manya-ji has fought for her place and earned it. She can cook like a goddess." Sara's tone was full of awe, and Micah snuck a glance at Manya's tiny form as she bustled around the kitchen, inspecting everything, tasting sauces, and snapping out orders. He was coming to believe Manya was capable of just about anything—the diminutive woman was clearly a force to be reckoned with.

The day passed in a blur, and Micah found himself pleasantly exhausted when it came time to go home. He dozed off in the car on the way back to the house and stumbled up the stairs to his room to collapse into his bed with a relieved groan. This level of activity was either going to save his life or be the death of him, and he was too tired to care which.

THREE WEEKS after he started working at the restaurant, Kali took Micah out to dinner.

"I barely see you anymore," she told him over drinks. "You're so busy now!"

Micah shrugged. "Your mother keeps me hopping."

"I was going to ask if you wanted to go to my club with me tonight," Kali said. "But if you're too tired, it's okay."

"Your... club?" Micah gave her a suspicious look.

Kali rolled her eyes. "Yes, Micah. It's a sex club."

Micah drew back. "Kali, I don't—"

"Relax," Kali said as she leaned forward across the table and pinned him with her dark eyes. "I know you don't do well in public-sex scenarios, Micah. They have private rooms. You need to sub. I can see it in your body language. It's been building up, and you need to let it out."

Micah slumped in his seat. She was right, and he knew it, but the thought of having sex with a stranger was... alarming. A thought struck him, and he glanced up. "Who exactly would I be subbing *for*?" he asked.

"Not me," Kali said immediately. "Too... messy."

Micah drew a relieved breath.

"I have a friend at the club. He's very good, very discreet. He'll respect your boundaries, but he'll take you out of yourself, and you never have to see him again if you don't want to."

Micah toyed with the stem of his glass and deliberated while Kali waited. As usual, Kali was right—Micah *did* need to sub. The urge had been welling under his skin for several weeks, making him twitchy, and he needed to get out of his head.

"All right," he said abruptly. "Let's do it."

Kali signaled for the check.

MICAH WAS a bundle of nerves as their car navigated the bustling streets of Mumbai, and his knee jiggled nonstop until Kali put her hand on his thigh.

"Relax," she said quietly.

"Why do I feel like I'm… cheating?" Micah whispered.

Kali's face softened as the car pulled up to the curb. "Because you're still in love with Devon. But you need this, Micah. You know you do. You need to let go, move on, all that happy crap."

Micah huffed an unwilling laugh, climbed out of the backseat, straightened his shirt, and smoothed his pants. He glanced up at the entrance to the club.

The door was solid oak, the lettering discreet above it—no flashing lights, no skimpily dressed women—which allayed Micah's nerves a bit.

"And you're sure about this place?" he asked as Kali joined him on the curb and took his arm.

"They're completely up to code and insist on a much higher standard of sanitization than any other club I've ever visited," Kali said. She tugged him toward the entrance.

Inside, it was dark, and a heavy bass line thumped through Micah's spine and out the soles of his feet. Kali pulled him into the hall and knocked on a door about halfway down.

"Come in," a deep voice called, and Kali pushed the door open.

"Micah, this is Sanyam," Kali said as she ushered him inside.

Micah stepped over the threshold and looked into the face of a strikingly handsome man with chiseled cheekbones and tilted eyes so black Micah couldn't see his pupils. He was wearing a plain white button-down shirt and black slacks, and his generous lips curved as he smiled. "Hello, Micah," he said, holding out a hand. "Kali's told me about you."

Micah hesitated but took his hand and glanced around. It was small, clearly soundproofed, and lined with a couch that ran all the way around the room. In the middle of the space hung black leather restraints, and on the wall there hung an assortment of riding whips and crops. Micah swallowed hard but said nothing.

"I'm going to leave you to it," Kali said. "I'll find you after, all right?" She left without waiting for a response.

"Have a seat," Sanyam said, gesturing to the plush sofa.

Micah sank onto it. He kept his knees together and his back straight, and Sanyam sat down next to him.

"I understand you're recovering from an ugly breakup," Sanyam said calmly. He leaned back against the cushions and draped his arm along the spine of the couch.

Micah nodded. He was terrified, but he didn't know how to say it. He was afraid that if he opened his mouth, he might burst into tears or tell Sanyam his entire life story. So instead he stayed silent and bit his lips.

Sanyam put a hand on Micah's knee, and Micah jerked, startled. Sanyam met his eyes steadily as the warmth of his palm soaked through Micah's pant leg.

"Before we do anything, what's your safeword?" he asked.

Micah floundered. *Manta ray.* Tears pricked his eyes. "Oh... cinnamon," he managed, plucking a random word from Manya's dinner menu.

"Good," Sanyam said, and a tiny tendril of warmth spread through Micah at the praise. "Mine is Crawford."

Micah lifted his eyes. "Like the market?"

Sanyam smiled. "Indeed. Like the market. Do you have any particular desires for how this evening should play out?"

Micah shook his head dumbly.

"A few rules first, I think," Sanyam said. "Hard limits?"

"Blood play, fecal play, watersports, breath play," Micah said. "And... shaming talk." Devon smiled at him in his mind's eye.

"Hitting?" Sanyam asked.

"That's okay," Micah managed. "I don't want to lay it out. I'd prefer to... wing it."

"Perhaps a kiss?" Sanyam suggested.

Micah's eyes fluttered closed, but he didn't argue. He could hear rustling as Sanyam moved closer, and then warm lips covered his.

Micah concentrated on his breathing as Sanyam kissed him, moving slowly so Micah could pull away if he needed to. Sanyam's lips were soft, his tongue gentle as he coaxed Micah's mouth open and slipped inside in soft, easy sweeps.

Devon. All Micah could see was Devon's blue eyes, sparkling with laughter as he and Devon lay on the floor together after the failed role-play attempt.

Micah squeezed his eyes tighter shut as Sanyam broke the kiss and pulled away.

"I'm sorry," he whispered.

Sanyam patted Micah's knee. "It's all right," he said in a gentle voice. "From now on, though, you will only speak when asked a direct question. Get on your knees."

Micah's eyes shot open, and Sanyam met his gaze.

"Now," he said, and Micah found himself sliding off the couch onto the floor without consciously thinking about it.

He landed on his knees, laced his hands behind his back, and took a deep breath as Sanyam stood up and circled him.

"You are a very attractive man, Micah," Sanyam mused, "and at some point I think I would very much like to fuck you."

Micah opened his mouth and Sanyam slapped him once across the face. Micah's head rocked back, and he blinked, stunned.

"I did not say you could speak," Sanyam said calmly.

Micah closed his mouth and took a steadying breath.

"Good," Sanyam praised, and Micah resettled his weight. His cheek stung, but he could feel himself sliding into sub space, easing into a more docile mindset.

Sanyam paced around him, ran a hand up into Micah's hair, and closed it suddenly, viciously, tight. Micah gasped at the pain in his scalp but didn't budge.

"You have discipline," Sanyam said. "This is good. I think perhaps I can work with this. Take your shirt off."

Micah obeyed with trembling hands. He was half-hard from nerves and anticipation, and terror and need choked him in equal measure. Naked from the waist up, he settled back onto his heels as Sanyam inspected him.

"Hands behind your back again," Sanyam directed. "Facedown on the carpet."

Micah balked briefly. Sanyam wanted him to put his face on the *carpet*? He wasn't any more prepared for the blow that time, and his head snapped back from the force of it. Micah tasted blood in his mouth, but Sanyam just caught a handful of Micah's hair.

"*Now,*" he said and pushed Micah forward.

Caught off-balance Micah toppled, landed on his stomach, and gasped for air. *This is wrong.* But he couldn't speak. Instead he closed his eyes, trying to sink back into sub space and find that delicate bubble that would protect him.

"Clasp your hands on the back of your neck," Sanyam ordered.

Micah obeyed numbly. *Devon.* Warm blue eyes, high cheekbones, laughing mouth—everything Micah had never known he needed until it was too late.

Sanyam struck the first blow across his lower back, and Micah jerked, crying out as the pain rocketed through him. Sanyam was using a crop or a whip of some sort, judging from the way the welt already burned sharply, but Micah kept his eyes shut and groped desperately for sub space again.

The next several blows landed in quick succession, but Micah didn't move except to suck in air. *I love you, Devon. I didn't deserve you, but I love you, and I always will.* Sanyam paused, and Micah used the respite to cautiously open his eyes. From his position, all he could see were Sanyam's bare feet as they moved around him.

Sanyam trailed a warm hand up his back and across the stinging lash marks. "You're doing so well," Sanyam murmured, and Micah's resolve broke.

"Cinnamon, *cinnamon,*" he choked out and flung himself away from the hand that was caressing his back so gently, almost lovingly.

He fetched up hard against the couch, and his feet scrabbled on the floor as he tried to push himself farther away from Sanyam's touch. But

Sanyam was frozen on the other side of the room, surprise and concern on his face.

"Scene over," he said, and he picked up Micah's shirt and held it out on two fingers.

Micah snatched it from him and yanked it on in short, jerky movements with shaking hands. Then he pushed himself to his feet. "I'm sorry," he managed. "I can't—I have to go." And he bolted out the door, tears blinding him.

He found his way out of the club by luck more than anything. His back burned, and his throat was so tight he could barely breathe. He fell into the car that was idling by the curb as Kali burst out of the club behind him.

"Micah?" she asked, breathless. Her top was undone, her hair a mess, and her eyes were big with worry as she climbed into the car beside him. "Sanyam found me. Micah, what happened?"

Micah turned, crawled into her lap, snaked his arms around her waist, and pressed his face to her stomach as he began to weep in desperate heaves.

Kali hesitated a moment and then wrapped her arms around him and murmured softly in Hindi as she stroked his flushed face with one cool hand.

"Take me home," Micah begged, unable to see through his tears. "Please—"

"All right, Micah," Kali said. "Hang on. We'll get you home."

"It was the wrong hand," Micah managed between sobs.

Kali was silent a moment. "What?" she finally said.

"He shouldn't have been… touching me," Micah whispered as he pressed his face harder against Kali's rib cage. "It was… the wrong hand."

"Okay," Kali murmured. "I'm sorry, Micah. I thought I was helping you. I really did."

Micah just held on and wept until he was wrung dry as the car wound its way through the city streets and up into their suburb.

Kali got him inside the house with an arm around his waist and muttered obscenities under her breath as Micah groped vaguely for each step, his balance wavering and unsure. She grunted in triumph when she finally toppled him into the bed, and Micah curled up with his pillow against his chest.

"Sorry, Kali," he whispered into the soft cotton. "Fucked it up… ruined your night—"

"Shut up. You did not," Kali said and touched his shoulder. "Go to sleep, Micah. You'll feel better in the morning."

CHAPTER TWENTY-THREE

ANOTHER MONTH went by, and Micah threw himself into working for Manya at the restaurant and learned everything she could teach him—both recipes and Hindi. He wasn't fluent, but he was beginning to understand her rapid-fire speech in bits and pieces, which made it easier to obey when she flung commands at him. She kept him so busy he couldn't think, which was exactly how he wanted it.

On the weekends, he went out with Kali, although they didn't scene again. They stuck to drinks and discussions about their love lives, and Kali accompanied him to his appointments with Parvati to have his tattoo completed.

The night before the Diwali festivities kicked into high gear, Micah waited until Ladli had gone to bed and the house was still before he slipped out the front door into the courtyard, clutching his pillow. He climbed the stone staircase to the roof and set the pillow down. Then he settled on it, drew his knees to his chest, and stared up into the night sky.

The smog from the city hung below him, and the stars above him were strung like fairy lights against black velvet. Micah took a deep breath and let the peace of the night steal through him.

"Devon," he said quietly. "I miss you, baby. Miss you so much. It's been a crazy couple of months. Manya's been teaching me everything she can think of. I can make dal now and palak paneer and poori like a champ, of course. I'm on permanent poori duty, apparently. I make the dough the night before, roll them into balls, and let them sit overnight to be fried in the morning. I'm pretty good at it too. Manya's going to teach me how to make masala dosa next. It took me a while to hear that stupid word without wanting to cry, you know? But I'm getting better, and my dosa are definitely better than the ones I made you."

He reached into his jacket pocket, pulled out Devon's button, and absently slid his thumb over the ridges.

"I'm sort of unofficially working in Manya's restaurant," he told the sky. "Three days a week that it's open and serving food, then another day for food prep, and a day for deep cleaning every week, because Manya believes in hands-on. It was kind of trial by fire—I wasn't sure I was going to survive at first, but now I love the hustle. Manya says she's going to let me take over the dinner service one night a week, if I keep improving."

A cricket sang over his shoulder, and Micah shifted his weight. The concrete was cold underneath him. Soft wind caressed his skin, and he took a deep breath. Time for the heavy stuff.

"I tried to sub a few weeks after I first got here," he said, and he could feel the flush of shame crawling up his neck. "I don't know why I'm only telling you now—maybe because I can't even think about it without wanting to hide under a rock. It was… a disaster. I safeworded, bolted. I'm sure I embarrassed the shit out of Kali, although she says I didn't. It just felt… wrong to do it without you. All I could think about was you the entire time."

He rubbed the button again and took a deep breath of cool night air.

"We're gearing up for Diwali. Do you know what that is? It's the autumn festival, and it's kind of a huge deal. So much cooking, apparently, and since Manya's the matriarch of the family, everyone's coming here. And I do mean everyone. Kali has a brother who has, like, a dozen kids, apparently. They live in the north, and Kali never sees him. But he and his family are coming in for Diwali, and I'm expected to help Manya with the cooking. Manya and Ladli and even Kali are cleaning like crazy, and I'm helping as much as I can."

The stars wheeled on overhead, frozen and silent, and Micah sighed.

"I wish I knew how you were doing, Devon. Celeste says she hasn't heard. I have to stop myself from texting or calling you every minute of the day, you know that?"

He rubbed his chest and the now-familiar ache that never really went away.

"But I guess you wouldn't be able to call me anyway. I changed my number a week after I got here. Those weird texts were getting worse—

coming in several times an hour—and I finally got sick of it. Got a new phone. A local number."

He sighed.

"Have you forgotten about me yet?" he asked the night sky. "Have you put me behind you, filed me away as a regrettable incident, and moved on? It'll be better for you when you do, Devon. I know you thought you loved me, but this was the best thing for you. Now you can find someone who fits you, who's right for you."

An owl hooted in the dark, and Micah hugged his knees tighter.

"I wish you could see India, Devon," he said. "It's…. God, it's amazing. So rich and vibrant and colorful. And smelly. Dear *God*, the smell." He broke off with a rueful laugh. "I want to show you everything. The Taj Mahal, Elephanta Island, the High Court. Oh, and I want to take you to Crawford Market. Manya and I do the shopping there. It's the most incredible place, Devon. Outside, it sort of looks like a medieval fort or something. But inside… inside it's this enormous, sprawling space that's just *packed* with vendors selling everything from fresh fruit to saris to birds. Dev, they sell not just chickens and goats but owls and even falcons, right there in the marketplace. It's crazy. I take hand sanitizer with me, of course." He smiled in the dark. "I'm better about germs, but I'm not stupid."

He fell silent, and the night wrapped around him, soft and comforting.

"Celeste says there's a restaurant for sale near where she lives… that the owners are moving away, but it's a great location. She wants me to think about buying it and hiring her to run my books for me. I don't know. The idea terrifies me, but I can't stop thinking about it at the same time. I've got enough set aside in savings for the down payment. My credit's good. I could get a loan easily enough. I could have my own place. Make my own decisions. Do what *I* want to do. I just… wish I could talk to you about it, Devon."

Crickets sang in the trees below him, blissfully oblivious.

"I thought about staying," Micah continued. "Finding a place here, maybe opening a little restaurant in the city or just staying on with Manya. I could make it work, I think. I could be happy here. But—" He took a deep breath and rubbed the button. "But it's not home," he whispered.

Finally he stood and picked up his pillow. Trailing it behind him, he made his way back down the stairs and silently let himself into the house.

Diwali

MICAH DODGED the shrieking child who ran past at top speed, holding the platter of *bhurta* over his head to avoid spilling it.

The house was packed with people, as Kali had warned him it would be. Her brother, Abed, and his wife, Saumya, had arrived two days previously with their horde of children. They only had seven kids, not a dozen, but it felt like three times that many when they played tag through the house.

Ladli smiled up at him from where she was crouched near the doorway, working on a complicated *rangoli* pattern. Micah set the bhurta on the table and knelt beside her.

"Show me?" he asked in his halting Hindi.

Ladli ducked her head but pointed at the containers of brightly dyed rice beside Micah's knee. Micah pointed at each in turn, until Ladli nodded and Micah handed her the bowl with the scarlet grains. Ladli smiled at him again and began adding red to the petals of the flower she was creating on the floor.

The process was slow and intricate, and Ladli was clearly a master at it. She pointed at the yellow rice next, and Micah handed it to her. That she added in spirals around the flower. It looked like tongues of flame licked at the edges of the design, and Micah was awestruck.

"She's won several competitions for her rangoli designs," Kali said from behind him.

Micah scrambled to his feet and dusted off his pants. "What do they mean? Do they *have* a meaning?"

"Of course they do," Kali said, arching an eyebrow. "They're considered good luck and will bring blessings on the household. They also welcome Lakshmi, the goddess of prosperity, and are an offering to her. Amma's looking annoyed. You might want to get your ass in gear."

Micah spun guiltily, to see Manya at the stove, not even looking at him. Still he hurried to wash his hands and join her with murmured apologies. She smiled up at him and pointed at the pot she was stirring. Micah took over and inhaled a deep breath of the savory contents. It was the potato curry he'd put together earlier for making the masala dosa.

The week had gone by quickly, and Diwali night was upon them. Kali explained that they'd be having *puja*—family prayers—that night and Micah was invited but not required to attend. In the meantime the feast was prepared and set out in advance, and the entire household was in motion.

A child shrieked, and Micah winced. He wasn't as bothered by kids as he had been in the past—not with so much to occupy his mind—but he still didn't particularly appreciate the noise they made *or* the messes they left in their wake.

He turned his attention back to the potato curry and stirred determinedly.

DIWALI NIGHT was an unqualified success. After the prayers, which Micah attended, they gathered at the table. Everyone in the family praised Micah's masala dosa in particular, and he found himself laughing and blushing as he fended off compliments and flattery.

"I thought these were Amma's!" Abed, a rotund man in his early forties, told him. He had dark, laughing eyes and a bushy mustache that hid the lower half of his face. Micah couldn't help but like him.

Dinner over, everyone piled outside to watch the fireworks. They gathered in the garden, arms around each other, and gazed into the night sky with awe as fiery flowers of red, blue, and green burst far above their heads.

Micah hung back and watched them with a fierce ache in his heart. He'd had a family of his own for a very short time, and then he'd lost it through his own stupidity.

Without looking, Kali reached a slim brown arm back, caught his wrist, and yanked him forward. Manya wrapped an arm around his waist from the other side, and Micah took a shaky breath, enveloped in love and surrounded by people who knew him and loved him anyway.

Maybe he still had a family after all.

Three months later

"ARE YOU sure about this?" Kali asked for the dozenth time.

Micah handed his bags to the claims attendant and passed his ticket over for inspection. "Yes, Kali. I'm sure," he said patiently. "It's time for me to go home. I can't keep sponging off your family forever."

"You paid for most of our food the entire time you lived with us," Kali pointed out. "If anything, keeping you here is financially viable for us."

Micah snorted a laugh, wrapped his arms around her, and pulled her close. "You have no idea how grateful I am for you," he told her. "You saved me, and I can never thank you enough for that."

Kali rolled her eyes even as she put her arms around his neck. "You saved yourself, Micah. Maybe I helped a bit, but it was you who took the first steps, you who pulled yourself out of that pit of self-hatred you were wallowing in."

"Are you saying it was inside me all along?" Micah teased, and she laughed and dropped a kiss on his mouth.

"Take care of yourself, Dumbo. Call me when you land and let me know when you and Devon fix things."

Micah let go and stepped back with a rueful sigh. "You're never letting go of that fantasy, are you?"

"It's not a fantasy," Kali informed him. "I can see the future."

"Yeah. You do realize you're not the actual goddess, right?" Micah said and ducked the mock blow she aimed at him.

"You bite your tongue, godless Westerner," Kali said, glowering.

Micah laughed and blew her a kiss. "I'll let you know when I land. You'll have to be satisfied with that."

HIS PLANE touched down without incident, and Micah sent Kali a text and then picked up his car and drove back to his condo. No one knew he was coming home, and he wanted it that way. He needed a few days to settle in, recover from the jet lag, and find his footing again.

The condo was quiet when he pushed the door open, and Micah took a deep breath of slightly musty air as he toed his shoes off and draped his jacket over the hook without bothering to see if it was hanging straight. Everything was exactly as he'd left it on his panicked flight out of the country, and Micah stood still in the kitchen and closed his eyes. Devon had made him amoeba pancakes right there.

Your pancake game is weak.

Micah touched his chest. "Devon," he said out loud, and the sound of his voice echoed oddly through the empty room.

He took a step forward, trailing a hand along the counter, and gripped Devon's button tightly in his fist. There, he'd given Devon that incredible blowjob with his hands laced behind his back and Devon's fingers in his hair.

A few more halting steps, and Micah stood at the edge of the living room. He stepped down into it and sat on the couch.

A promise made under orgasmic duress is not actually legally binding.

Micah rubbed his chest and fought the ache, but he smiled through the tears in his eyes.

"I'm so glad I met you," he said.

He smoothed a hand against the leather of the couch and then stood up and took a deep breath. Time to face the bedroom. He stopped just outside the door and gathered his nerve.

Devon breathed a quiet laugh over the back of Micah's neck, his lips gentle against the bumps of his spine, and Micah shivered.

Finally Micah managed to push the door open, and it swung slowly inward. Dust motes gleamed in the late sunlight slanting across the hardwood floor from the high windows. The ache was worse than ever, and Micah pressed his hand flat against his breastbone as he struggled to breathe around it.

The first tear fell as he stepped over the threshold. The restraint system still hung from the ceiling. Micah touched it with one finger and set it swaying gently.

He turned, avoiding the bed for the moment, and crossed to the bathroom. The bathtub stood empty, but Micah could barely see it through the tears that hazed his vision, and he sat down abruptly on the rim and gripped the edge to steady himself.

Devon shifted his weight into a more comfortable position and stroked Micah's thigh with slow, hypnotic motions under the water.

"You were the best thing that ever happened to me," Micah whispered, his throat thick.

He stood up, swaying, and stumbled out, heading for the bed. There, he rummaged in the drawer and came up holding his collar. The leather was supple and soft in his fingers, and he clutched it tightly as he crawled onto the mattress and pulled Devon's pillow against his chest. It still smelled like Devon—pine and snow and that fancy shampoo he liked so much—and Micah's tears fell faster and soaked into the pillowcase.

"Thank you," Micah managed between sobs. "Thank you for... loving me, Devon."

When the tears finally slowed, Micah pressed his face into the pillow and took a deep breath. He felt much as he did after a particularly hard subdrop—cored out, scoured clean, and purified. Somewhere in there he'd taken another step toward forgiving himself, and he wiped his eyes with a trembling hand.

No matter what happened next, somehow he knew he was going to be all right.

When he was sure his voice was steady, he picked up the phone and called the bank.

CHAPTER TWENTY-FOUR

MICAH STOOD outside the tiny restaurant and held the keys to the front door with a death grip.

"Come on, boss," Celeste urged as she gripped his arm. "Let's get inside and look over your kingdom."

"I've already looked it over," Micah protested. "It's why I bought it, remember?"

"Prime location, lots of tourists, sound business with a history of turning a profit, yada yada," Celeste recited. "Come *on*. You're officially the owner, Micah. Let's go."

Micah laughed and let her tug him inside. It had been twelve nerve-wracking weeks of applying for the proper permits, getting the building inspected, and making sure everything was squared away, and he was ready to open on time. He trailed a finger along the mahogany of the hostess's podium and looked around the small, welcoming foyer.

He and Celeste had painted it themselves, with some help from Alan, who'd been more than happy to quit trying—and failing, as he put it—to be a headhunter. Alan had come to be a busboy for Micah, despite the necessary pay cut, and Kevin, one of Celeste's best friends and, according to her, "a damn fine waiter," had pitched in as well, painting and decorating as Micah directed.

Celeste danced through the small dining room and twirled between tables laid with cloths of cream with gold wings embroidered on them. There was only room for about twenty patrons at a time, but Micah liked it that way. That was more than enough to keep him busy, but not so many that he'd be overwhelmed, since he was the only one working the kitchen for now.

The phone rang, and Celeste stopped dancing to grab the receiver off the wall. "Farishta House. How may I help you? No, ma'am, I'm sorry. We're booked until two weeks from Sunday. Would you like something then? Yes, ma'am, absolutely." Her eyes sparkled at Micah as she wrote the name down, and Micah grinned at her as he went into the kitchen.

He'd spent most of the last month getting it perfect and laying everything out exactly as he liked it. It was a small space—perfect for one or two people at most—with a huge walk-in refrigerator and an even bigger pantry. Every surface gleamed from Micah's obsessive cleaning. He picked up the rolling pin Manya had given him, slapped it against his palm, and felt its heft as he looked around the room.

They would open the next week. Micah had spent every spare moment he had over the past months refining the recipes Manya had taught him and adding to his book. He tested and experimented on Celeste and Alan and Kevin and added the winners to the roster. He was confident in his ability to turn out delicious food, and he was happier than he'd ever been. If he still sometimes clutched Devon's pillow to his chest when he fell exhausted into bed at the end of another long day and breathed deeply of the scent that was beginning to fade, well, no one had to know.

Celeste burst into the kitchen and startled him. "Another reservation," she sang.

Micah smiled. "You're determined to make this place a success before we've even opened, aren't you?"

"It's my livelihood on the line here too," she pointed out as she leaned against the stainless-steel counter. "Got everything ready for tomorrow?"

Micah nodded. "Did you really have to take a wedding-rehearsal dinner for my opening night?"

"Hey, the lady was really nice," Celeste protested. "And they're the only patrons for the first half of the night, so that's not too bad, right? You can totally handle eleven to twelve people for a couple of hours."

"Yeah. I can," Micah said. "I *can*."

"That's my boy," Celeste said and patted his shoulder.

MICAH SPENT the day in the kitchen. He obsessively checked his ingredients to make sure he had everything the wedding party might conceivably order, and he made the conscious decision not to look into the dining room when the guests arrived. Kevin seated them, since

Celeste was at the store picking up several things Micah had realized at the last minute he wanted, and Micah waited with food prepped and ready for the first orders to be placed.

It didn't take long for Kevin to bring him the order tickets, and Micah swung into action. He was relieved to see all the entrees were easily prepared, and he went into autopilot as he churned out rice, ladled sauces, and arranged things to his satisfaction. Then he shoved them at Kevin, who picked up the trays one at a time to carry them through.

Micah checked the temperatures of his curries, fried several quick batches of poori, and readied the masala dosa for the second course. He didn't note the passage of time, and it barely even registered when Celeste staggered in the back door, laden with groceries.

"Fresh mangoes, saffron, and the raw almonds you wanted, boss," she said cheerfully. "Did you want the mangoes in the pantry or fridge?"

"How ripe are they?" Micah asked, wiping sweat from his forehead under his cloth cap.

"Still need a day or two," Celeste said judiciously.

"Pantry," Micah said without looking up as he stuffed the masala dosa.

"Everything going smoothly?" Celeste asked as she emerged.

Micah nodded absently. "No hiccups so far. They're not too demanding."

"Good. In that case I'm going to make sure I have the computer in order. It was giving me fits earlier."

Micah waved vaguely as Celeste headed for the office. Kevin put his head through the swinging door about twenty minutes later. "Hey, boss, they're about to leave. They were wondering if you'd come out so they could tell you how much they liked it in person."

"Oh," Micah said as he lifted his head. "I… sure. Yeah."

He washed his hands and dried them on his apron as he shouldered his way through the swinging doors. The party was seated around his two biggest tables pulled together, and Micah tugged his cap off and ran a hand through his sweaty hair.

And then he froze because Devon-fucking-Mallory was sitting across the table, laughing at something Sean had said to him. Micah couldn't move, couldn't remember how to make his limbs work or even how to draw in air, and then it was too late. Devon looked up, his eyes snagged on Micah's, and the mirth slid off his face. He stood up so abruptly that the chair he'd been in went over backward and several people gasped.

"Devon?" Irene said, and she looked over to see Micah, who had turned to stone in front of the door. "*Oh*," she said.

Sean shot to her feet too, her mouth working in fury, and she clenched her fists. "You son of a bitch," she hissed. Fallon laid a calming hand on her arm, and Sean gave her a frustrated look.

Micah couldn't look away from Devon. It had been over eight months since he'd seen him, and he drank in the sight like cold water on a hot day. Devon had lost weight. It showed in the planes of his cheeks and the shirt that hung loosely on his broad-shouldered frame. His hair was shaggier, his sideburns longer, and Micah ached to touch him.

Instead he squared his shoulders and took a deep breath.

Irene spoke before he could. "Everybody but Devon and Micah, out of this room right now."

"But he—" Sean protested.

"Sean, *shut up*," Fallon said and pushed her toward the door.

Irene herded them all in front of her, glancing over her shoulder at Devon as Jim rolled her wheelchair out.

Devon didn't look at her. He hadn't taken his eyes off Micah since Micah had appeared in the doorway. He seemed rooted to the floor.

Only their harsh breathing broke the quiet of the room, and finally Devon swallowed hard.

"This... is your place?"

Micah nodded dumbly.

"It's... it's nice," Devon managed. He touched the back of the chair next to him with an absent finger. "I knew you were home, of course. Celeste told me, but I didn't know about... this."

"Devon," Micah whispered, and Devon flinched.

"I wouldn't have come if I'd known," he said, and it was Micah's turn to jerk as though he'd been hit. "I have to go," Devon continued, and he bent to pick up his coat from the chair still on the floor.

"*Wait*," Micah said desperately.

Devon stopped and straightened, and Micah took a halting step toward him.

"Please," he said through numb lips. "Please... just wait a second? There are... things to be said."

Devon just looked at him, but he didn't move, and Micah took that as permission.

"I'm so sorry," he said. "I was... I was wrong, Devon. I was *so wrong*, and I'm so sorry. I know you can't forgive me. I'm not *asking* you to forgive me. I just... I need you to understand."

"Oh, I understand," Devon said harshly. "You don't love me. You never did. You didn't *want* to love me."

Micah wanted to weep at the look on Devon's face. He wanted to wipe the hurt and anger away and beg his forgiveness all over again. Instead he clutched his apron, twisting it in his hands as he struggled to breathe.

"I fell in love with you at the aquarium," he blurted, and Devon's eyes widened. Micah let go of the apron and flattened his hand over his chest as the old, familiar ache spread. "You wrapped your coat around me, and I never wanted to be anywhere else but in your arms."

"Then why—" Devon broke off and rubbed his mouth with a shaking hand.

"I didn't deserve you," Micah said and took another step forward. "I hated myself. I thought I'd—God, it's stupid, but—Devon, everyone's always left me. All my life. Starting with my *mother*, the one person who's supposed to be there for you, no matter what. She *left* me, Devon, because I wasn't worth loving."

"That's not true," Devon started, but Micah held up a hand to stop him.

"I bounced around foster homes, developed into a neurotic mess, and I *learned*. I learned that no one wanted me, that no one ever would. I put up walls to defend myself because it hurt so much, Devon. It was like my heart was being ripped out of my goddamn chest every single time someone sent me back or told me I wasn't good enough."

There was grief on Devon's face, but Micah forged on.

"And then you walked into my life. You were everything I was afraid to want. I thought you were perfect. You were *good*. And I... I wasn't."

"That's not *true*," Devon repeated.

Micah blinked away tears. "So when you told me you loved me, I panicked. I was going to drag you down—*sully* you. I couldn't risk it."

"You put me on a pedestal," Devon growled, his voice raw with frustration. "I'm not perfect, Micah. I'm nowhere *near* perfect." His voice rose. "And you didn't even give me a *chance*."

Micah closed his eyes and pressed harder on his sternum. "I know," he whispered. He looked up into Devon's tear-sheened eyes. "I should have trusted you, and I didn't. I was too afraid. I won't ask you to forgive me, Devon. But I have never loved anyone the way I love you. And I am so, so sorry. That's... all." He searched Devon's face, but Devon was utterly still.

"Okay," Micah whispered. "That's all." He looked at Devon one last time to memorize the shape of his mouth, the tilt of his eyes, the way his nose tipped up the tiniest bit at the end, and the soft hair that fell forward over his high brow. And then Micah turned and walked away, through the swinging doors into the kitchen with his shoulders back and his head up.

He headed straight for the bathroom, braced his hands on the sink, and rested his forehead against the mirror as he took deep, gulping breaths.

It was several minutes before his hands stopped trembling and his breathing eased. He looked at himself in the mirror and grimaced at his reflection. He was pale and his hair stuck to his forehead and stood up in little clumps. *Bet that made a great impression on your ex-lover.*

A tentative knock came at the door. "Boss?" Kevin sounded worried. "Boss, the next customers are here, and I've got their orders and umm... any chance of you coming out and maybe cooking for them?"

Micah sighed and washed his hands. He took the orders from Kevin and set them on the counter. Then he moved to the door and peeked through the small window into the dining room. Devon was gone. The chair was righted and back in its place, and the room had begun to fill with new patrons.

That was it, then. It was really over. Micah took a deep breath and squared his shoulders. He'd done the right thing. He'd apologized and cleaned the slate. Despite the grief that wanted to crush him at the thought of never seeing Devon's face again, a sense of peace stole through Micah's soul. Now... now he could move forward with a clear conscience.

He threw himself into making food. The familiar motions were easy as breathing and allowed the hum of his mind to fade into white noise as he stirred, poured, and plated, and arranged everything perfectly before sending out each tray.

He made it through the second rush of patrons without incident and leaned against the counter to take a quick breather.

Micah's eyes were closed when he heard the doors swing open. "Put the tickets on the rack, I'll be right there," he said without looking.

"I don't have any tickets," Barrett said, and Micah jerked upright and nearly fell over. Barrett stood just inside the doors with his hands in his pockets as he smiled at Micah. "This place is *amazing*," he said and took a step farther in.

"No customers back here," Micah said automatically. He suppressed a slightly hysterical laugh as Barrett predictably ignored him, prowled along the steel table, and inspected the room. "What are you doing here?" Micah asked.

"Having dinner," Barrett said. He looked up and smiled brilliantly. "I heard this place was opening, and then I found out it was *yours*, and well... I just had to. I gave that snarky bitch Celeste a fake name when I made the reservation, of course, or she never would've given me a table."

"You're *really* not allowed to be back here," Micah said again. He clenched his fists in a vain attempt to stay calm, but Barrett didn't even seem to hear him.

Instead he rounded the table and advanced on Micah, who swallowed and backed up until his hips hit the stovetop behind him. Barrett came right up on him until their chests were nearly pressed together, and Micah turned his head away and prayed desperately. Celeste was in the office, and since she hadn't come out to investigate the strange voice, she probably had her headphones on or was buried in her mysterious computer workings. Kevin was in the front, dealing with customers. Micah was on his own.

Barrett held on to the edge of the stove on either side of Micah's hips and pinned him in place. "I've missed you," he murmured, his breath hot against Micah's neck.

"I haven't missed you," Micah snapped before he could stop himself.

Barrett pulled back, and his eyes narrowed. "I tried to call you," he said, still right up in Micah's space. "All those flowers, the texts—why did you change your number?"

Micah froze. "The... that was *you*?"

Barrett inclined his head, and a smile curved his lips. "Honestly, Mike, you were never this slow when we were together. The *type* of flowers didn't clue you in?"

"I didn't recognize *any* of them except the marigolds," Micah sputtered. He tried again to pull away, but Barrett stayed right with him.

"Petunias for anger, marigolds for jealousy, larkspur because you're so fucking *fickle*—" He took a deep breath and composed himself. "The orange lilies I sent Devon signified hatred. Didn't *that* at least clue you in?"

Micah's head spun. "Just let me go," he whispered.

Barrett cocked his head as though considering for one brief moment. "No," he said and licked a wet stripe up Micah's throat.

Micah jerked away, repulsed, but Barrett grabbed his arms. His fingers bit in cruelly, and he crushed their mouths together.

No. Micah struggled desperately to break free, but Barrett followed his movements without effort.

Finally Barrett broke the kiss, his pupils blown and lips reddened. "Fuck, you're hot when you fight," he growled. He pressed his hips forward and ground his pelvis against Micah's abdomen. Micah choked back a sob. "I've had enough of you playing hard to get," Barrett continued in Micah's ear. "I think I'm going to bend you over this counter. I'm going to fuck you right here until you scream, with all those customers out front knowing you're having the best sex of your life."

Terror roared through Micah. "Kevin," he managed. "He'll be coming in soon."

"I slipped him a fifty and told him I was your boyfriend and to leave us be," Barrett murmured, and he pulled Micah's shirt aside enough to bare his collarbone. "You've lost weight, Mike. Did you do that for me?"

Fury suddenly spiked through the fear that had choked Micah. How *dare* Barrett? How dare he? Kali's voice echoed through his mind. *No one's going to save you but you.*

He was vaguely aware of the door swinging inward as Barrett shifted his weight so he could drop his head and suck a mark into Micah's neck, and Micah gritted his teeth.

"*Don't call me Mike*," he snarled and brought his knee up as hard as he could into Barrett's crotch.

Barrett staggered backward with a howl, cupping his abused genitals, and Micah lunged sideways, grabbed his rolling pin, and swung it with as much force as he could muster at Barrett's head.

Barrett went down like a sack of potatoes, and Micah dropped the pin and looked up into Devon's shocked face.

"*Devon?*" he whispered.

Devon crossed the kitchen in a few long strides, stepped over Barrett's limp body as though he weren't even there, and took Micah's face in his hands. "Did he hurt you?" he asked.

Micah closed his eyes and reveled in the feeling of Devon's hands on his skin, Devon *touching* him, but then he shook his head and pulled away. He felt giddy, high on the adrenaline coursing through his system. He took a few steps back, and Devon let him go and watched him with worried eyes.

Celeste appeared in the doorway to the office with shock on her face at the tableau in front of her. "What the *hell* happened?"

"Call the police and go back in the office and stay there," Micah snapped. He rounded on Devon and drove a finger at his chest. "*I deserve love, Devon Mallory!*" Then he blinked, startled. He hadn't actually meant to say that.

"I know you do," Devon said quietly.

"I'm hardworking, I love with my whole heart, I'm a damn fine chef, and I'm *loyal*," Micah continued. He was light-headed, but he'd started and he had to say it—had to get it out. "I may not win any prizes in the looks department, but I don't care because I'm funny, I'm smart, I'm kind, and I *know* that now. I do. And no one can take that away from me!"

"I don't want to," Devon said, his tone still low. "It's what I was trying to get you to see the entire time we were together, Micah."

Micah realized with a shock that Devon was smiling even though there were tears in his eyes. He rubbed his face with a trembling hand, his knees weak, and felt for the counter to brace himself. "What are you doing here?" he asked.

"I thought about what you said," Devon said. He took a step closer. "I left because I didn't know how to process it. But then I did, and I... I needed to come back and talk to you. I needed you to know...." He took another step.

Micah swallowed hard, caught in Devon's bright blue gaze. "Know what?" he whispered.

"I still love you, Micah," Devon said with a hitch in his voice.

Micah covered his mouth and stared up at him.

"I can't stop," Devon continued. "God knows I tried, but it's like you're a drug, you're under my skin. You wormed your way in, and I can't pull you out. I love you so much. I will go to my grave loving you, and I don't regret a *second* of our time together. Okay? You were the best thing that ever happened to me. I need you to know that, Micah. I need—" He searched Micah's face with anxious eyes. "Can we try again?" he whispered.

Micah stifled a sob, hurled himself forward, and wrapped his arms around Devon's neck as Devon caught and lifted him so Micah could lock his legs tightly around his waist and bury his face in Devon's throat.

He wept, his shoulders shaking. He could feel the tremors running through Devon's body as well as he whispered broken words into Micah's hair.

"I'm so sorry," Micah choked out. He lifted his head. "I'm sorry, Devon. I love you so much. *I'm so sorry—*"

Devon slid a hand up into Micah's hair and stroked the back of his neck. "I know, baby," he said, smiling through his own tears. "I know, and it's okay. It's over and done, yeah?"

Micah blinked hard and tried to focus on Devon's face. His lips were a scant inch away, and all Micah had to do was lower his head the barest amount... and then they were kissing. Their mingled tears were salty on Micah's tongue as he pressed forward.

Devon opened for him and moaned as Micah deepened the kiss and licked into Devon's mouth—pushing, invading, and *claiming*. Devon gave as good as he got, snagging and tightening his hands in Micah's hair to the point of pain. Micah shuddered at that, caught between arching into Devon's hand and kissing him even harder. Devon laughed breathlessly into his mouth and pulled him closer.

Several long minutes later, they came up for air and Micah pressed their foreheads together.

"I missed you so much," he whispered.

"Missed you too," Devon murmured and tugged him into another kiss. "Don't ever do that again. Okay?"

"Never," Micah promised. "Never, Devon, I promise." He glanced over Devon's shoulder at Barrett, motionless on the floor. "Do you think I killed him?"

Devon snorted a laugh and let Micah slide to the floor. "I kind of hope not, if only because conjugal visits in prison are nowhere *near* as good as the real thing."

Barrett stirred and moaned, making Micah grimace in distaste. Several large police officers burst into the kitchen, and things got very noisy for the next few minutes. When the din died down, Barrett was kneeling on the floor in handcuffs, Devon and Micah were holding hands, and Celeste was beside them as a kind-eyed officer asked questions.

"He *assaulted* me," Barrett shouted.

"An ambulance is on its way, sir," one of the policemen said with no discernible sympathy in his voice.

Barrett groaned and swayed on his knees for effect, and Micah rolled his eyes.

"*He* actually attacked Micah," Devon said. "And it's not the first time. Douche bag's got a history of stalking him. I was there for a lot of it, and Celeste can probably corroborate as well."

Celeste nodded fervently.

"He threatened to rape me," Micah said. "I was defending myself. Can I get a restraining order?"

"Absolutely," the officer said. "We'll need you to come to the station in the morning to make a full report."

"I'm okay, then," Micah said. "I just want him out of here and to never come back."

He sagged against Devon's side and Devon wrapped his arm tight around his waist. Micah closed his eyes and let the clamor whirl around him. He was safe and secure and *home*.

CHAPTER TWENTY-FIVE

THE COPS finally left, and Barrett shot him a venomous look as the officer dragged him to his feet and pushed him out the door. Next to Micah, Devon waggled his fingers at Barrett and then turned and pulled Micah against him.

"I don't know about you, but this is about as much excitement as my poor heart can take," he said.

Micah rested his head against Devon's chest and breathed deeply of his scent—pine trees and snow. "Take me home," he whispered.

"I'll lock up," Celeste volunteered. "And have a word with Kevin about never letting people into the back *ever again*."

Micah sent her a smile and followed Devon out the back door. He was drooping from exhaustion as the adrenaline rush faded, and Devon pulled the keys from his grasp with ease.

"I'm driving. You're resting," he said firmly.

Micah blinked and tried to focus. He swayed into Devon's side, and Devon laughed quietly.

"Do I need to carry you?"

"I'm fine," Micah said automatically. He straightened and made for his car with steps that wavered only slightly. Devon held the door for Micah and then he hurried around to get in the driver's seat. Micah rested his head against the cool glass and watched Devon as he drove with quick, economical movements. He was asleep before they'd gone three blocks.

A gentle hand on his shoulder startled him awake.

"We're here," Devon said, and Micah sighed and rubbed his face.

Devon stayed behind as they climbed the steps to Micah's front door. They were close but not touching as Micah unlocked the door and then stopped to face him. Devon tilted his head with confusion on his mobile features.

"Are we... not going inside?"

Micah just reached out, caught Devon's wrist, and pulled him closer. Devon went without protest.

"Hey," he murmured as he smoothed Micah's hair out of his face.

"Hey back," Micah said, his throat suddenly tight and his eyes pricking with tears. How had this happened? He'd been sure he would never see Devon again, and now he was about to walk into his house with him and Devon was *smiling* at him, love in every line of his body, and Micah thought maybe he was dreaming.

"Oh baby, no," Devon said, thumbing away the first tear that spilled over. "Sweetheart, don't cry. I'm here. It's okay now. It's all okay."

"I know," Micah managed around the lump in his throat. "I just—"

Devon's eyes softened. "Yeah, I know." He cupped Micah's face in his big hand and leaned down. Their lips met again in a slow, gentle slide, and Micah went up on his tiptoes to wrap his arms around Devon's neck. The kiss heated quickly, and it was several minutes before Micah finally tore away, panting.

"I have something of yours," he said.

Devon raised an eyebrow, and Micah pulled the button out of his pocket and held it out on the palm of his hand.

"It fell off your coat when you... I kept it. I'm sorry. I should've given it back, but I needed to...." He bit his lip. "It was the only thing I had of you."

There were tears in Devon's eyes too, and he smiled tremulously as he folded Micah's fingers over the button.

"Keep it," he whispered. "And open the damn door so I can take you to bed."

Micah blinked and felt for the doorknob. They stumbled through to his kitchen as Devon pushed Micah's jacket off his shoulders. Micah shrugged it down impatiently and left it in a crumpled heap on the floor as he kicked his shoes off and jumped into Devon's arms.

Devon staggered back and his shoulders thumped against the wall as he grunted under the onslaught of Micah's mouth.

"Don't you...? Jesus, Micah," he panted. "Don't you wanna... hang up your jacket and put your shoes away?"

"Fuck the shoes," Micah growled against Devon's lips. "No, don't fuck the shoes. Fuck *me*."

Devon huffed a laugh and felt his way through the kitchen as Micah attacked his neck. He clung like a limpet and kissed up and down the column of Devon's throat.

"Been so long," Devon gasped as he fumbled for the bedroom door and very nearly fell through. "Missed you—*ah*." His breath hitched as Micah sucked a bruise into his collarbone and scraped his teeth lightly over the spot. "*Jesus*—"

Micah let his legs loosen and landed on the floor with a thump. Devon's hands covered his when Micah reached to unbutton Devon's shirt in quick, jerky movements.

"Not a race," Devon said gently.

"Speak for yourself," Micah said. "It's been way too long since I've seen you naked, Mallory."

Devon laughed again and tugged at Micah's shirt, pulling it out of his pants and undoing each button in turn until it fell open and Devon was able to take a step back and look him up and down.

"You've lost weight," he said. There was a furrow in his brow.

Micah shrugged, tossed the shirt in the laundry basket, and yanked his singlet up and over his head. "Turns out that'll happen when you're on your feet and moving nonstop ten to twelve hours a day," he said. He reached for his belt buckle and stopped. Devon was still staring.

"You... don't look happy," Micah said. He crossed his arms over his stomach, suddenly self-conscious.

"I miss your belly," Devon admitted.

Micah glanced down at his stomach. "It's still there. Look." He rounded his shoulders and hunched over a little, pooching his belly out, and Devon burst into a startled laugh. Micah grinned up at him and Devon pulled him in for another kiss.

"My God, you're adorable," Devon said when Micah was breathless and clinging to him.

"I kind of am, aren't I?" Micah said, and Devon grinned and dipped his head to kiss him yet again.

"I like you this way," he said, his lips curving.

Micah returned the smile, suddenly swamped with love. "I do too," he admitted. He turned to rummage in his nightstand for the lube. "Do we need condoms?" he asked over his shoulder, but Devon didn't reply.

Micah straightened to see Devon staring at him with shock and something like awe on his face.

"What?" Micah demanded, alarmed. "Is it my hair? Do I have something on my nose? *What?*"

Devon finally found his voice. "Turn around," he said, and Micah shivered and pivoted in place so his back was to Devon.

He dropped the lube onto the mattress and rubbed his arms as Devon approached and touched Micah's spine between his shoulder blades.

Oh. Micah had temporarily forgotten all about the tattoo that stretched across his shoulders—the gold-and-black wings that flexed with his movements, his permanent acknowledgment of the claim Devon had staked on him over a year before.

Devon was utterly silent as he slid one reverent finger across each perfectly inked feather, making Micah shudder and lean back into his hand. He turned to see tears in Devon's eyes.

"Micah," Devon said, his voice thick. "You... did this... for me?"

"Well... yeah," Micah said. He lifted one shoulder. "I was your angel. No matter what, I wanted to remember that you saw me that way."

Devon grabbed his arm, pulled him around, and yanked him into a hard embrace. "I love you," he managed and kissed him. "I love you so much, I'm so *proud* of you, oh, Dosa—"

There it was, that stupid nickname Micah loved and had missed so much. He slid his hands into Devon's hair, plastered himself against Devon's frame, and fervently kissed him back.

"It's gorgeous," Devon said after a minute as he let Micah go to take off his pants. "Fuck *me*. It's stunning."

Micah snorted a laugh as he shoved his own pants down over his hips. "As if *that* would ever happen."

Finally naked, Devon tilted his head, and that little furrow appeared on his brow again. "What's that supposed to mean?"

Micah stepped out of his pants and shoved Devon backward onto the bed. Devon landed with a bounce and propped himself on his elbows as Micah crawled on after him.

"Seriously," Devon insisted. "What did you mean by that?"

"Nothing. Do we need condoms?" Micah asked. His mouth watered, not an inch from Devon's erection, and all he could think about was tasting him again.

"I haven't even *looked* at anyone else," Devon said, but when Micah tried to take him into his mouth, Devon's hand was there, blocking his descent, and Micah *growled.*

Devon grinned at that but tugged until Micah glowered and slithered up Devon's long body. He wriggled and felt Devon's hard length rubbing against his abdomen. Devon gasped and closed his eyes.

Encouraged, Micah did it again and then again until Devon gripped Micah's ass with both hands and his fingers bit into his flesh so hard Micah couldn't stop his whimper as he dropped his face onto Devon's chest.

"Micah, what did you mean, 'as if'?" Devon asked.

"God, you're not letting go of that," Micah managed. He lifted his head and gazed down into Devon's earnest blue eyes. "It means Doms don't bottom, Devon. That's all. It was a stupid throwaway comment, and I really, *really* need you to fuck me now." He leaned in for another kiss, but Devon frowned and Micah stifled a moan and dropped his head to Devon's chest again. "I'm not getting sex tonight, am I?"

Devon cupped Micah's elbows. "Yes, you are, but first we need to talk about this… this bizarre notion that because I dominate you in bed, that means you can't top me."

Micah rolled off Devon's chest, sat up, and crossed his legs. "It's true," he said with a shrug.

Devon followed him upright and leaned forward to take Micah's hands. "And who told you that?"

"Barrett—oh," Micah said.

"Exactly. What'd he say?"

"He said… only subs get fucked, that I was sick for suggesting it but he… forgave me." Micah took a shaky breath as the old remembered shame rushed over him.

Devon stopped smiling, and he gripped Micah's hands almost to the point of pain. "Look at me, baby."

Micah looked up into Devon's eyes.

"I want you to fuck me," Devon said.

Micah sucked in a startled breath, but Devon looked serious, his voice steady as he continued.

"I've done a *lot* of reading since you left," he said. "But this is one thing I knew without research. You could fuck me in a dozen different positions—and I kind of hope you *do*—and it wouldn't change the fact that I'm the Dom and you're the sub in this relationship. That's a mental thing, not a physical one. You're not sick for wanting to top, baby. Have you ever done it before?"

Micah shook his head, briefly lost for words. "I mean…. Kali and I… had sex, but not— She didn't like—"

Devon leaned forward to cup his cheek. "Oh, you're going to love this," he murmured. "Get the lube, and let's get me prepped." He lay back as Micah scrambled off the bed.

When Micah turned back, he was struck dumb by the sight of Devon with one arm tucked under his head, his long legs splayed as he slowly and casually stroked himself back to hardness. He was beautiful—a feast spread out for the taking—and Micah couldn't breathe for wanting him.

"Not getting any younger." Devon sounded amused, and Micah shook himself, but then he hesitated.

"Dev, there's something else…."

Devon arched an eyebrow, and Micah swallowed hard. Concern settled over Devon's features and he sat up and took Micah's hands again.

"You can tell me anything, Dosa," he said. "You know that, right?"

Micah nodded and inhaled a steadying breath. "While I was in India, Kali and I…."

"Did you have sex with Kali?" Devon asked gently.

"No," Micah said, startled. "No, Dev. But she took me to… a club." Devon waited.

"She said I needed to sub," Micah continued. "She was probably right, so I went and I tried. I tried to sub, but I ended up… panicking. I couldn't stop thinking about you, and I… bolted." He looked up into Devon's face. "But I nearly subbed for someone else, Dev. I feel like I… cheated on you."

Devon framed Micah's face in both hands. "You didn't cheat on me, baby," he whispered. "We weren't together at the time. You needed to scratch that itch. I understand. Okay?"

Micah searched his eyes as awe suffused him. "How are you so perfect?" he breathed.

Devon huffed a startled laugh and kissed him. "I'm so very *not* perfect, my love," he said. "I just… get you. Now can we please move on to the sex-having portion of the evening?"

Micah blinked. "Right. Sorry," he said and settled himself between Devon's legs as he leaned back against the pillows again. Micah looked up along the hard planes of Devon's stomach and into his eyes. "Are you... sure?"

Devon grinned at him. "Do you want me to prep myself while you watch?"

"*No*," Micah said hastily, and Devon laughed outright.

"Then get on with it," he said, affection and amusement rich in his voice. "I've got a good hard-on going to waste here."

Bright laughter bubbled out of Micah, and he scooted closer as he flicked open the lube and coated his first finger.

Devon spread his legs as Micah touched him gently, circling the flexing knot of muscle with the pad of his index finger.

A thought struck Micah, and he glanced up. "Have *you* ever done this?"

Devon shook his head, already a little breathless. "First time for... *ah—*"

Micah had sunk his finger in up to the knuckle and stopped. He closed his eyes briefly as he slid his other hand down and wrapped it around his cock, already back to full hardness. Devon took a deep breath, and Micah inched farther in and watched Devon's face.

"Okay?" he whispered.

"Just... keep going," Devon managed through gritted teeth. "Feels amazing, love."

Micah obeyed, sliding his finger in and out several times, and then squeezed out more lube and added a second finger.

Devon arched his back and stroked himself quicker as a groan ripped from him. "Harder," he gasped.

The room was silent except for the slick sounds of Micah's fingers inside Devon's body and Devon's labored breathing.

Micah added a third finger, and Devon very nearly sobbed, chest heaving.

"Feels... so good," he groaned. "See... why you like it so much."

Watching Devon come undone at the seams, feeling the way Devon writhed on Micah's fingers, was one of the hottest things Micah had ever experienced, and his death grip on his own cock was the only thing keeping him from falling apart.

Devon ground down on his hand and sweat beaded on his chest. Micah squeezed his dick harder as he struggled to keep from losing it. When he looked up again, Devon was laughing.

"You gonna fuck me or what?" he taunted.

Micah narrowed his eyes, and he thrust his fingers in deep and crooked them sharply upward. Devon arched up off the bed with a strangled cry.

"Okay," he managed when he had his breath back. "So maybe teasing you when you have the upper hand—"

"Literally," Micah pointed out.

"Wasn't the smartest thing I... could've done," Devon finished. "Micah, please will you fuck me now? *Please*, before I cry manly tears of utter despair?"

"You beg so pretty," Micah told him, and he went to his knees as he watched Devon's eyes darken.

Micah slicked himself up and pressed forward, with his tongue between his teeth, as he watched his cock slide inside Devon's body and disappear by increments. He caught his breath as he sank deeper. Silken heat surrounded him, and he couldn't breathe, too caught up in the sensations that roared through him.

"You're so *tight*," he whispered.

Beneath him Devon groaned encouragement and stroked himself in sharp, short movements. His hips moved in tiny circles as he pulled Micah farther in.

"That's it, baby," he said breathlessly. "That's it. Come on, Micah, *fuck me*. Come on—"

Micah bottomed out and Devon's ass came to rest firmly in the cradle of Micah's hips. Micah ran his hands up and down Devon's legs, delighting in the shift and flex of muscle and skin. Devon looked up into his eyes. His pupils were blown and his lips bitten red, and Micah smiled at him.

He pulled almost all the way out and leaned forward with one hand in the sheet beneath Devon's shoulder and the other pushing Devon's leg up, bending him almost double as Micah slammed home over and over with hard thrusts.

He could feel the familiar pressure building almost immediately as warmth spread through him, but he held it back, eyes locked on Devon's face.

Devon's hand moved faster on his shaft, and his eyes were unfocused as he chased his own orgasm, and his breath came in sharp gusts.

Micah was so close—balancing on the razor's edge—but he gritted his teeth. His rhythm never faltered, and Devon rewarded him by stiffening as his mouth fell open.

"Micah... I *love you*—"

And then everything was tight, shuddery heat as Devon's back bowed. He came in long, hot pulses, painting his belly with streaks of white while Micah spilled helplessly into Devon's core, feeling as though he were being turned inside out—taken apart and remade with joy. Finally he collapsed on top of Devon's motionless form, struggling to breathe. Devon brought one hand up to cradle Micah's skull and laced his fingers through Micah's damp hair.

They lay that way for several minutes before Micah stirred and pulled out and his awareness slowly filtered back. He was still sprawled across Devon's chest, and Devon was tracing absent patterns across Micah's shoulder blades with his free hand. It took Micah a while to realize Devon was following the outline of the feathers with one long finger.

Micah lifted his head and Devon smiled up at him.

"Hey there, gorgeous," he murmured. "How do you feel about a nice hot bath?"

THEY SETTLED into the tub together. Micah nestled securely in Devon's arms as the warm water covered them, and Devon rested his head against the rim and sighed. For some time Micah said nothing. He was content to rest and let the sub space take him, with his head on Devon's shoulder as Devon rubbed tiny circles on Micah's thigh with his thumb.

"So, wedding party, huh?" Micah finally said.

Devon opened his eyes and smiled. "Rehearsal dinner, basically."

"Who's getting married?"

"Oh.... Fallon and Sean," Devon said. He shifted his weight and the water sloshed. "That's what they were going to tell us that weekend."

Micah hummed as he closed his eyes and snuggled closer. "How bad does Sean want to kick my ass?"

There was a smile in Devon's voice. "Pretty bad. You saw her in the restaurant."

"How much free food is it going to take to get her to agree to leave me my dignity?"

"A lifetime's worth, I'm guessing," Devon said, and Micah smiled.

"Worth it. So how's the shop doing?"

"You didn't hear?" Devon asked. "We moved. Found a place downtown, and we've got more business than we know what to do with."

"That's awesome!" Micah said. He tucked his head under Devon's chin and pressed his damp cheek to Devon's throat so his face was hidden. "How'd you afford the move?"

"Some 'mysterious benefactor' bought us a three-month ad run in the biggest newspaper in town," Devon said. His voice vibrated in Micah's ear as he continued. "We started with a trickle that turned into a steady flow once they saw how good our customer service is. All our existing clients followed us when we moved downtown, plus we pick up more almost every day."

"That's really incredible," Micah said. "I'm so happy for you, Devon."

Devon pulled away, put a finger under Micah's chin, and tipped his face up. "Thank you," he said quietly.

"For what?" Micah said, blinking up at him.

Devon rolled his eyes. "The 'innocent' act doesn't work on me, pal. You saved our asses. So… thank you."

Micah lifted a shoulder and made the water ripple. "It was kind of the least I could do, honestly. I'm just glad it worked."

"Me too," Devon admitted. "Oh, there's one more thing."

Micah waited and Devon kissed his nose.

"You 'may not win any prizes in the looks department'?" he said. "Total bullshit."

Micah laughed out loud.

"Seriously," he continued. "You're *still* the most gorgeous man I've ever seen, and I can't believe you're mine."

"*Meri jaan*," Micah said as warmth spread through him.

"What?" Devon asked.

Micah ducked his head, suddenly shy. "It means… my life."

Devon smiled so widely it had to hurt. Then he leaned in and kissed him softly and Micah settled back under Devon's chin with a happy sigh.

One month later

MICAH HUNG up the phone, unable to stop the smile that spread across his face. He started to dial Devon's number, but stopped himself. He wanted to deliver his news in person.

"Celeste," he shouted as he hastily stuffed several dosa with potato curry and shoved them into a carton.

"You bellowed?" Celeste inquired, poking her head out of the office.

"I'm going to the garage," Micah told her. "Stir the masala for me every ten minutes or so, would you?"

Celeste looked dubious. "Fine. But there'd better be some shrikhand in it for me."

"Extortionist," Micah said. He kissed her cheek. "Back in a few."

HE MADE it through downtown traffic and pulled up outside the brand-new offices of Mallory Automotive in record time. The garage bay doors were open, and Sean was half under the hood of what looked like a very expensive Mercedes.

Micah thumped the hood with his fist and laughed as Sean jumped and whacked her head. She emerged rubbing her scalp and glaring in Micah's direction.

"What the fuck do you want?" she demanded.

"Your brother, most days," Micah said cheerfully. "If it helps, I come bearing potato curry." He held out the carton.

Sean took it and jerked a surly thumb toward the back of the bay. She went back to work, muttering under her breath, and Micah headed into the garage.

Sure enough Devon was elbow-deep in an old pickup truck's engine, his coverall smeared with grease and oil. He glanced up as Micah came around the corner, and his face lit up.

"Hey, you," he said as he straightened. "Let me get cleaned up and I'll greet you properly."

Micah ignored this. He took a quick running step, jumped into Devon's arms, and wrapped his legs around Devon's waist as Devon grunted and caught him.

"Babe, I'm *filthy*," he protested.

"Don't care," Micah said and kissed him hard. No matter how often they did this, Micah never got tired of the way Devon's eyes slid shut and he held on to Micah as though he were afraid Micah would vanish if his grip slackened.

Devon took a step forward, deposited Micah on the hood of the car beside them, and pushed until Micah leaned back flat against the sun-warmed metal. He braced an elbow on either side of Micah's head and arched an eyebrow as Micah smiled up at him.

"So, Mr. Ellis, what brings you to my door?" Devon asked.

"You left your dishes in the sink this morning," Micah said. He twined his arms around Devon's neck and leaned up to plant a kiss on the only clean spot on Devon's jaw.

Devon winced and turned his head to catch Micah's mouth. "Sorry," he said against Micah's lips. "I was in a rush, and I forgot. I'll do them the second I get home."

Micah kissed him again. "I already took care of them. And I wanted to tell you that Manya and Kali invited us to India for Manya's birthday next month. They both want to meet you. I want to show you everything, Dev. There's so much to *see*. What do you think? Can you take the time off?"

"I'll have to ask Sean, but I'm sure she'll be okay with it," Devon said and pulled him upright. "Do you think they'll like me?"

Micah snorted and pushed until Devon stepped back so Micah could slide off the hood. "They're going to like you better than they like *me*," he said. "Give Manya that smile of yours, and she'll be eating out of your hand." He cast a disparaging glance at the grease stains on Devon's skin. "Although maybe wash it first."

"Micah Bartholomew Ellis, you come into *my* place of business," Devon said with mock outrage, "on this, the day of my daughter's wedding, and you call *me* dirty?" He lunged suddenly for Micah with his hands outstretched, and Micah yelped, twisting away, and dodged to put the car between them.

"Okay, you are *way* cuter than Marlon Brando," he informed him over the hood. "But there are still *limits*, Mallory!"

Devon grinned at him, and Micah gulped as Devon slid around the car with his eyes intent on Micah's much smaller form. He was so screwed.

Michaela Grey told stories to put herself to sleep since she was old enough to hold a conversation in her head. When she learned to write, she began putting those stories down on paper. She and her family reside in the Texas Hill Country with their cats, and she is perpetually on the hunt for peaceful writing time, which her four children make difficult to find.

When she's not writing, she's knitting while watching TV or avoiding responsibilities on Tumblr, where she shamelessly ogles pretty people and tries to keep her cat off the keyboard.

Tumblr: greymichaela.tumblr.com
Twitter: @GreyMichaela
Facebook: www.facebook.com/GreyMichaela
E-mail: greymichaela@gmail.com

COFFEE CAKE

MICHAELA GREY

Coffee Cake: Book One

Bran Kendrick never expected to fall in love. He's asexual, after all. What chance does he have of finding someone who'll see past that? So when Malachi Warren catches his eye, Bran tells himself his crush will pass. Malachi disagrees. He has been attracted to Bran for some time, something he is delighted to find Bran reciprocating. They begin to date and feel their way through an intimate relationship that meets both their needs.

Suddenly Bran finds himself juggling a new boyfriend, a demanding job, and a college degree he's not sure he wants, but he couldn't be happier—until a series of seemingly random accidents befall Malachi. When they escalate, Bran realizes someone is trying to take away the best thing that ever happened to him, and he must scramble to keep Malachi safe while they search for the would-be killer.

www.dreamspinnerpress.com

BEIGNETS

MICHAELA GREY

Coffee Cake: Book Two

Malachi Warren barely survived a series of assaults on his life. But survive he did, though not without baggage. Now, Malachi must pick up the pieces of his shattered life—the most important piece being his boyfriend, Bran Kendrick, who is dealing with problems of his own.

Stagnating at his job at a small-town café, Bran's pride keeps him from asking Malachi—or anyone—for help. Desperate to do something, Malachi secretly pays a celebrity chef with a bakery in New Orleans to take on Bran as his apprentice.

As Malachi and Bran begin to make a new life in New Orleans, the specter of Malachi's PTSD and the growing stress over the secret he hides from Bran threaten their relationship. Before it's too late, Malachi must confront his past and face his fears about the future, all without losing himself—and Bran—in the process.

www.dreamspinnerpress.com

Also from Dreamspinner Press

www.dreamspinnerpress.com

CPSIA information can be obtained
at www.ICGtesting.com
Printed in the USA
FFOW01n1651220117
31579FF